A WILLFUL GRIEVANCE

A LILLIE MEAD HISTORICAL MYSTERY

LISA ZUMPANO

FIELDING HOUSE PRESS

A Willful Grievance

A Lillie Mead Historical Mystery

PROLOGUE

Somewhere in England

T he list had five names on it.

EACH NAME HAD BEEN CARVED into the thick paper with the fine, smooth tip of his pen. He was left handed, but his penmanship was meticulous.

Each name, four males and one female, had been placed there over the last five years, beginning that dark October of 1918 and culminating in the folded, dirtying paper he now held in his hands.

It didn't look extraordinary by any stretch of the imagination. If someone were to pick it up, it could have been anything —a dinner party perhaps, or a church committee. Maybe even the employee list of a munitions factory, although unlikely as the war had been over for a year now and most of the factories had been mothballed.

As it was, none of those things applied to this particular list. No, this particular list had taken a good degree of painstaking research, a hefty number of bribes—*the English were easily bought*—and a bit of diligent detective work.

The man glanced at it now as he stood huddled against the North Atlantic wind that had cut its way across Scotland, blowing in from the ocean and hurtling itself over the frozen landscape of Dumfries and Galloway, across the Irish Sea and on towards the Midlands until it pushed through the back of his impeccably tailored wool coat and settled on this most northern tip of Oxfordshire. Or was it Warwickshire? Everything had started to look the same.

The writing on this particular list was unmistakably his, with its carved Cs and his Rs, the bone coloured page was of thick, fine stock and his pen had created small indents at the top of his letters. Two of the first names had been crossed off. It was remarkably satisfying to see the letters sliced with a black freehand line, each a celebration of a job well done. Each a step closer to the end of the list.

The first had been no trouble—everything had gone as expected. The second had been a little messier. The man didn't like it when things didn't go according to plan, but in his line of business, some things couldn't be helped.

Three more to go.

He despised England. But there was a job to do and he was the man to finish it.

He leaned down and patted the head of an Irish setter, his eyes never moving from the horizon. The hill on which he stood had a perfect vantage point from which to survey the little town below. It was a world apart from where he had grown up. His home had been a depressing corner of a large and unforgiving city thick with poverty, sickness and crime.

This village, by contrast, looked as though it had leapt off the illustrated pages of a children's novel. He stuffed down the familiar feeling that he got when he looked at it. That melancholy sensation of always being on the outside looking in— never belonging, never having a chance. It was a simple thing, really—one's station and opportunity were nearly always defined by the circumstances into which one was born.

He looked down at his new, but temporary, companion and thought of him as another example of something he hadn't ever had the luxury of having.

"Come on, boy, may as well get back to work."

The dog looked up at him, letting out a tremendous yawn and stiffly getting up to stretch. He was obviously an old dog, although the man, having just met him, had no idea of his actual age. The setter yawned again and trotted after him, perhaps hoping to be fed. The man was taking long strides down the hill now and not looking back.

1

SUPERINTENDENT FELIX PETTERS

Chipping Norton, West Oxfordshire
Christmas Day, 1919

A deep, biting cold had blanketed itself over the Cotswolds that year. The ground had frozen into whatever impressions had been there before the temperatures dipped drastically—a hoof imprint here, deep furrows where a car had tried to pass through the once muddy ground, the paw of a naughty fox creeping dangerously behind the hurried foot print of a startled hen. The skies had thrown off their usual winter blanket to deliver a glorious, blinding aquamarine, and the slightest whiff of crystalline snow delicately layered its lace over the frozen limbs of a long row of hornbeam hedging.

Any birds that would have been seen in these parts this time of year had long made their way to warmer locales —*thankfully*, thought police Superintendent Felix Petters. Seeing animals in wintertime without food or water, pecking at the unyielding landscape or anxiously attempting to dig or burrow in search for nourishment, caused him the most enormous angst. Had they been where he was now, his focus on the frozen bloated body entombed under a prickled mess of blackberry bushes and a thick thatch of frigid crabapple leaves would certainly have been diverted to the more altruistic measure of saving God's creatures. The dead man before him was long gone. There was nothing that could be done now to help him.

Felix was wearing his usual layers: three sets of gloves—one for cold and two for germs; two pairs of wool socks—the thinner ones next to his skin, the thicker ones glued to the inside of his boots which were soft French calfskin, weathered almost to the point of comfortable perfection; and a wisely chosen thin layer of silk long underwear, over which his dark brown corduroy trousers were beginning to feel a little snug. He would have to take his evening intake of food down by an eighth; he wouldn't be able to stand seeing an extra layer of flesh around his middle. *A pound here quickly becomes ten there.* As usual, he had layered well for the inadequacy his uniform presented—a new cotton undershirt, a perfectly pressed striped oxford shirt over which he wore a thick, but finely knit, navy blue sweater.

His coat was standard issue, black, wool, buttons too large for their holes, and never warm enough or dry enough to be considered suitable.

It was Christmas Day, but Felix had never really minded working the holidays. In fact, he often volunteered to be on call. Every year it was the same rigamarole. His mother would attempt to persuade him to join her at his aunt's house, a cold and unwelcoming thatched cottage at the corner of the village which was overgrown with creeping ivy and smelled of pickled cabbage. He disliked his aunt—a prematurely old woman with a narrow mind and an even narrower heart. His uncle had died years ago, God rest his soul, in an ingenious maneuver which, in hindsight, was probably planned in order to escape his miserable reality. At least Felix thought of it as such. The poor man had decided to go fishing with a few of his friends. One of the men had brought some homemade whiskey along for the rowing, and, so the story goes, they drank more than they fished and ended up getting their boat stuck on the wrong side of a particularly deep loch. His uncle died in a valiant attempt to set it free. Drowned, as it were, although the other three managed to escape with only some waterlogged clothing and a few scrapes and bruises. Felix liked to think his uncle had preferred it that way, and was now free as bird. He smiled to himself as he readjusted his gloves and wiggled his freezing toes in his boots.

He sighed and peered down at the frozen body before him. Male, middle aged, dressed for country living—tweed trousers, dark leather boots, a warm oilskin coat. His scarf was still neatly wrapped around his neck, his cap clutched in his right hand. What was that beside him? Felix knelt down to get a better look. Nestled in the long grass and frozen mud was a leash: woven leather with a brass clip. Where was the dog? Felix stood again and looked around.

He was at the far northern end of an unkempt church yard. The town council had tried to get something done with the grounds, but the reigning vicar was a muddled old man with a penchant for birding and thus had lobbied arduously to keep the vicarage as natural as his parishioners would allow. Brambles encouraged grey partridge, he had argued, to say nothing of skylarks, peregrines, red kites, nightingales, turtle doves, and spotted flycatchers. He had wisely stopped promoting the survival of buzzards, realizing even in his own affected state that his congregation winced whenever he mentioned that particular species.

Felix motioned to a couple of constables who were standing, frozen and miserable, awaiting his instruction. They probably actually enjoyed being with their families on Christmas Day and resented the intrusion of a dead body on a day of celebration.

"Let's get him down to the morgue, fellows." Felix carefully peeled off his outer layer of gloves as he spoke, careful not to touch them on his coat or anything else he wore. To do so would require an enormous undertaking of disinfection—an eight step program he had developed himself, which was something he had little time for today.

He watched as the men jostled the body onto the stretcher provided by the ambulatory service, rigour mortis inconveniently getting in the way of the man's dignity.

"For Christ sake throw a sheet over him, would you?" Felix hollered as the dead man's arm tipped dangerously and threatened to overturn the whole stretcher.

A small crowd of onlookers had huddled together at the base of the churchyard behind the iron fence, their whispers evaporating into the thin winter air, their breath puffs of grey against the whitewashed landscape. Shivering at the forefront stood the boy who had found the body that morning. His mittens were moth-eaten, and his thin coat was doing little to insulate him against the biting weather. Yet he had stayed there, for the past three hours, watching every movement Felix made. Poor kid. He too, must be escaping some miserable Christmas celebration, or lack of it, back home.

"Son." Felix was now standing before him. The boy looked up at him with round dark eyes, his pale face expectant and nervous. There wasn't a freckle to be found on his alabaster cheeks.

"Yes sir?" His voice trembled.

"Need you down at the station—official business. *You* are a very important witness." Felix was putting on airs for the crowd in the hopes of giving the boy some semblance of status in a world that had likely cruelly passed him over.

The boy's eyes widened and he pushed out his chest proudly. "Sir, yes sir."

Felix thought for a moment that he might even salute him.

"There's a good lad." He steered him toward the awaiting vehicle and whispered to him as they cleared the crowd behind them. "Peppermint sticks and hot cocoa all right with you?"

The boy looked at him, confused.

"That is what we feed all our witnesses. Helps them...uh... recall details in a more coherent way."

"Oh yes, please, sir."

2

JACK

Oxford, Oxfordshire
New Year's Day, 1920

"Is this where you want it?" Did the ensuing silence mean she didn't care, or did she not hear him? "Up here? On this...." Jack teetered precariously atop the box he had placed on an old wooden chair in a dangerously ill-thought out plan to reach the highest shelf in the cramped cottage kitchen.

"Lillie!"

Where on earth was she? *Oh, to hell with it.* He reached out to place the handful of dishes he was holding on the aforementioned shelf. As he did so the chair wobbled, causing him to drastically correct his position—or *overcorrect,* as it happened—and he and the handful of dishes came crashing down hard onto the flagstone floor. Each and every piece of pottery shattered into hundreds of tiny pieces.

"Dammit!"

He couldn't be sure if he had sworn out loud or not and he

remained there for a moment, taking stock of his limbs and hoping he hadn't been heard. He appeared to have escaped unscathed, although he felt like an imbecile there on the stone cold floor. He wondered why on earth that frustrating woman upstairs had ever thought this cottage was quaint. It was cold— although, admittedly, it was he who had let the fire go out; damp, even though the walls had been sealed and painted year after year with layers of chalk paint by a fastidious former owner, and if he was being honest, the only residual water was from a kettle he had left to boil; and the wind rattled the leaded glass windows, although who had windows that weren't being rattled today? This wind would make a golden eagle cry, if there were any about that were idiotic enough to leave their nests today. It wasn't lost on him that he was being unreasonable. He looked around at the mess he had created, wondering if he had time to get it cleaned up before she noticed.

"It's a good thing those were a flea market find and not my grandmother's best china." Lillie stood at the door, her eyes assessing the scene on the kitchen floor and then moving on to him. She bent down and offered Jack a hand up, which he took thankfully, rubbing at his knee as he got to his feet. Perhaps an injury would gain him some sympathy and, truthfully, he could feel the beginning of a bruise beginning to swell underneath his trousers already. He wondered if he should feign a sprained ankle and be done for the day.

He had grown tired of moving, having done so much of it over the past few years for his work in intelligence; and although this wasn't his move, it gave him the same feeling of melancholy he always got when a change was underway.

He brushed off his pants as he got to his feet and retrieved a broom and dustpan from the linen cupboard off the kitchen.

"Let me," Lillie said, mockingly. "You have done enough, I think."

She took the broom from his hands. Who was he to resist?

Nodding, the pretence of defeat painted on his face, he took his semi-wounded body to the chesterfield in the small warm sitting room off the kitchen. He marvelled, not for the first time, how a faded floral overstuffed sofa could feel so inviting. Just yesterday he had taken a restful nap here after he had attempted to put together an iron bed in Lillie's room upstairs and had accidentally hit himself in the forehead with the wrench; he hadn't been required to use homemaking skills much in his line of work. Hardly his fault given the shoddy workmanship of the manufacturer—a blacksmith could have made better furniture. In the end Lillie had finished the job for him while he nursed a bruised head, a hot cup of sweet tea, and a damaged ego.

He really made a better spy than a labourer.

He watched her as she swept up the shards of pottery, bits of white and yellow littering the kitchen floor like shells on a beach, the swishing sound of the pieces being moved about the floor as though an ocean wind were moving sand.

"You could just marry me and we could buy a proper house." Jack was smiling at her from the sitting area. The type of smile, even as he tried to hide it, that was more of a cringe than a genuine smile. The type of smile that anticipated a good thrashing.

She didn't stop sweeping or even look up at him. This thread of conversation was hardly new for them.

"This *is* a proper house."

"You know what I mean, something bigger, more grand."

"I don't like big houses. This cottage is perfect for Penny and me. Quaint, warm, and in the right location at the edge of the village, so I am not bothered by the high street noise. It has a perfect little nook for writing while overlooking the fields. I am told by the estate agent that in the spring the view is an explosion of wildflowers—ox-eyed daisies and meadowsweet for as far as the eye can see."

"I just thought..." Should he really be hounding her again? He struggled to find the right words. "I just thought that I have to go back to London, for work, and wouldn't it be nice to come home on the weekends?" Even to his ears it sounded pathetic.

"You can come home on the weekends. We don't have to be married for that."

He sighed. His relationship with Lillie would always be complicated. Separated for two years during the last half of the war, she had believed he was dead until relatively recently. He had gone off due to a foolish misunderstanding and, not that he had ever told her, also for her own safety. It wasn't until she had taken a job with a newspaper in Oxford that they had reunited, albeit shakily.

Lillie was an American. Raised in New York City, she had attended Oxford at the same time as Jack and his best friend Harry. The three of them had become the best of friends and Lillie and Jack's more romantic feelings had developed slowly and often tumultuously over the course of the last five years. He wondered if she would ever forgive him for allowing her to believe he was dead.

"I don't have a home to come to here. And I can't very well stay with Harry at Tynesmore—not now that he is soon to be married. I would be like a fifth wheel, banging around the place as surely as a lonely swallow in search of a nest."

"So you want to marry me so you can stay in my delightful cottage? Incidentally, swallows know perfectly well where their nests are, year after year." She was teasing him now.

Lillie had bought the cottage just a week prior. Without him. She planned to live there with her sister Penny who was in the midst of a messy divorce from her husband, who was now on trial in New York for his part in a corporate fraud scheme that had culminated in the death of a very important English socialite.

Jack frowned at her and didn't answer.

"Listen, there are three bedrooms. Penny and I are each taking one of the upstairs ones and the one on the main floor can be yours for when you come 'home', as you put it."

He allowed himself a little smile. Perhaps she did love him after all.

"Won't that be...improper?" He only said it because custom necessitated him to.

"Having a man stay with Penny and me? Probably. I am sure we will be the talk of the town. Although you know me, I really couldn't care less."

"I'd like that, very much." His voice was soft and he reprimanded himself for it.

"Good, why don't we see about getting a bed for that room. It isn't large so we will have to find something on the smallish size, but I think we can still eke out some space for a chest of drawers and a wash stand." She looked at him, knitting her eyebrows together. "You can leave your gun and all your identities here when you aren't using them at work. Happy?"

"Tremendously." Of course he knew she was making light of what he did for a living. "And you know I don't carry a gun."

"Ah, but you say nothing of aliases. Now, are we finished? Can I get back to it?"

He nodded, finally satisfied. "When is Penny back? It seems a shame you have to do all this on your own—get this place furnished and set up."

"Not for a couple more weeks. Shutting down the house in Manhattan proved to be more work than she thought. I'm not surprised. They had a ton of furnishings and with Floyd about to go to prison—thank God for miracles—she has quite a lot to get sold. She is threatening to bring some of her favourite pieces back with her but I can't imagine where we would put them." She glanced around the room.

"And the divorce?"

"In progress, so I hear. She is working with an attorney in

the city who doesn't anticipate any holdups, but you never know, it's still a man's world out there, no matter how far we have come. Anyway, I don't mind getting the cottage set up without her, I rather like it actually. And it will be nice to have it all done before I return to work next week. Jeremy is wanting me to get started right away on a story about a couple of bodies found in North Oxfordshire."

"Hm." Jack didn't care for Lillie's job as chief crime reporter for the Oxford Daily Press. The last story she had covered had very nearly gotten her killed. "Pity," he mumbled under his breath.

"If we are finished making a mess here, how about helping me with some odds and ends at Tynesmore? Harry has given me a bunch of things he has stored in the attic—some linens, a rather good set of Chippendale dining chairs, and," she said, smirking at him, "a few more dishes I hope."

"Mm. Yes, of course."

Were there not people one could hire for all this?

THE DRIVE to Tynesmore from Orchard Cottage, as it had been aptly named for the abundance of apple trees planted in the garden, took ten minutes. Jack's Lagonda, now at least seven years old, still drove as beautifully as the day he had bought it. Of course it had hardly been on the road. During the war, it had languished instead at Harry's estate under a tarpaulin. Harry had thought Jack was dead and gone but he hadn't ever relinquished control of the tawny coloured car. For all Harry's posturing and flippancy, he was deep down a nostalgic. Jack was thankful to be behind the gleaming burled walnut steering wheel once again, wishing only that the top could be down. He didn't think Lillie would enjoy an open air experience with the freezing temperatures they were having in Oxford, though.

Reaching across the seat he placed his hand on her leg and

gave it a little squeeze. He had seen so much in his time at the front, and he knew many men of his generation had been forever changed because of it. And so he, as so many of his fellow soldiers did—at least those determined to survive— grabbed hold of whatever he could to love and cherish.

For life and peace, as sure as the sun rises, were fleeting.

3

THE HUNTER

Bracknell, Berkshire

T he third name on the yellowing paper was that of a retired university professor living in Berkshire. His specialty was political theory—he wasn't sure what kind, exactly, but it didn't really matter. The professor wouldn't live long enough to discuss Friedrich Engels ever again.

It was all a load of rubbish anyway. The world was a pawn for rich, propertied men who thought nothing of throwing their citizens into war or starvation if it served whatever ignorant and simple goals they had in their pea-sized brains. Theory—real thought and deep reflection on the state of civilization—had no place in politics.

This third name surprised him—or the man's former occupation did. He would have thought an educated man would have had the morality to see what had happened those few years ago was horrifically wrong.

He let out an enormous sigh. It was his way of releasing

nervous tension; that, and cracking his knuckles. It had been taught to him by his former mentor. *Former.* He supposed he should be saying *deceased,* but he could never actually bring himself to use the word. And he had been so much more to him than just a mentor. Under his tutelage the hunter had not only survived his early life, but he had grown into a successful young man—one capable of not only surviving the war, but also of commandeering the great, profitable ship of business relationships that his mentor had built from the ground up. His memory would be honoured now, in a way he thought fitting.

The High Street of Bracknell that late afternoon was bathed in the rose pink light of the setting winter sun, making it appear as a false front of a child's puppet stage would. The chalky brick of his hotel walls glowed rouge while the sidewalk pavers bled into the clay of the road. He headed south at a good pace towards the public library, and found himself missing the Irish setter.

Normally he would clean up anything left over—a product of his elite assault training—but the dog had made a good impression, and thus he should be allowed to live and prosper. The man had quietly left him in the boot room of a farmhouse not far from where he was now. The smells from the kitchen would hopefully let him know someone would be home to care for him. He couldn't very well take him from job to job.

Reaching the front door to the library, he strode past it without glancing in. Turning the corner and scouting the side street, he confirmed he was alone over the course of another half block, then turned and doubled back to the intersection. Here he had a good vantage point to watch the comings and goings of the local library book worms. The library was housed in an old building and its most recent refurbishment appeared to have been hastily undertaken. Someone, in their less than infinite wisdom, had thought it appropriate to shore up its aging brick facade with a combination of white paste and ugly windows.

The hunter sighed discontentedly and retrieved a cigarette from inside his coat pocket. It was relatively easy to renovate a building—one just had to follow the cues of the original architect—yet so often these later generations managed to so incompetently botch things up. He cupped his hands to keep his match from being extinguished and, inhaling deeply, he settled into his watch post.

He didn't know how long the professor would be in the library, only that his daily visits here were habitual and he often remained inside anywhere from thirty minutes to three hours. At least it wasn't snowing. There was no shortage of things to watch as he waited for a sighting. A steady stream of people came and went. Old women dressed in black overcoats, hats pulled down low to shield their heads from the cold. Young women dressed in faded wool clothes, scarves wound tightly around their tired faces. Dirty faced children, unwashed and shivering with the cold, hurrying their parents into the warmth of the building.

The hunter glanced at his watch. It was nearly five o'clock. The library would be closing soon, so he hadn't much longer to wait. He thought of his mentor—*Kapitan,* as he had liked to be called. The hunter wondered now if that title was a nod to his love of boats. His mentor had never referred to his real birth name. He had abandoned it as neatly as he had his childhood and his abusive parents, making his way to Chicago as a young man and then on to New York to live out middle age. There he had prospered, as sometimes the children of misfortune are able to do, and his business had made him a tidy sum. It wouldn't be until many years later that he made the fatal mistake of traveling through England en route to the Netherlands. Although they should have known better and picked a neutral country instead of this hellhole one.

Now he was here because he needed to be, because he wanted to be. For revenge. To avenge. For *Kapitan* was his mentor, his employer...his best friend.

That trip they'd made in 1915 was a stupid mistake that cost him his life. *But how were they to know...*

What was taking the professor so long? Had he missed him somehow? The hunter stubbed out his cigarette with a polished boot and retrieved his calf skin gloves from his coat pocket, pulling them over his long, elegant fingers. Dusk danced around him, greens became grey, whites glowed in the street lamps, trees became eerily shadowed skeletons.

At last the professor emerged though the front doors. He carried an armload of books he would never get to read. The professor pulled his collar up around his face and started down the road in the opposite direction of the hunter.

The wind had picked up, its faint whispers rustling the skeletons, and sending what people were left on the sidewalks scurrying as startled mice would scatter in a storm.

Now seemed as good a time as any.

The hunter began his stalking.

The man laboured under the weight of his books, stopping often to readjust his load, then carrying on at a good clip into the biting wind. He didn't live far from the town, just a little way down the road, but it would feel like twenty miles with the weight he had in his arms.

The professor was larger than the hunter had expected. He didn't have the hunched physique of a crusty ivory tower dweller. Nor did he seem as old as the information the hunter had bought suggested. He was at least six feet tall, and his way of moving suggested he spent more time outdoors than his resume let on. It was disconcerting, to be sure, but not insurmountable. The hunter, after all, was well versed in his art and had come up against far more formidable foes than the one he had in his sights now. He remembered with distaste a particular German officer stationed in Belgium near the end of the war.

The hunter and his prey had left the lights of the village behind now as they carried on into the enveloping darkness. The hunter fell back slightly and allowed the professor to put some distance between them. It wouldn't do to announce his presence quite yet. The cottages that had dotted the road, their chimney smoke curling and layering smells of cedar and peat onto the air, slowly vanished as they walked on. Small farms took their place, and what animals couldn't be seen could be faintly smelled instead; pigs, sheep, horses, chickens. The smell of fowl disgusted him. A winter moon rose tentatively on the horizon, its blue light illuminating the stone road. The air was at once colder, hollower.

They continued on this way for a time, the stalker and his unwitting target, along the rarely traveled road, deeper in the countryside. Finally, the professor turned off the main road onto a short but steep smaller road that would take him to the front door of his thatched cottage. The hunter kept closer now, skimming the edge of the road's blackthorn hedging. He kept to the shadows as much as possible, silently cursing the cold light of the moon. He could hear the professor labour slightly in his breathing. Not as much as the hunter would have expected for the terrain he was covering at surprising speed.

He wondered if the man knew he was being pursued and wasn't letting on. He may have been a professor once, but his previous occupation was hardly that of a benign shopkeeper. It wouldn't be unusual for him to have some awareness and training in this sort of thing. That thought disturbed the hunter but he pushed it aside. He was close enough now to see the glint of gold lettering on one of the books the professor carried. *Leviathan*, it read, in all capitals. Perhaps that was what the hunter was, he mused. An enormous sea creature, sent to wreak havoc and chaos on a system needing accountability. A cosmic fugitive serpent who would impose order—by force, coercion and death—and the result would be a new rebirth. Order. Justice. Vindication.

The professor was rattling his key in the lock now. It sounded forced, artificial. The hunter stayed poised, hidden in the shadows, his body pressed against the frozen hedge, waiting, his breathing muted, body numb. He had planned to wait until the professor was inside and then surprise him from behind. Doing it this way lessened the chance they would be seen by anyone and his research told him the professor lived alone.

Finally the lock gave way and the professor pushed open the door to the cottage. The hunter shifted his position, crouching, waiting for the right moment. Into the cottage the man went, books still in hand, and disappeared rather too quickly behind the door.

The hunter crept out of the shadows, and made his way towards the open door. From the blackness into the light he emerged, zeroing in on his kill.

He was, however, not the least bit prepared for what happened next.

4

LILLIE

Oxford, Oxfordshire

Tynesmore was a delightful rambling estate not far from the village of Oxford. It was the family home of Harry Green, friend to both Lillie and Jack. As Lillie stared out the attic dormers, she marvelled again at how it looked, set amongst rolling fields, now frosted in silver and dotted with wooly horses moving about in search of what little grass they could find under a dusting of snow. Colossal bales of hay had been placed out every few acres, their green highlighting the colourless landscape. Ignoring them, the animals searched for a fresh blade of grass where they could find it, leaving the piles of hay untouched, monuments to their protest of domestication.

Harry resided alone on the estate, his parents having left the country for their London townhouse and his brother deciding to stay in Switzerland after the war.

"You have enough furniture up here to furnish an entire

house, Harry, why are you keeping all of this?" Lillie was
sorting through the attic in search of the chairs Harry had
promised her. Finding them was proving a difficult
undertaking.

"I haven't a clue really, things just end up here and I seem to
forget about them. Looks a bit like a furniture graveyard."
Harry pushed his flaxen hair back from his face and wiped his
hands on his perfectly pressed pants, leaving a long smear of
white dust down the front of them. He gazed around the attic
with a look of confusion on his face. "I know they are here
somewhere, I saw them last year..."

He moved a large pile of papers out of his way and an enormous cloud of dust engulfed him. "Or was it the year before
that..."

"I'll find them, don't worry." Lillie wasn't so sure.

The sight of the always dapper and pristine Harry
attempting to help her sort through this mess amused her.

"I notice Jack has escaped all this moving chaos and made
himself scarce," Harry said, looking distractedly looking
through a pile of old books.

"Mmm," Lillie agreed.

Jack really hadn't proved to be much help with the move.
She knew he didn't want her to move into the cottage and his
incompetence was his method of silent resistance. She also
knew he wanted to marry her but, after all they had been
through—his disappearance during the war, her long years of
grief, and now their reunion—she wasn't ready. Jack didn't
approve of her new role as lead crime reporter for the local
newspaper and deep down she didn't want him to have any
influence over her decision to work in an occupation that
could, at times, be rather dangerous.

"You'll have to forgive him one day you know..." Harry was
across the attic now, attempting to peer under a dust cover at
the mammoth contents beneath.

Lillie didn't answer. Was it about forgiveness? Perhaps it was...

"He loves you. It was war after all, and the strangest things happen during wartime. None of us could have predicted the way things would go."

She inhaled deeply, attempting to release the tension building inside her.

"He pretended he was dead," she stated, more bluntly than she intended. "For two years," she added a little more gently.

"Yes, because...he had to. He was an intelligence agent during a war. He was one of the very elite few who dared to travel into occupied Belgium for God's sake—the rest of them languished in neutral countries, sipping martinis and hoping for tidbits of information from their dinner parties on Lake Geneva. He was the real thing, not some trumped up version of a gentleman spy. It was safer that way—for everyone to believe the same thing."

"Or convenient."

"It's the same thing."

"No, it isn't. And you're missing the point entirely. He left because he saw me dancing with another man and thought I was in love with someone else. Not only does that make it seem as though he hardly knew me, but he obviously didn't trust me enough to tell him the truth before he just ran off. Ultimately he chose to marry the Service, not me."

Harry frowned at her. "You really must work on letting it go."

"Yes, trying..." Not with much success though, she had to admit. Perhaps there was too much water under the bridge, as they say.

Apparently giving up, Harry released the dust cover to settle again over furniture that wouldn't be seen for another fifty years.

Changing the subject, she asked, "Where is Rumple today?

Maybe he can shed some light on the case of the lost Chippendale chairs?"

Harry's manservant was usually ubiquitous, and it had just dawned on Lillie that she hadn't seen him yet today.

"He went to Chipping Norton. An old friend of his turned up dead in some swamp and Rumple went to find out the circumstances and pay his respects."

"That is terrible news. Drowned then?"

"Not sure. Either that or something more sinister. He should be back by suppertime. If we haven't found the chairs by then, perhaps he could enlighten us as to their whereabouts. Either that or rescue us from this horrific attic."

"How go the wedding preparations?" Harry was marrying Lillie's friend Primrose, although she hadn't heard much of the wedding plans lately she realized.

"Oh, fine..." Harry's sigh alluded to something else.

"'Oh fine?' That doesn't sound very promising."

"Primrose doesn't want to rush things. I had rather hoped for a January wedding but she is pushing things off until at least February or March. And she has taken a new job, which surprised me. She has gone up north with the family. I'll not jest, I wonder seriously if she is having second thoughts."

"Nonsense. January was overly ambitious anyway, you've only just asked her. Why not take the time to plan things properly? After all, what's the rush? You have the rest of your lives."

"I suppose." He sounded unconvinced.

"And how has your mother reacted to the news?" The last time Lillie had met the matriarch of the Green family there had been no doubt she expected Harry to marry someone of the family's choosing. Primrose, for all her attributes, would not be considered the suitable choice.

"Don't even ask, my mother is frightfully disagreeable with any decision I make without her consideration. A more difficult woman you have never met."

Lillie smiled, remembering a dinner she had once attended with Mrs. Green and nodded her silent agreement. Spotting the chairs, she exclaimed, "A ha!"

"Sorry?"

"I've found them!"

"And not a moment too soon. I couldn't take another minute of this dust. Let's go have a drink. You'll stay for supper won't you? And Jack of course, wherever he is."

"That would be nice actually. The kitchen at the cottage isn't at all set up and I can't imagine trying to cook anything there for at least another few days. Give me a hand with these would you?" She was pulling the dining chairs two at a time across the attic but they were heavier than she anticipated. Harry relieved her of one and went back for another.

"Where will you have the reception?" Lillie asked, breathless from her efforts.

"I think here, in the great hall. It never gets used otherwise."

"Will you have many guests? Or will you keep it small?"

"You are full of questions. Come on, leave these for now and let's go find your fiancé."

"Jack isn't my fiancé."

"Whatever you say. I hear a whiskey bottle calling."

THE HUNTER

Outside Bracknell, Berkshire

T he hunter stepped into the dim light of the professor's cottage, his eyes taking a minute to adjust.

The small sitting room smelled of lemons and dust and the furniture was shabby in the way English furniture is supposed to be. The rugs were obviously of good quality, worn and faded on the edges but still thick in the middle, and the oak side board must have been last century at least.

He didn't see the professor anywhere and wondered in passing why he had left the door slightly ajar. The cold night air rushed past him, diffusing the scent of old books and furniture polish. Perhaps the man had gone into the kitchen? Or the boot room?

The hunter didn't like these old cottages. At just over six feet tall, his height caused his head to graze the ceiling. The sharp messiness of splintered beams plucked at his short cropped hair, and he immediately felt claustrophobic. The hunter fingered the knife in his pocket, preparing. He carried a small hand gun also but he preferred the silence of a blade. It would be satisfying to get number three over with. A list of five was daunting to even the most seasoned professional.

The room was absolutely silent, the air holding the suspense of an opera before the soprano sings her final note. If the professor was in the kitchen, or anywhere in the tiny cottage, would the hunter not have heard him? He barely had the time it took to ponder this question, for at that precise moment, the professor stepped out from behind the door and hit him hard in the face with a book.

The hunter reeled back, startled, with a distant ringing in his ears. He tasted the metallic tinge of blood, probably from his nose. He shook his head and lunged forward. The professor nailed him neatly again with the same heavy book and the hunter lost his balance and fell to the floor. He felt a kick to his stomach and one to his head, and saw a threatening cloak of darkness begin to fall. Fighting it, he grabbed hold of the professor's leg, his hands slipping over the soft wool of his trousers and settling onto his boot where he was better able to get a grip.

He pulled the scholar to the floor, overestimating his own ability to recover from the two harsh blows to the head. The hunter had lost his strength and with his vision now blurred, he wasn't able to accurately read the professor's next move. The man still held the book in his hand and attempted again to hit him with it but the hunter, by some miracle of intuition, avoided the swing and grabbed the professor's throat. He held it, hearing the man splutter and wheeze. He supposed choking was as good as any other method of killing and increased the pressure while pushing on the man's chest with his knee. The professor continued to struggle, moving this way and that, and eventually was able to bring his palm up and hit the hunter in the nose a second time.

Blood splattered the sitting room walls and the hunter, momentarily startled, groaned in agony. The professor was on his feet now and making for the door. If he reached the blackness outside the hunter was sure he wouldn't see him again. Wiping his nose, he got to his feet in pursuit. He grabbed the professor's coat and attempted to tackle him to the floor once again, but the man slithered out of it, not adjusting his pace in the slightest. The hunter lost his balance and fell across the threshold of the cottage, the shed coat in his hands. He felt the throb of his head and the soft wool of the man's coat under his fingertips and he didn't have to look up to know that the professor was gone.

The hunter shook his head, attempting to clear the spots from his vision and the hammering from his skull. The book the professor had hit him with was lying beside him, its gold lettering a glaring tribute to the survival of political theory across the ages.

Leviathan. An enormous and laborious tome. A worthy weapon.

The hunter had always preferred the brevity of Machiavelli.

LILLIE

Oxford, Oxfordshire

"Will you have any more dessert, Miss?"

Lillie looked at the silver tray Rumple was holding in his hands. On it were the remnants of what once was a perfectly laid out assortment of cakes and puddings. Jack and Harry had made quick work of demolishing it, each of them taking at least three, while Lillie was finishing the last of a vanilla and bourbon custard. She swirled her spoon around, toying with the last of it, but eventually put her silverware down in defeat.

"Thank you, but I better not."

"As you wish." Rumple placed the tray on the sideboard and began clearing their plates.

"Shall we?" Harry motioned in the direction of the library. "The fire is going and I have some port we should try. I've only just purchased a few bottles of this particular vintage and I want your opinions."

"I can't say I know a thing about port, Harry." Lillie frowned at him and then glanced up at Rumple's back, noting his exceptional efficiency as he set about his work. He was middle aged, but hadn't lost any of his musculature, and his livery jacket strained across his shoulders as he moved—a physique he likely got as result of his military training during the war. Not for the first time, Lillie wondered exactly what he had been tasked to during his time in the army.

"I was sorry to hear about your friend, Rumple," she said, raising her voice slightly to be heard above Harry and Jack's chattering.

Rumple turned to face her and Lillie noticed the strain on his face.

"Yes, thank you. A loss, a terrible loss."

"And was he a good friend?"

"He was more of an acquaintance, someone I had worked with during the war. Although I admit we hadn't kept in touch much lately. Still, a shame I won't be seeing him again…I rather liked him."

His gray eyes took on a glassy haze, and he looked as though his thoughts were far from the dining room in which he now stood.

"Was it an accident?"

"Oh no, certainly not." Rumple looked as though he would say something else, but then apparently decided against it.

"So the police suspect foul play?"

"Yes, and as well they should." His back was to her now and he fussed with the dishes on the sideboard.

"If you don't mind me asking, how was he killed?"

"Stabbed, I'm afraid. Multiple times."

"Were you able to speak to anyone, about what happened? Now that I think of it, I believe your friend's death is one of the cases I am meant to be covering for the newspaper. There were two recent deaths in Oxfordshire apparently. Both in the North, but a few villages apart, if I remember correctly." Lillie was trying to remember the details of her conversation a few days ago with her editor, Jeremy Winston.

"I tried to get in touch with the Superintendent in charge while I was there today but he wasn't available."

Harry and Jack had stopped their conversation and were now listening to Lillie and Rumple's exchange.

"Why don't you let me see what I can find out. I will travel to Chipping Norton tomorrow and see if I can't find this Superintendent—"

"Petters."

"Good. Superintendent Petters. Were you aware of the other death in the same area? It may just be a coincidence, two deaths in a few days, but it is strange. Come to think of it, I believe that one was a stabbing also."

"Lillie...." Jack's voice was quiet and pleading and she was acutely aware of his disapproval.

Silencing him with a glare, she looked back to Rumple inquiringly.

"No, I wasn't. Are you suggesting the two are connected?"

"I haven't a clue, not yet anyway. But it does seem odd there are two so close together."

"A serial killer perhaps?" Harry mused, spooning the last of his dessert into his mouth. "Or they could be completely unrelated and of no consequence to each other."

Lillie wondered. Two deaths, in the same area, at the same time of year. Both male, which was unusual for a serial killer.

"Possibly."

"Well?" Harry pushed his chair back.

"It's late Harry, I should probably get back to the cottage."

"Just stay for a quick nightcap. I won't keep you long, and then Jack can drive you home."

Conceding, Lillie got up from the table and followed Harry and Jack into the warmth of the library. It was a large room but cosily furnished with thick velvet upholstery, wool carpets and leather bound books. It smelled now of wood smoke and unlit tobacco dispersed with the heady scent of newly budding hyacinths from the resident greenhouse.

"Mmm," she sunk into a deep, feather down chair by the fire. "This really is my favourite room in the house, Harry."

Harry handed her a ridiculously large glass of port and she sipped it steadily, feeling it warm the back of her throat as she swallowed. For all she didn't know about port she was enjoying this one enormously.

A knocking interrupted her thoughts.

"Is that someone at the door? At this hour?" Harry glanced at the clock on the mantel. "It's nearly midnight, how odd."

Annoyed, he put down the bottle he was holding with a thump and stalked out of the room in search of the offending culprit.

Jack smiled at Lillie over the firelight. "Probably someone wanting to be paid for a gambling debt."

"You don't think Harry has a problem, do you? With gambling I mean?"

Jack shrugged. They remained in silence for a few moments straining to hear what the voices that were now in the hallway were saying. Lillie was only catching snippets but she was feeling warm and relaxed enough by the fire to not to want to get up and investigate.

The door to the library was opened and Harry reentered the room ahead of a man who seemed to be limping and holding onto his side. He was without a coat and was wet and shivering. Lillie jumped up from her chair.

"Please come and sit here by the fire, you will catch your death!"

On closer inspection she noticed the man had red rings across his throat and the outside of his eye was bleeding as well. Rumple rushed into the room behind them carrying an armload of blankets which he threw over the man haphazardly and then rushed to the sideboard to pour him a large glass of brandy.

"Who is this?" Lillie whispered to Harry, standing back out of earshot.

"Apparently somebody Rumple knows, although how I have no idea. I am as in the dark as you are."

The man was shuddering now, attempting to get comfortable. It was obvious from the way he moved his ribs were likely broken and he could very well be suffering from hypothermia.

He attempted to speak but finding it difficult to do so, chose instead to gulp the drink Rumple had given him, his thin fingers, skin white with cold, wrapped around the crystal glass like claws.

"Shouldn't we call a doctor?" She was astonished none of them had thought of it.

"No, please..." Lillie hadn't thought the man could hear her through his shuddering, and while his voice was weak, he was insistent.

Eventually, after what seemed like an eternity, the man stopped shivering and looked up at the four faces that were watching him. The white of his injured eye was filled with blood and he looked almost terrifying in the light from the fire. If it weren't for his intelligent face, Lillie would have escaped from the room immediately, citing some excuse. As it was though, she was intensely curious.

"I....I'm sorry to intrude..." the man began.

Rumple interjected, saving him the difficulty of introductions. "This is Professor Hargreaves. He and I once worked together."

"Oh?" Harry prodded.

The Professor nodded, adding. "On a project, although it was some time ago now."

"What has happened to you? Did you have an accident?"

Shouldn't they be asking him why he was here with no coat, injured and bleeding, in the middle of the night?

"I am terribly sorry to come here, but I ... I was attacked and I needed to leave immediately. I got away, obviously, but I wanted to warn..." Here he trailed off, as though unsure of his audience.

"Warn whom?" Why was the man being so secretive?

"Theodore. I wanted to warn him..." Who on earth was Theodore?

"Thank you," Rumple said.

Oh...Theodore was Rumple. Theodore Rumple. Of course. She had never asked Rumple's first name, oddly, and now she felt badly somehow.

"I should have come earlier—I was going to, and then I wasn't sure—but with both Reginald and Patrick gone, and so quickly, I realized we might be next."

"I'm sorry, I don't understand. Who are Reginald and Patrick?" She was trying to play catch up with this haphazard train of thought but it seemed a convoluted sea of swirling confusion.

The Professor looked towards Rumple, who nodded his approval.

"Reginald and Patrick were two men we also worked with, during the war. Both of them were recently found dead, up north, and tonight, I believe whoever killed them came for me also. I managed to fight him off, this time, but he will be back. Of that I am sure."

"Was one of these men the friend of yours in Chipping Norton that turned up in that swamp?" Lillie looked to Rumple for confirmation.

He nodded. "Patrick. I didn't know Reginald was the other man."

The professor swallowed another gulp from his glass, then

added, "He changed his name a few years ago. Went by the alias John Staine, but Reginald Blackwater was his real name."

"I wouldn't have even known it was him who had died, had Professor Hargreaves not told me when he arrived this evening."

"So we have two dead men, likely murdered..." Lillie began.

"Certainly murdered," the professor interjected.

"Right, two dead men, both murdered, by an unknown man who tried to also kill you tonight. And you think that this murderer is, therefore, killing a group of people, you included, Professor, because...why exactly?"

Rumple and the Professor exchanged a glance.

"Neither of us is one hundred percent sure, but there are theories." Professor Hargreaves shrugged, apparently not about to elaborate.

Harry, Jack and Lillie looked warily at each other.

A foreboding heaviness settled over the room. At once the air felt too hot, the scent of wood and flowers nauseating, the books lining the walls claustrophobic. Time seemed suspended in a haze of uncertainty, tobacco smoke, and nature's perfume.

Lillie wondered if she wanted to know the answer to her next question. For certainly once it was asked and answered, they would be all be set on a rolling course, with Rumple their reluctant captain and this broken professor their navigator.

"Which are...?"

Some things couldn't be helped.

THE HUNTER

A Train Car, Somewhere in Northern England

The night train rattled along the tracks, the steady hum of its steel wheels a softly reassuring lullaby. An occasional lonely whistle punctuated the frigid night air. From the open window of his sleeping car the hunter gazed out at the stars and the tops of barren trees, feeling the rush of crisp January air cool his skin, listening to the creak of his rail car as it swayed this way and that. An eternity of frost blanketed the dark hills beyond and as the hunter watched the frozen landscape pass, lit only by a frigid moon, illuminating miles of nothingness in both earth and sky, he felt a sudden sharp twinge of homesickness.

He reached up and gently rubbed the swelling on his forehead and ran his fingers over his broken nose feeling bits of crusted blood around his nostrils. His headache had subsided, although his frustration had not. He was in a far from an ideal situation. Two targets dead and a third on the run. Four and five were in entirely different geographical directions, and although it would have made sense to do the one in Oxford next for expediency, the wiliness of the professor caused him some concern now.

Did the academic realize the entirety of the situation? Or did he believe he had been attacked by a thief, or a psychopath? If he did realize what the hunter was there for, it wasn't impossible to believe that the professor would in turn warn the next two targets, assuming he knew who they were. As he rolled the situation over in his mind the hunter had the uneasy feeling that the professor was more intuitive than he had given him credit for. Which meant, of course, the hunter should anticipate more resistance waiting for him.

All this had helped make the hunter's decision simpler. Target four would be the one farthest away from Bracknell and Oxford. If he could get out ahead of the situation, and of any potential amassing of forces, surprise could still be his ally.

Which was why, after stumbling out of the professor's cottage, bleeding and injured, he had cleaned himself up the best he could and made his way steadily through the darkness, stopping only to pick up his things at the hotel, and then on to the nearest train station.

He couldn't sleep now, on this murmuring train, even though it was the middle of the night and he was dog-tired. Giving up, he pushed back the sheets on the narrow bed and sat up. He sighed, deeply inhaling the fresh air into his lungs, and reflected on why he was here, miles from home, on a train destined for the Scottish frontier.

The hunter hadn't come about this way of life easily, being poor and alone as a young man was a journey devoid of options. He had worked at many trades in many cities—carpentry, steel work, factory hand—before he had fallen into the life he had now. He had always known he was destined for greater things. He hadn't planned on being poor forever and he wasn't a man to accept either societal or legal limitations. His tutelage had come, years later, after being picked up for a number of petty crimes; theft, assault, and forgery were but stepping stones to more profitable ventures. Unbeknownst to him, his life of crime happened to be in a city, and even more specifically, an area, that was under the control of a faction he was unaware of. Looking back on it, he was amazed he had been so naive, thinking he could carry out his own brand of petty crime in someone else's domain.

He was lucky, at that time, to be taken under the wing of a competing organization, and eventually, he ended up working side by side with its patron. And that man changed his life, irrevocably. Had he not met him then, he would now be in a prison workhouse, or very possibly dead. Some called it organized crime; but the hunter, having no family of his own to compare it to, thought of it as just that—*family*. And, as with all families, sometimes one becomes so deeply embedded that it is impossible to find a way out.

THE TRAIN LURCHED SUDDENLY, bringing the hunter's attention back to the present. He looked out the window at the lightening landscape, the tops of the hills now sharper, the outline of a town in the distance the first sign of life he had seen all night. Something about it, the stone buildings, their haphazard rooflines, reminded him of somewhere his mother had taken him before she died—he couldn't remember where.

He began to gather up his things, placing them in his leather case. Pulling on his coat and shoes, he watched the city of Edinburgh through the window. Its spires and mossy crags emerged like a storybook scene out of the morning haze.

From there he would travel northwest to Stirling and then

deep into the countryside. The information he had on his next target wasn't entirely clear. Her coordinates had been more difficult to come by and, by virtue of her remoteness to the other four, she would likely be more difficult to find.

But, the hunter reflected, if this job were easy, everyone would be doing it. And he was used to hardship.

8

LILLIE

Chipping Norton, West Oxfordshire

"And the primary evaluation of a corpse, irrespective of suspected foul play or not, involves which four initial steps? Before you answer, think of what we covered last week with regards to blood splatter trajectories and the implication of blunt force trauma..."

The door to Superintendent Petters' office was slightly ajar, but Lillie paused at the threshold. The man's voice was efficacious and soft, with a slight nasal whistle that could have been inherent, or due to a winter cold. She didn't want to interrupt. He must be conducting some sort of a tutorial, although the receptionist hadn't indicated he was with anyone.

Spying a worn wooden bench across the hall she sat down, folded her hands in her lap, and prepared to wait. A voice was answering the Superintendent's question, although she couldn't hear what he or she was saying from where she sat.

"But what of the coroner's autopsy?" Petters again, questioning his pupil.

Again a reply that couldn't be properly heard.

"Aha yes, you are correct. Yet again. Shall we leave it for today? Don't go though, I have some work for you on a cold case—strangulation. Or was it? See what you can make of it. I won't tell you what I suspect—a fresh set of eyes is just what it needs. And remember the adage I taught you at the start—coincidence is synonymous with what?"

A tiny voice responded, and this time she heard it. "Rubbish."

"Good work. You are a fine student."

Lillie heard the scratch of a chair as it was pushed back at the lesson's apparent conclusion. Petters' voice came again, louder this time.

"Hello out there! Please come in now."

Surprised, Lillie hastily got up and crossed the hallway. She didn't think anyone knew she was out here. The door squeaked on its hinges as she hesitantly pushed it open and looked in to the most immaculately clean office she had ever seen.

"Superintendent Petters?"

She gazed around the room, noting the exceptional symmetry of the space. The Superintendent sat behind a glistening steel desk. Behind it, lining the wall, was a large wooden filing case, each drawer labeled with a typewritten face, upon which sat an identical line of picture frames, each sepia photograph offering differing views of the same landscape. There were eight of them. Photography was obviously a budding hobby for the Superintendent.

"I am, yes."

Lillie stepped forward and was startled to see the author of the diminutive voice she had had trouble hearing from the hallway. The boy couldn't have been a day over ten. He had clear skin the colour of Dover chalk and intelligent shadowy eyes that watched her closely as she stepped forward.

"Lillie Mead. Oxford Daily Press. May I...?"

"Please." Petters was standing now and motioned to a chair beside the window.

She noticed he didn't come forward to shake her hand but there was nothing in his demeanour to make her think he wasn't being polite. The Superintendent opened a desk drawer, retrieved a pristine white dusting cloth from inside and set to work polishing the top of his already gleaming desk. He rubbed the metal top in large, circular motions, each an exact replica of the one before it, not missing an inch of the surface while the boy and she watched, neither of them speaking. When he finished he put the cloth back into his drawer and pushed it shut with the sleeve of his left arm.

Satisfied with this obviously important exercise, the man sighed contentedly and re-focused his gaze on her.

"Miss Mead, how can I help?" His smile was charming and completely unguarded. "Oh, terribly sorry, where are my manners, please let me introduce you to Sergeant Noble." Petters nodded towards the boy.

"Oh...uh...." Lillie was confused, but not wanting to appear startled she quickly overcame her hesitation. "Pleasure to meet you, Sergeant."

Surely he couldn't be serious? The lad was still a schoolboy.

Petters' face gave away nothing. He was the epitome of seriousness and tact and not the slightest hint of sarcasm sullied his features.

"Sergeant," Petters said, nodding at the boy, "you may carry on with your work."

"Thank you, sir." The boy gave Lillie an awkward little bow of acknowledgment and left the room, closing the door quietly behind him.

Lillie looked at Superintendent Petters, who now gave her a small smile.

"I know what you are thinking," he said, the smile now morphing into a grin.

"I'm sorry?"

"How can a boy that age be a sergeant in the police force? And of course, you would be right."

"I..." Not finding the words, Lillie supposed staying quiet was the best option.

"That lad is terribly bright. He found the body last week—the one in the church yard—which presumably is why you are here?"

Lillie nodded.

"Anyway, poor boy lives in the orphanage outside town, terribly depressing place, to say nothing of the hygiene of the nuns who administer it. I thought he could use an occupation —in a manner of speaking—and he likes to hang about the station. I often take him with me to the pub for dinner after work, or the shop for our tea in the afternoons. Gives him something to look forward to, I suppose, although I rather think it makes my day a little cheerier as well."

Superintendent Petters was quickly becoming one of Lillie's favourite people.

"But enough of that," he said, leaning forward. "Tell me about your newspaper."

"The Oxford Daily Press? Yes, well, I head up the crime section and wanted to talk to you about your recent finding of two deceased males. The one you have just mentioned, and also the other one who was killed prior."

"Hm, yes. Both male, middle aged, causes of both deaths were stabbing. From what we can tell the same knife was used in both homicides. You may as well know this, and preferably print it—if it can help bring out anyone who knows anything. I don't think the killings are random."

"Were there any other distinguishing similarities?"

Petters didn't immediately reply. He swivelled his chair to look out the window instead, lost in his thoughts.

Lillie waited.

Petters swivelled back to look at her and slowly, almost imperceptibly nodded.

"There certainly were." He seemed reluctant to elaborate.

"I am assuming you don't want me to print what you are going to say next." It wasn't her first encounter with the police and she understood the need for discretion.

"You assumption is correct. It isn't exactly a secret per se. Everyone in Chipping Norton seems to know, but I personally would like to know more about it myself before I announce it county wide."

"Of course, I understand. What you say next won't be on record."

Petters sighed. "Our killer inked two small letters onto the back of both victim's hands."

"Oh, someone's initials perhaps? His own?"

"It's possible. But why would he do that? It doesn't make any sense."

"What were the initials?"

"S.D. And I have run them, on every male in the area—Sam Dunn, Solly Davenport, Sigmund Dahl, you name it, I have looked it up."

"Unlikely anyone would leave that sort of a calling card, isn't it?"

"Precisely. I don't think finding and investigating males with the initials S.D. is a good use of resources. He did it for a reason, he wants us to know why he has targeted these two men. It's a message, a code if you will, I just don't happen to be all that swift at code breaking."

Petters folded his hands on the immaculate desk in front of him. He leaned forward, the smell of his lavender soap faintly discernible as it crossed the air between them. He had a kind face, his small and narrow features were pinched somehow, but not unpleasant. He was beginning to bald but kept what was left of his fair brown hair short and clean. Lillie noticed his fingernails were spotless and perfectly filed. He was an efficient man, and seemed an intelligent one.

Moreover, he was open to outside thinking.

"Miss Mead, have you any theories a frustrated police constable might need to hear?"

"If and when I do, Superintendent, you will be the first to hear them."

9

LILLIE

Oxford, Oxfordshire

Except to bathe, Professor William Hargreaves hadn't moved from his chair by the roaring fire in the Tynesmore library since the previous evening. He now wore a paisley dressing gown, underneath which were a pair of expensive silk pyjamas, both borrowed from Harry's wardrobe. In front of him on a small round side table lay the remains of a bowl of soup and a plate of half-finished soda bread. Rumple had wrapped the professor's broken ribs with flannel bandaging. Although the wounds around his eye were now clean and doused with medical ointment, they had begun to swell, giving his face a lopsided look.

The room was full of the hushed whispers of a planning session. Both Rumple and Professor were animatedly discussing something by the fire, while Jack and Harry on the other side of the room were drawing up what looked like a large flow chart on Harry's desk. Lillie's entrance went unnoticed by all except Constance, Harry's large and friendly Irish wolfhound, who, getting up from the rug in front of the fire, sauntered over to her and leaned into her legs.

"You're back." Jack gave her a wave from the desk and Rumple and the Professor stopped their conversation, turning their anxious faces in the direction of hers.

"Yes." She unwound her scarf and removed her coat, throwing both over the back of an empty chair. "And I have some information."

"Tell us, please." Harry drew out the words dramatically. "Because at this point, we haven't much new to add, other than the two men knew each other."

"They were killed by the same knife," Lillie told them.

"Well, I suppose that isn't really a surprise, is it—but the question still remains, why?" Harry rubbed his unshaven chin. It was rare to see him with facial hair. Obviously the intrusion into his household had upset his normal morning routine.

"Perhaps this will help. The killer penned initials onto the back of both of the men's hands. S.D."

"What sort of a murdering fool leaves his initials behind?" Harry scoffed.

"Presumably someone who wants the police to know exactly why he came calling. Someone with an axe to grind. Revenge, likely." Lillie replied.

Rumple and the Professor exchanged a long look. Their faces told Lillie they knew exactly what the initials stood for.

"They aren't the killer's initials," said the Professor, putting his face into his hands and rubbing his forehead in defeat. "Are they?" He looked up at Rumple, perhaps hoping to dispel his own fears.

Rumple was slowly shaking his head. "I daresay not."

"Please dispense with the suspense, Rumple. What do the initials stand for?" Harry's impatience threatened to bubble over.

"I am having a hard time believing it myself but I think they refer to something—some*where* actually—that we met during the war."

"I don't understand." Harry again, prompting him.

"When I worked with the Defence of the Realm—D.O.R.A. as it was known commonly—along with the Professor and the two other victims, Patrick and Reginald, we would often meet at a requisitioned country house just outside London. We used it as our planning headquarters. From 1914 to 1917 we held weekly meetings there, just the five of us. Although the house's name was Summerdyne, we gave it the acronym S.D. It was in named in the minutes of our sessions, and would have been fairly easy to find in any of the files."

"But why would a killer reference it? What happened there that would warrant killing two men and gunning for a third?" They were just getting snippets and Lillie wanted a fuller picture. "And you said the *five* of you. If you are the fourth, Rumple, who is the fifth man?"

"The fifth is a woman. Florence Millicent-Marks. And to answer your question about what happened at Summerdyne— well, I suppose it is hardly classified information anymore, so I can tell you. We reviewed intelligence reports on suspected German spies working within England during the war. We were the final review panel, the five of us, and it was our mandate to..." Rumple paused, clearly uncomfortable. He shifted in his chair, the leather groaning its objection, and eventually abandoned it to instead pace the length of the room. Lillie hadn't ever seen him so agitated. "It was wartime, and things were different then, you see..."

"It was your mandate, the five of you, to do what exactly?" Although she had a suspicion, Lillie wanted it confirmed. They had alluded to it all the night before when the professor had arrived in his ghastly state. Lillie had asked the tough questions that a reporter should ask—but they had danced around, trying out different theories, and never actually getting to the heart of the thing. Who wanted these people dead, and why? Whatever the shrouding secrecy was, it was time to do away with it.

Rumple sighed, as though he could wish it all away. The Professor stared at the fire, watching the flames dance, a faraway look of regret in his eyes. He too waited for Rumple's answer, although he obviously knew what it would be.

"Our mandate was to decide which people would be *executed* at the Tower of London." Rumple winced as he said the words.

Despite the warmth of the room, Lillie felt a chill pass over her and she looked at Jack and Harry, standing by the desk as though frozen in wax. Jack's face wore a neutral expression and Lillie couldn't tell whether he was surprised or not. Had he known about Summerdyne already? His business *was* intelligence after all.

"Oh sweet Jesus," Harry said quietly after a moment. Apparently he had been in the dark as much as she was.

His voice was but a pin drop in the quietest room in Oxford.

10

THE HUNTER

Edinburgh, Scotland

T he morning sky was the colour of spun fairy floss, its pinks and blues dotted with white cotton, its reflection on the hills creating the surreal landscape so craved and celebrated by the impressionist's brush.

Even the hunter could appreciate the beauty of Scotland as he emerged from the Edinburgh station and headed west along the cobblestone street towards the post office. A porter had given him directions, and, glancing at his watch, he hurried his pace a little. He had some research to do before the regional train's one o'clock departure to Stirling and it wouldn't do to miss it.

The wind was bitterly cold and it blew through the city with an unrelenting force quite in contrast to the peacefulness of the sky. At least he was out of England for the time being. He hadn't been in the Scotland for five minutes and already his spirits had lifted. He wrapped his herringbone scarf high up around his nose and mouth. Not only did it hide his wounded face but it mellowed the sharp bite of the January air on his skin.

Although he hadn't slept, the brisk morning awakened his senses and brushed any fatigue from his body. The city was just coming alive and the hunter felt the rebirth of a new morning, a new place. The smell of coffee and fresh bread swirled in the wind and he was suddenly hungry. He couldn't remember the last time he had eaten, but there wasn't time for that now.

The post office was housed in a baronial building that dated to the late 1860's. The last fifty years hadn't been kind to it. Haphazardly thrown together, its dirty stone facade was a riot of differing shades of ashen yellow and red, one of its two feeble turrets had a broken window, and the building's asymmetrical slate roof was missing many of its shingles. The entire disheveled effect wasn't encouraging for a supposed bastion of record keeping. And records were why the hunter was here. He needed to see the directory for Stirling and the post office was said to house all the directories for the entire country in its Edinburgh branch.

As he pushed open the front door a small chime echoed above his head and an old woman behind the front counter looked at him over top of her spectacles.

"Yes?" It was a demand more than a question and the hunter was instantly annoyed.

"I am looking for a directory, for Stirling. I am trying to track down a farm."

"They are all in there. Agricultural and domestic. Mind you put it back where you found it." She pointed to a room off the main lobby and went back to reading whatever it was when he came in, promptly ignoring him.

The hunter nodded and followed the direction of her finger. He almost laughed out loud when he saw the state of the room. At the center of it was long, black, worn table upon which were scattered numerous directories, some open with the pages torn out, others in a heap, and more than a few cast aside on the chairs and floor. Stupid woman. Was it not someone's job to sort this mess out? He rated his odds at finding what he was looking for at slim to none.

Each directory was for a particular council area and he sorted through them quickly—West Lothian, Inverness, Ayr, Fife, Clackmannan—he wasn't having any luck, and pushed them aside. The shelves along the wall housed a few more and he was encouraged to see that some counties had duplicates which would increase his odds of finding Stirling. Moray, Renfrew, Forfar, and then Moray again.

An elderly man came into the room as the hunter was pulling an armload of books off the shelf and nodded to him. The hunter could smell him from where he stood, urine and faded scotch. He wrinkled his nose in disgust. The old man sat at the end of the table and pulled a little flask out from his coat. He set about taking small sips, his eyes opening and closing as he did, and the hunter concentrated on ignoring him. Eventually the man fell asleep, small choked snores willfully escaping from the sides of his wrinkled mouth. Apparently he was a man with nowhere else to go, as nobody would willingly choose this room as a place to spend any time.

The hunter sat down as far from the man as he could possibly get and dropped the pile of directories onto the table in front of him. Exhaustion was catching up with him and for a moment he felt an overwhelming sense of defeat, depression, and loss. Pushing the feelings away he focused his tired gaze on the books in front of him, dirty from years of fingers sorting through them, people looking for relatives, friends, industry...*enemies*. Kirkcudbright, Selkirk, Lanark, Nairn, *Stirling*...eureka!

Although the cover was torn, the rest of the directory looked relatively intact, and the hunter greedily turned the pages searching for her name. *Florence Millicent-Marks*. Not finding it, or her father's name, he turned to the agricultural pages. Although he didn't know the farm name, the hunter's intelligence told him Ms. Millicent-Marks had taken over her father's dairy farm after the war. Scotland didn't have many varieties of dairy cows, primarily only Shetlands and Ayrshires, so finding a farm that bred and raised either of these would be a first step towards finding her. He knew she was within the Stirling area so he focused his search on any dairy farms within fifty miles of the town's center. There were three. He hastily scribbled down their names and addresses and got up from the table. He didn't bother putting the books back on the shelves— a match and some gasoline would do a better job of cleaning up the place.

The hunter left the old man snoring at the table and made his way from the building. His relative success had improved his mood and he was further pleased to see he had time to stop for some breakfast before his train departed for Stirling, *Gateway to the Highlands*. Gaelic for "place of battle," the hunter found its etymology fitting. According to historical folklore from centuries ago, when the city was being invaded by the Vikings, a lone wolf howled into the night, waking the residents in time to defend the town.

The hunter gave this some thought as he took his seat at a small, impeccably clean cafe on the Royal Mile and ordered a coffee and a full Scottish breakfast of bacon, sausages, black pudding and beans.

When *he* came to call in Stirling, he hoped that wolf was dead.

11

LILLIE

Oxford, Oxfordshire

"So this...this...murderer...is tracking you all down? For something you participated in—as part of a government agency—years ago?" Lillie had never noticed the incessant ticking of a colossal grandfather clock in the hallway, but it was now beginning to irritate her.

She walked across the room and closed the library door in an attempt to clear her thoughts.

"It would seem so," Rumple agreed.

"So, either he is on his way here for you, Rumple, or he is on his way to kill Florence. He doesn't know where the Professor is after that botched job, presumably."

Rumple gave a grave nod.

Lillie bit her upper lip and rubbed a small scar on her forehead. She needed to think very carefully. "I suppose," she began, cautiously weighing her words. She was cognizant that while what she was about to say was meant to be directed at the current situation, her words could also easily relate to her and Jack's stalemate. She glanced at him across the room. "War has affected all our lives—those four years put us on different trajectories; paths we wouldn't have taken otherwise. One can hardly judge or take back what happened during that awful time, we must instead live with it—whatever *it* is—and try to move forward."

Jack nodded and gave her a small smile. "Harry, I think the first order of business is to get some security around Tynesmore." He was always quick to react with logical solutions and this time she was grateful for his input.

"Of course, I will call a friend in London and ask for some recommendations."

"And we should get in touch with Superintendent Petters to let him know what we have discovered. I'll do that." Lillie spun to face Rumple. "And you and I need to pack. Quickly. It's urgent we get on the road."

"Why, are we going to Scotland?" This surprised her. She stopped and looked at him. Was Florence all the way in Scotland? That was a bit more difficult than she anticipated.

"I'll come." Professor Hargreaves was, with some difficulty, attempting to get up from his chair as he spoke.

"Sorry Professor, you are in no shape to travel. Stay here, coordinate with Superintendent Petters. Get him whatever information he needs based on the past history of D.O.R.A. And start compiling a list of those people who were executed at the Tower."

"Lillie..." Jack crossed the room toward her, his eyes pleading with her not to go.

"Hurry up." She glared at Rumple, willing him to move. She took Jack's hand and squeezed it reassuringly. "I won't be gone long," she whispered, kissing him gently on the cheek. "And don't overpack!" she hollered to Rumple's retreating figure. He had a tendency to be quite a clotheshorse.

"I'll drive you to the station," Harry said, moving quickly towards to the door. "I'll have the car out front in five minutes. Incidentally, where in Scotland are you going?" Harry looked at the Professor.

"Stirling. That is where Florence's family farm is. At least I seem to remember it as Stirling..." He pushed himself up from his chair with difficulty. "Harry, if you don't mind my using the telephone, I should get busy on putting together that list—after you call the Superintendent, of course." He nodded at Lillie, and they started towards the small room off the main foyer that housed the telephone.

"Please, help yourself—Lillie, why don't I have my aunt meet your train in Edinburgh. She lives just outside the city and can get you to Stirling faster than you having to take the Caledonian line." Harry was calling to her over his shoulder as he hurried off to retrieve the car.

"I didn't know you had family in Scotland!" She called back.

"Just my aunt Mildred. She must be nearly seventy now."

"Harry, I don't want to put anyone out...." Especially a seventy year old woman, Lillie thought. *What was he thinking?*

"Balderdash, she loves this sort of thing, ferrying people around and being useful. She's a stout old thing, plenty of life left in her. I'll ring her after I drop you and Rumple. Now hurry up! The train from Oxford leaves at five sharp and if you miss it, you'll be waiting until tomorrow morning."

With everyone getting ready for their departure, there were just the two of them left now in the library. Jack inhaled deeply and gave her a sharp, uncompromising stare. "Just what the hell do you think you are doing?"

Lillie rarely heard him use such terminology, and never with her. He looked furious, and she had to admit she was startled by his delivery. She instantly felt her spine tingle. Who did he think he was?

"My job," she stated flatly.

He nearly hissed his response. "Your job? Your job is to write articles! Not chase down a bloody assassin. He's a murderer! What do you think he is going to do when you two show up? Have tea and biscuits and discuss the future of the monarchy?"

She was getting irritated now. And she was late. She certainly didn't want to miss that train. She stepped forward to show she wasn't going to back down and tried appeasement instead, although what she really wanted to do was blast him. "I know you love me," she started through gritted teeth, "but I'm going, regardless of what you think I should do." She took a deep breath. "I love you Jack, but you can't dictate my actions."

He stared at her and said nothing. His face softened slightly, but his eyes remained hard.

"Now, I really must get on." She picked up her bag.

"Lillie..." he tried again, but she gave him a brief shake of her head.

"Goodbye Jack. I'll let you know when we get there."

The clacking of her shoes on the library floor put a brisk end to their argument.

12

SUPERINTENDENT PETTERS

OXFORD, OXFORDSHIRE

L ater that evening, Superintendent Petters and Jeremiah Noble stood in the foyer at Tynesmore feeling like two fish out of water. So *this* is how the wealthy live, Petters mused, glancing at the magnificent staircase that circled elegantly to the second story. The parquet marble floors were inlaid with oak and polished to perfection over which thick carpets were thrown, banishing the echoes of their whispers. Jeremiah, his white skin almost translucent from the cold, moved closer to Petters for security and warmth. His intelligent dark eyes roamed the room.

The house smelled of supper, a roast perhaps, and the garlic and onions of a soup stock, along with dessert. A vanilla cake? Or was it marzipan? Petters's mouth was watering and his stomach reminded him he had missed dinner—again. He wondered about Jeremiah. Had the orphanage fed him the usual measly dinner of broth and bread? The more time he spent with the boy the more he realized how much he liked him, but also how poor his living conditions and prospects were. Who would adopt a boy of ten? He was destined to be a fixture at Abbey Memorial Orphanage until he could find work and leave. People wanted babies, not grown children. And the state of country's economy hardly helped matters; post-war stagnation for the traditional English products—cotton, steel, coal, iron—meant rising unemployment and massive deflation. Although none of country's troubles appeared to be reflected in the Green household, Petters mused, glancing around at its opulence.

The sound of shoes on marble interrupted his thoughts and announced the arrival of the patron of the house. Petters was surprised to see a youthful looking man standing before them, his flaxen hair flopping over one eye, his perfectly tailored clothes slightly out of sync with the pleasingly mischievous face.

"Harry Green, delighted to make your acquaintance. I can't thank you enough for coming tonight." The man had impeccable manners, yet his demeanour was instantly disarming, his casual and relaxed attitude quite out of context with the surroundings.

"Superintendent Petters, nice to meet you. And this is Jeremiah," Petters said, smiling at the boy as he introduced him. The two men shook hands.

"Please come into the dining room—the Professor is having his dinner and he isn't very mobile, as you will see. Much better we go to him."

Harry led the way to a beautiful yellow, silk-walled dining room. At its center was an enormous mahogany table laid with silver vases of greenhouse flowers, beside which was a long buffet draped in white linen and proudly displaying a line of steaming warmers. The smell of fine food filled the room, taunting Petters and the boy.

Harry made polite introductions and Petters noticed that the Professor had not only a bruised face, but showed obvious signs of having at least a few broken ribs.

"Have you had supper?" Harry was addressing Jeremiah,

and the boy slowly shook his head, eyeing the buffet table as a lion would a gazelle. "Well, you must sit down, there is enough here for an army. I wasn't expecting to have a house devoid of guests, so it is a lucky thing you are here, my boy. Can't see good food go to waste." Harry retrieved a warm plate from the buffet and handed it to Jeremiah while motioning to the food. "Please, take as much as you possibly can eat. You too, Superintendent."

Petters and the boy thankfully did as they were told and once their plates were full they sat down at the table.

"Please, Professor, tell me about what you know thus far." Petters had already spoken to the Professor briefly on the phone that afternoon but had chosen to travel to Tynesmore that evening to continue their conversation. He understood from the Professor the situation was not only grave, but a matter of national importance—not something that should be overheard by a switchboard operator. "I understand Ms. Mead and Mr. Rumple have already left for Scotland?"

"Yes," the Professor wiped the edges of his mouth carefully and placed his napkin back in his lap as he spoke. "They have gone to try to find Florence. We believe she is the next target. There were only five of us, and he has already killed two and maimed one." He winced as he shifted in his chair.

"Tell me, how do you think he found you all? Surely it wouldn't be a matter of public record—who made decisions on executions during the War?"

"There would have been some record of our meetings at Summerdyne, but quite right. Many details, such as our identities, would be classified."

"So this someone who is killing your group, or attempting to, is either part of the government apparatus and has a relatively high security clearance, or he is acting with information specifically supplied by someone in the that realm."

"Yes. I suppose that would be correct."

Petters mulled that over while he speared a large Brussels

sprout, smothered it in gravy and put it in his mouth. He chewed thoughtfully, glancing over at Jeremiah who had finished his plate of food and was sitting quietly with his hands in his lap.

"Son," Harry said, addressing Jeremiah again, having clearly noticed his empty plate and the speed with which the food on it had been devoured. "Please help me out and have some more supper. I really don't care for leftovers." He motioned with his chin towards the buffet. "And don't forget the dessert tray when you are finished. Some terribly unhealthy things there that really need to be finished up or I shall find them tonight at midnight and my waistline will pay for it. I am counting on you." Harry gave him stern look. Jeremiah leapt up, gleefully following his orders.

"Was there anyone in the agency, or in the intelligence service who had it in for you?" Petters was toying with a theory.

"I can't think of anyone. We were just doing the job assigned to us."

"Mmm, perhaps...anyone who was, how shall I put it..." Petters searched for the right words. "Scorned? Jilted? Passed over for promotion? A lover maybe, or a wife or husband angry about an illicit romance?"

"Are you suggesting that the killer is an active civil servant —someone still working within the government?" Harry was leaning back in his chair assessing the two men across the table.

"Not necessarily. It could be that the killer is angry about an execution and is being fed information by a civil servant. Someone who is still there, in the halls of Parliament, and has access to files. Either way, in order to find the killer we need to track the flow of intelligence."

"Or do as Lillie and Rumple are doing and find his next target, wait him out," Harry suggested.

"Perhaps, but he won't be easily caught. Whoever is doing

the killing is a professional. He operates with precision, and, with the exception of the Professor, he doesn't make mistakes. No, I should say a two-pronged approach may be our best bet. One arm tracks the killer by following his assumed target. The other tracks his information flow."

Harry and the Professor nodded.

"I hope Ms. Mead and Mr. Rumple know what they are getting themselves into," Petters carefully put his fork down while he fought the urge to lick his plate clean. "Had I known they were going to Scotland, I would have sent an officer with them."

"So do I," Harry said, furrowing his brow. "So do I."

13

THE HUNTER

STIRLING, SCOTLAND

The late afternoon light, infused with the gauze of mist and fog, descended quickly on the town of Stirling. Its elevated castle, as though painted with strokes of ashen blue, somehow served to soften the hills of the highlands beyond. It was a land of lakes, marshes, forests and mountains and the hunter was impressed by its rugged and impenetrable beauty.

The regional line chuffed slowly along the river Forth, a winding ribbon of partially frozen water the colour of midnight, and painstakingly wound itself past bare vegetation to the town's center.

The hunter thought for the first time in a long time about painting. He had once dabbled in oils, even creating a few admirable pieces, and the future of art was enticing. New. Pared down. Minimalist. Gone was the stuffy old Victorian methodology and the hunter celebrated the new visionary work of Kandinsky, O'Keefe, and Munch. Perhaps he would pick up a brush again when this was all over, he thought, committing the pleasing scene before him to memory. As stunning as this landscape was, however, he still looked forward to returning to America.

Stepping onto the platform, the hunter was surprised by the ferocity of the North Sea wind, its harsh hand a slap against his skin as it blew its way west along the river. The railway building was a small one story hut, its brick facade weathered by years of savage winters and parched summers. Rail stations, no matter where they were in the world, had a tendency to be unsightly, and this lack of attention to aesthetics always irritated the hunter. They were often the gateways to magnificent cities or charming towns yet they were so often overlooked by architects and planners.

Making his way towards King Street, the hunter's mood improved with the arresting visual of Stirling Castle. Perched precipitously on its hill, a watchful eye cast over the huddled winter town, its facade was illuminated by the setting sun. The castle and the highland hills beyond looked as a haystack would, the gradations as it climbed higher and higher reminding him of how insignificant they all were.

He would be noticed here. His accent, his way of dress, the way he carried himself. A different identity wouldn't be a bad idea, just in case he was being tracked. He was good with aliases: he could be French, German, or Russian with ease. He hadn't the general look for anything very colonial so he would stick with what he knew and what would be logical given his locale. He quietly ran a few words over his tongue, brushing up on his accents. He rolled his r's, he pursed his lips, he brought up guttural sounds from his diaphragm. Italian wasn't out of the question, he mused, nor was Spanish, and he enjoyed those accents. People here wouldn't like the Germans, so he abandoned that idea, deciding instead on French. That would be the safest, and although no one really cared for the French either— imagine charging the allies to use their railways during wartime—at least they were tolerated. Albeit sparingly and only for their cuisine.

The hunter was now frozen to the core and in need of supper and a warm drink. He put his case down on the cobble-stones, and rubbed his hands together in an attempt to feel his fingers again, wiggling his toes in his boots. The street ahead of him culminated in a clock tower and the road forked left and right on either side of it. To his immediate right was the chalky facade of The Golden Lion Hotel. This would be a good a spot as any to rest tonight and begin his inquiries. He picked up his case, thankful he didn't have to carry it much longer, and made his way to the front door.

The hunter's chosen pseudonym, Pierre Dumont, would be an agricultural attache to the French Government who had been sent to Scotland to research dairy cows. As such, he would need extensive information on farms in the area, some of which, of course, he would be visiting during his stay. It was a good cover, and he would only need it for a few days.

That would be enough time to find the needle he was searching for in this proverbial frozen haystack.

14

North Yorkshire, England

My Dearest Harry,

I am writing to you from the windy dales of North Yorkshire. I wonder at my own insanity taking a temporary job with this family. They may be well to do and own a frightfully large country home outside Easingwold but it is in dire need of funds, not to mention a roof, paint and stone mason who is permanently on staff to attend to all the crumbling blocks. The rooms are damp and cold, the cook they have brought with us seems intent on killing us with her food, and the children are unhappy at being taken away from their friends for a 'holiday'. A misnomer if I have ever heard one. It is far too cold here for anyone to spend much more than a few minutes outside so we are relegated to hovering around the fireplace in the drawing room, all five us, attempting polite conversation or reading any number of the dusty and outdated books

Lord Bracken has in his wanting library. So far I have found them as frightfully dull as he is.

I miss you, and Lillie, and Tynesmore in general. How is Lillie's move coming along? I just adore her new cottage and can't wait to see it blooming with wildflowers once this horrid weather turns warm.

I have given more thought to your proposal, and more specifically the timing of our wedding. I had hoped, I suppose, to be married in the spring, outside on a lawn under the blossoming trees, but the more I think of the way life goes I wonder why I want to wait? It doesn't matter when we get married, just that we *get* married. So please, let's set a date. Imminently. In fact, how does the beginning of March sound? You have plenty of flowers in your hot house so I know we can certainly adorn the church and I like your suggestion of hosting the reception at Tynesmore.

I have decided also that you were right when you proposed I quit my job as a governess. No more lonely locales with families I barely know and who don't appreciate me. I am ready to be a wife and mistress of your beautiful home. And, perhaps, I might try my hand at writing a romance novel. I know I shall never write anything earth shattering or world changing as our friend Lillie will do, but what is wrong with wanting to entertain just for the sheer pleasure of it?

Yours lovingly and forever,

Primrose

TYNESMORE, *Oxfordshire*

Darling Primrose,

I cannot tell you my exhilaration at receiving your letter. All at once the clouds lifted and the sky was the most majestic shade of blue and all the world seemed to be sunnier.

I cannot wait to marry you! And March sounds terrific. How

is the first of the month? Am I betraying my enthusiasm? It only gives us a few months to plan—find a caterer, book the church, harvest the greenhouse—but with my energy and your beautiful presence we can certainly have it all done in time. Incidentally, when do you return from that horrid country house? The Dales in winter? What is the family thinking?

In answer to your question, Lillie's move was somewhat interrupted. I will explain all when you arrive home but suffice it to say that duty calls and she has gone out of town for work.

Jack wasn't happy at having to return back to London either. But as you know, this country needs...well, a letter is hardly the place to reveal classified information now is it?

I await your arrival home with the utmost anticipation. As I await our happy life together forever.

Yours always,

Harry

TELEGRAM to STIRLING, Scotland

January 3, 1920

Aunt Mildred. As discussed, please meet the morning train from Oxford with a car. Rumple arriving 6:05 a.m. And save the date, March 1. I am getting married! Please let Rumple and Lillie know.

Your nephew, Harry

TELEGRAM to LONDON

January 3, 1920

Jack. Getting married March 1. Be my best man? With luck Rumple's situation will be resolved by then. They should be arriving Edinburgh by morning light. Have sent my aunt to collect them.

Harry

. . .

TELEGRAM

to Oxford

January 4, 1920

Dear Harry. My heartfelt congratulations on your impending nuptials. I shall be delighted to be your best man.

Jack

15

LILLIE

EDINBURGH, SCOTLAND

"She was always frightfully intelligent," Rumple said.

He was gathering up his things around the train car as he spoke about Florence Millicent-Marks. He picked up a book, some cologne, and a warm Russian style fur hat with ear covers that leaned towards the ridiculous. Lillie wondered if perhaps he held a torch for her, or had done once. The sun was making an appearance over the frost salted hills, giving a false promise that this day would be warmer than the last.

"She wasn't like other civil servants at the agency." He wound a clashing multicoloured scarf that looked as if it had been knitted by a colour-blind old woman around his neck before pulling on his overcoat. "She questioned everything. Why were we in the war? Who benefited from it? How should it be carried out? She was constantly quoting Thucydides, and hashing out the true foundations of Utilitarianism. Honestly, half the time I had no idea what she was going on about. She didn't mind being in hot water with the rest of us peons—me, the staffers, our superiors. Amazing she was never fired, now that I think of it." Rumple gazed out the window at the morning landscape as he did up his buttons. When he was finished most of the scarf was thankfully hidden beneath his collar.

The night had given way to a crisp and clear pink-tinged morning and Lillie could see the city of Edinburgh in the distance. Neither of them had slept a wink.

"Was she married? Children?"

"Not at that time, no. She was being courted by a staffer in the Prime Minister's office. I can't remember his name, but she never married him. Last I heard he was pining over her and she left to go back to Scotland. I didn't like him really, he was...oh I don't know, controlling, I guess, and more than a little narrow minded," he sighed, and smiled. "Florence wasn't a women who could be tamed. Not with that mind."

Not for the first time that week Lillie wondered how Rumple had gone from being on an important wartime committee to being Harry's manservant? Surely after the war he could have gone on to do almost anything else. She knew he had been in the Green family employ in one capacity or another prior to the outbreak of war, but to come back, after all he had seen, all he had done? In their letters Harry had once mentioned Rumple's erratic behaviour, something about a persistent rage to do with a seemingly innocuous situation— Lillie couldn't remember what, exactly—but she wondered now if he hadn't been affected in the way so many men had been after what they had seen and done. They were like ghosts, some of them, empty hollowed out shadows of men fighting demons in their dreams and the futility of everyday life while they were awake.

The train had slowed and wound itself carefully through the outskirts of the city.

"Will you recognize Harry's aunt Mildred?" Lillie asked, changing the subject.

"Oh yes. I haven't seen her in a few years but I doubt she has changed much."

"Have you got any other logistical information on Florence? Other than she is on a farm somewhere around Stirling?"

"She described it to me once. We were having a drink after work—a few actually..." Rumple smiled at the memory. "She spoke of a lake that she used to swim in when she was young, on the farm, Lindon or Lochdon, something or other. Also, it took some time to get to. It wasn't immediately near Stirling, but north-east of the city if I remember correctly. It's been a long time though, so I am hardly going to be a good navigator."

"He may not already be there, the killer. It's possible he is looking for you right now instead and we will have some time."

"If that is the case, he will be in for a fight. Harry has hired a very good security firm from London."

"Well, that is a relief anyway. Now, once we find Florence and warn her, do you expect to just wait for him? Trap him? We should notify the Scottish authorities, of course."

"Hmm," Rumple said, thinking. "In the army, we tended to just look after these things ourselves."

"Yes, well, we aren't in the army are we? We are in a civilian society and I think we should involve the police. It's a moot point anyway, I've no doubt Superintendent Petters has already called the Scottish authorities ahead of our arrival."

They fell into silence as the train entered the sleepy station. The few people waiting on the platform were bundled in hats and scarves and Lillie realized it would be even colder here than it was in Oxford. She shivered and pulled her gloves out of her pocket, wondering as she did if she wasn't quite recovered from the radiation poisoning she had experienced a month ago as a result of her last assignment.

"There she is." Rumple was pointing to a stout looking woman at the mouth of the platform.

Mildred looked every inch of her seventy years, but was strong and weathered. She wore sturdy hunting boots that engulfed her calves and a heavy oilskin coat. Her hat was pulled firmly down around her ears and she wore lined calfskin work gloves. Lillie could have almost mistaken her for a man if it wasn't for her height. At barely five feet tall, she should have looked much more frail than she actually did. Instead she gave the impression she could wrestle a bull if she had to. She was the complete opposite of the other members of Harry's family.

"Mildred!" Rumple called to her as they exited the train, waving his arms in an unusual display of exuberance.

She gave a hearty wave back and rushed forward to embrace Rumple. "Bloody train is late again. I wondered if you would ever arrive." She stood back to look at him.

Turning her attention to Lillie, she held out a gloved hand. "I'm Mildred, nice to meet you."

"Lillie Mead. I can't thank you enough for meeting us."

"Pleasure. It isn't often I get called into action. Now, car is out that way," she said, pointing briskly with her polished bamboo walking stick. "There is a hamper full of food, and plenty of blankets. I am ready to drive you wherever you need to go." She had already started walking and called back over her shoulder.

"Oh, and Harry is getting married I hear. Wanted you both to know the wedding is a little over seven weeks away! Better hope to heavens all this mess is finished by then because if I know my nephew, he will want all of our energies focused on him."

16

SUPERINTENDENT PETTERS

LONDON, ENGLAND

The War Offices were housed in a dignified, five story neo-baroque building on the corner of Horse Guards Avenue and Whitehall. Its stone-white facade was damp from the morning rain but its waterlogged walls did little to diminish its otherwise magnificent existence. It was a building that looked as though it could withstand even the most determined natural disaster.

The London morning air wasn't nearly as biting as that of Oxfordshire and Superintendent Petters revelled in the moderate marine mist that blanketed the noisy city, dampening the sounds of cars and hurried conversations.

He hadn't slept much the previous evening. Having dropped Jeremiah back at the orphanage after their supper at Tynesmore, Petters had returned home to pack a day bag and await the morning train to the city. He wasn't sure he was in the right place now, but he figured he had to start somewhere, and the Committee of Imperial Defence seemed as good a place as any. Their role during the war had primarily been dealing with foreign espionage and while D.O.R.A. had many tenets, the one he was interested in had to do with the eleven executions at the Tower of London.

"Mr. Tupper will see you now." An ageing secretary interrupted Petters's thoughts and he got up to follow her down a long, brightly lit arched corridor. They went past throngs of identical offices, each of their doors painted in a glossy red finish, the larger offices walled with opaque water glass through which he could see only shadows. It was a grand, stately building and Petters imagined what it must have felt like during the four perilous years they were at war with Germany —what these walls must have witnessed as a hub of wartime government activity.

The secretary showed him into a small office off the main corridor and as they entered, a tall, thin man in a grey Savile Row suit got up from behind a bulky wood desk and came around to shake his hand. His shoes were impeccably polished, his hair pushed back with the just the right amount of pomade. He held out a perfectly manicured hand.

"Charles Tupper, pleased to meet you."

Surprisingly, he had a handshake that could crack granite. Petters winced involuntarily and silently reprimanded himself for judging a book by its cover.

"Superintendent Petters, Oxfordshire Constabulary." He was thankful the feeling was coming back into his hand. "Thank you for taking the time to meet with me."

"Not at all. What can I do for you, Superintendent? My secretary told me it has something to do with one of our wartime committees?" Tupper sat back down and clasped his hands together on his desk. His heavy French-paste cufflinks clinked the top of the desk as he leaned forward.

Tupper's physical presentation caused Petters to be acutely aware of his own ill-fitting uniform. He wished he had taken the time to brush his coat. He caught sight of a thatch of white cat hair on his lapel and realized the strays he had been feeding that morning must be becoming less and less feral if they were now leaving their hair on his clothing. This thought pleased him to no end.

Realizing he had once again become distracted by the thought of animals, Petters re-focused his attention on the matter at hand. He looked long and hard at the chair he was meant to sit in and found he was relieved that it wasn't upholstered—nothing retained odour and germs like fabric did. He reflected briefly on his aversion to human as opposed to animal filth—the latter of which he did not mind in the least.

Sitting down he carefully placed his briefcase in his lap and pulled out a file folder. He slid it across the desk towards Tupper.

"We've had two murders in North Oxfordshire over the past month and a third attempted murder. All three victims worked together on the same committee during the war." Petters snapped the briefcase shut and decided to keep it in his lap. For all the grandeur of the building, the floor looked as though in hadn't been cleaned in some time.

"Oh?" Tupper had the file open and was glancing through the pages as Petters spoke. "Which committee was it?"

"It was under the auspices of D.O.R.A. An oversight committee responsible for the final review of German spies apprehended in England. Essentially, they decided whether a jailed spy would live and be useful or be executed at the Tower."

Petters watched as the man peered closer at the pages in the file.

"Did it have a name, this committee?"

"Nothing official, but its participants referred to themselves as 'Summerdyne' after a house that was requisitioned for the war and which they made use of for their meetings."

"Mm. Haven't heard of it but there must be a record of it

somewhere." Tupper was turning the picture he held in his hand this way and that in attempt to see something. "And what is this?" Petters didn't have to look to see what it was.

"The initials S.D. Our killer writes them on the victims' hands."

"Ach," Tupper said, pushing the photo with timidity back towards Petters. "A little morbid isn't it?"

In spite of his handshake, Tupper was in all likelihood more of a paper pusher than a soldier. He was a bit of dandy and had probably practiced that handshake over and over again in order to make himself appear more like one of the boys.

"Indeed."

Tupper was trying to recover his composure as he neatly put all the papers back into the file and pushed it, in addition to the photo, across the desk.

"Just because I haven't heard of it myself doesn't mean someone doesn't know of it. I do know that Basil Wilkinson was the man responsible for rounding up many of these foreign spies, so I would suggest you try him first. He was the assistant Commissioner of Crime during the war but they promoted him to Director of Intelligence last year. You can find him at Scotland House, in Westminster. In all likelihood, he would have been coordinating with your committee on a daily basis during the war."

"Thank you, I'll do that. I appreciate your time."

Petters gave Tupper an efficient nod and stood up, transferring his briefcase into his right hand. There wasn't a chance he would be caught unawares in a handshake with this charlatan again.

"Oh and Superintendent..." Tupper called after him, "between you, me and the wall, mind your step with Wilkinson. He doesn't like to have his authority questioned—*by anyone.*" Tupper gave him a hard stare, ensuring Petters understood him.

"Thanks, I'll keep that in mind."

If there was one thing Petters didn't like in a person, it was an unbridled, non-discretionary assumption that he was able to do as he wished regardless of legal checks and balances.

He should enjoy meeting this Mr. Wilkinson, if only to remind him of what it meant to be a civil servant.

17

THE HUNTER

STIRLING, SCOTLAND

"**S**eems odd they'd send you here in the dead of winter."
It was a good point the hotel keeper made, and it vexed the hunter that he hadn't anticipated it.

Buying himself some time to reply, he glanced around the lobby at the makeshift breakfast room and found he was distracted by the mouthwatering scents of smoky steeped tea and fresh bread. It took a few seconds for him to reluctantly refocus his attention on the vaguely disgusting hotelier behind the reception desk. He was a fat man and had a face that was the most unnatural shade of red. Purple spider veins criss-crossed his cheeks and nose like a road map; he was balding slightly, he smelled of last night's liquor, and he didn't appear to change his clothes very often.

The hunter let his eyes crinkle with the forced smile he now painted on his lips. Adjusting the wire-rimmed glasses he did not need to wear, he thought carefully before he spoke.

"Oui, yes, it is strange timing I would agree. However our ministry is so terribly busy during the spring and summer that we must conduct much of our research during the winter," he drew out the word 'terribly' as he knew a Frenchman would do.

"Of course it isn't nearly as cold in France as it is here right now."

Although it pained him to do so, he gave the man a jovial wink for good measure and wondered fleetingly if he should kill him.

The hotel keeper shrugged and retrieved a map from a glass cabinet behind him. A nauseating waft of cigarette smoke filled the air as he did so.

"Here's where you would find the feed store." The hotelier pointed with a plump and dirty index finger. "About a ten minute walk or so from here."

The hunter nodded.

"They'll be able to tell you what farms in the area are in dairy cows, and those that are beef. Will be able to give you an overview of farming in general, for these parts, so it isn't a bad place to start your forays. How long do you intend to stay?"

The hunter put on his cap and smiled. He already knew of the three local dairy farms from his research in Edinburgh but didn't want to seem overly competent. He only needed to narrow things down a little.

"Only two days, not long. After this I am on to Ireland and then to the continent. I still need to see Switzerland and Belgium before I head back to Paris." He was making up everything as he went but by the suitably impressed look on the hotelier's face his cover was terribly convincing.

"I see, still seems like an awful time of year to go looking at cows."

The hunter nodded his benign agreement. He asked his next question carefully.

"I understand there was quite a successful dairy farm in the area, but the man who used to own it passed away and left it to his daughter to run. Millicent-Marks was his name I believe? Raised an enormously successful herd of Ayrshires, something we don't have in France. I am especially interested in that particular breed." The hunter had no idea if France had Ayrshires or not and was betting the hotelier wouldn't either. "I wouldn't mind starting there, if you know where I could find it?"

The stupid man had no inkling of anything untoward when he answered. "Oh, yes, of course—Alastair's place. Well, it's a bit of a walk, but if you can find a ride it would only take about ten or fifteen minutes by car." He smoothed the map on the counter and used the tip of his pencil to trace the route.

Listening to the scrape of lead on the paper, the hunter couldn't believe his luck. By tea time he should be finished his number three job and on his way back to Oxfordshire. He accepted the map with thanks and began his journey by hailing a taxi outside the hotel.

Giving the driver directions, the hunter sat back in his seat and wondered if he shouldn't have brought his belongings with him. If things went according to plan, stopping back at the hotel on his way to the train station would be an inconvenience. Of course that would be only a very small irritation on an otherwise perfect day so he supposed he shouldn't mind too much.

The town of Stirling soon gave way to fields and streams and thickets of forest and the road narrowed, its surface becoming holed and rough. The hunter sighed, wishing he could go home. He longed for a real city and all the amenities it provided. Good food, nice hotels. Pavement...

The taxi turned off the main road and onto a long fenced drive whose surface was even more uneven than the road they had just left. This must be it, the hunter thought, and he silently practiced his cover as the car ambled along slowly, eventually pulling up in front of a large two story barn.

"Here we are." The driver swivelled in his seat, craning his neck to look back at the hunter who was already reaching for the money in his pocket. He would return to town on foot. It was a risk having a witness and he wondered if he wasn't being foolish for taking a taxi in the first place. As with everything, the hunter calculated the risk—time to the farm versus giving his target an opportunity to escape—it was a necessary risk.

"Thank you," he said, paying the man and exiting the car. It drove away the way it had come, spitting and crunching along the frozen drive, leaving the hunter to his thoughts.

Standing in the open, he had a good look around to get his bearings. It didn't appear as though anyone had noticed the car pull up. A stone farmhouse could be seen in the distance, a small swirl of smoke escaped through the chimney and he wondered if he was being watched from any one of its dark windows. He would search around the barn first, he thought, and turned on his heel in the direction of its big sagging double doors.

"Hello." The voice was to the left rear of where he stood.

The hunter was startled—he had thought he was alone. He turned around to find himself face to face with a young farmhand. He sized him up quickly—mid to late twenties, stocky build, mousy hair that hadn't been combed in some time, a hole in his left boot although his coat appeared new.

"Oh! You surprised me." The hunter hadn't forgotten his accent and now played it with perfection.

"What do you want?" It was abrupt—not unfriendly, but not welcoming either.

The hunter, speech at the ready, stepped forward to shake the man's hand, realizing too late it wasn't offered. The farmhand stepped back, putting a wary distance between them, and the hunter dropped his hand awkwardly to his side.

This man was odd somehow. It wasn't just the abrupt way he spoke, but his eyes darted this way and that, hesitant and fleeting, never meeting his own.

"I am part of a committee here from France investigating dairy farms and I hoped to meet with the farm owner."

The farm hand twitched his shoulders in an odd and unpleasant manner. Still he didn't look at the hunter.

"Cows." He said bluntly after a moment.

"That's correct, dairy cows specifically." The hunter replied and searched the farm hand's face for some semblance of acceptance. He found none. Instead the man looked down and kicked at the frozen ground with his boot, stopping every few seconds to examine the hole over his left toe.

"You are French?" he asked, finally, still kicking at the snow and ice.

"Yes."

"You aren't." The kicking stopped suddenly, and with finality.

"Pardon me?" The conversation was becoming disconcerting and the hunter felt the tingling sensation of doubt seeping up through his spine and into his face. It felt hot against the crisp air. Was he being caught out?

"You aren't French. I can tell."

"Well..." The hunter stalled, searching for an answer that for now seemed elusive.

"French people pronounce their vowels more. You don't do that."

Initially, the man had appeared to be a simpleton, but the hunter was quickly realizing that while he was socially awkward, he was, regretfully, as sharp as a hawk.

"I travel quite a lot, perhaps I have lost some of my 'Frenchness'." The hunter smiled. His thoughts were whirling now. He could possibly attack the man, but as they were standing out in the open and he didn't know if anyone was watching from the farmhouse, it was too risky a move for a situation he hadn't properly assessed.

"No. I don't think that is it."

The farmhand was backing away now and the hunter feared he would start to run. He hadn't encountered this type of situation before and it perplexed him. He had great conviction in the stupidity of the human race, but this seemingly simple man was a great deal more complex than he appeared.

"Perhaps I should return when the farm owner is available?" the hunter asked, attempting to stop the man.

The farm hand didn't answer. He had put at least forty feet between them now and the hunter realized he would have to run and tackle him if he was to stop him. It was no good. He would have to come back another time. Sometimes retreat was the only option.

"Well, good day—I will begin with a tour somewhere else and try again another time. Could you tell me where I might find the Ballymeade Farm?" He was thankful he remembered one of the names from the directory in Edinburgh, although whether it was in dairy cows or beef escaped him.

The farmhand shook his head and turned towards the house, moving quicker than the hunter had anticipated he could. It was a good thing he hadn't tried to stop him, for he likely would not have caught him.

Turning on his heel, the hunter wrapped his scarf around his face and started back down the long driveway to the main road. He didn't really plan on leaving. He would circle back and hide out in the barn, using it as an observation point.

And then, as soon as Florence Millicent-Marks revealed herself, he would kill her.

18

LILLIE

THE SCOTTISH COUNTRYSIDE

Aunt Mildred drove like she was on course at Brooklands Motor Circuit. Her sturdy car leaned heavily into the corners as she accelerated into the apex of her turns, its whining engine at full throttle, its protests vehemently ignored. Rumple was holding on to a leather strap suspended from the ceiling in an attempt to steady himself and Lillie had pushed her body back into her seat as far as it would go, her legs and back clenched against the swaying of the car. She was beginning to feel motion sick and rolled down her window in an attempt to stop herself from vomiting as Mildred accelerated again down the bumpy road at an unnatural speed.

Lillie's thoughts drifted back to her row with Jack the previous evening. With the long train ride and lack of sleep, she had spent much of the trip fretting about their recent reunion and what it meant for their careers. He, it seemed, planned to carry on as though it were business as usual. His work in the intelligence department wouldn't change—long nights, covert travel, treacherous missions, and an avalanche of secrets would stamp their lives. She, presumably, would continue to work for the newspaper and that would be fine with him so long as the stories she worked on weren't dangerous.

Never mind that she was lead crime reporter. Of course there was the possibility of danger!

"Won't be long now," Aunt Mildred called back to her, hollering over the rush of wind.

Lillie nodded, attempting to bring her thoughts back to the present, a fresh wave of nausea engulfing her as she breathed in the cold air from outside. Aunt Mildred couldn't have been more different than the rest of Harry's family. Lillie questioned whether she could even be related to the upper class, buttoned down, snobbery of Mr. and Mrs. Green. Harry, granted, was a bit of a rogue himself, but still, in manner and presentation, he was the polar opposite of Mildred.

"There's a supply store not far out of Stirling," she continued, taking her eyes off the road to look at Lillie. "Services all the farms in the area. We will stop there first and get our bearings. They will know the Millicent-Marks farm, I'm sure of it."

Lillie nodded again, not daring to speak. She was fearful if she did, she might be sick all over the seat.

The small town of Stirling appeared in the distance and soon they had circumvented it and were heading north into the country. Cottages and stores shortly gave way to rolling farmland, the highland hills looming in the distance as though painted on a canvas. It was a startling landscape and one unique from that of anywhere she had ever seen. The wild ruggedness of its melancholy setting reminded Lillie of why the Scots were so fiercely independent. Even the sky seemed to protest the intrusion of foreigners, its blue hue blackened with the threat of rain, wind and resistance.

Barely reducing her speed, Aunt Mildred turned abruptly off the main road into the lot of the feed store. The car came to a screeching halt inches from a new tractor that was parked to the left of the front door. Lillie breathed a sigh of relief and watched in amusement as Rumple carefully extracted his hand from the leather strap.

Pushing open the door of the car, she was met with the blissful rush of fresh cold winter air. She felt instantly better with two feet on the ground.

"I'll get directions," she announced to a rather green-looking Rumple, who nodded his tacit agreement.

Mildred hopped out of the car to follow her, looking as sprightly as a gazelle. "I'll join you. Could use a stretch."

Lillie nodded. Other than her driving, Aunt Mildred was proving to be a nice addition to their little group.

"With any luck, we will be there soon and find Florence as safe as a diamond in a vault."

"I certainly hope so, my dear," Mildred agreed.

Lillie pushed through the door of the feed store, ready to embark on their journey into uncharted territory.

19

SUPERINTENDENT PETTERS

London, England

"I am sorry you didn't call before you came, Superintendent. Mr. Wilkinson isn't in the office this week. He has taken some of his holiday time."

Superintendent Petters was trying, with some difficulty, to keep his face neutral as he felt the heat of frustration creep up the back of his neck. What a waste of a day this was turning out to be.

"When do you expect him back?"

"Not for another week."

"Do you know where he went?"

"I'm sorry sir, I really couldn't say."

Of course not, that would be unprofessional. But it was worth a try.

"Very good, here is my card. Please have him call me upon his return." Petters gave the woman a false smile and turned to leave the reception desk.

He remembered something as he reached the door and turned back around to face her. As he did so he thought he caught the briefest whiff of nervousness on her face but she recovered her composure so quickly that he must have imagined it. "Incidentally, when did Mr. Wilkinson leave for his holiday?"

"Three days ago, sir."

"I see." Petters was hesitating, wondering if there was any way for him to coerce the receptionist into revealing anything more about Wilkinson's whereabouts.

Three days ago he had two bodies and an assault on the Professor. A lot could happen in three days. He looked around the sparsely furnished office and decided it would be best to come back another time. Intimidating the man's receptionist was hardly worth the effort.

"Good day." Petters tipped his hat and started the long trek back to Chipping Norton.

20

THE HUNTER

THE MILLICENT-MARKS FARM, SCOTLAND

The inside of the dairy barn smelled of clover and manure infused earth. The milking stations were prepared for the evening with fresh alfalfa in the mangers and a new layer of straw the colour of burnished brass on the floor. Presumably this had been the farmhand's doing prior to his interruption. The barn was large, with fifteen stalls aside and an open area likely used for sheltering most of the herd at one far end.

The hunter hurried down the aisle way, brushing his fingers along the cold metal of empty galvanized jugs, each lined up at attention, ready for their next filling. Various hoses were hung from hooks placed strategically between stations and the hunter noticed a rudimentary looking machine with an assortment of different sized hoses attached at the end of the aisle on a rolling metal cart.

He wondered what time the cows came in and hoped he could find somewhere to watch the house without being watched himself. The higher the better, he thought, remembering his marksman training in the early war years, and located a wooden ladder situated under a hay drop in the ceiling. He scuttled up it and emerged into a long low loft with exposed rafters and shuttered vents at either end. A field mouse scampered across his path and the hunter stifled a sneeze. He'd always despised allergies in a person, and now felt irritated that he himself might be the one falling prey to hay fever. This knowledge did little to improve his mood.

The sound of a car traveling down the gravel drive interrupted his thoughts and he rushed to the far end of the loft to watch it through one of the vents. It approached the barn at a startling clip and then carried on past the courtyard and towards the farmhouse gathering speed until it finally drew up, with some notable skidding, in front. Had the ground not been so frozen the hunter imagined it would have been swallowed in a cloud of dust.

Three people emerged and the hunter examined them as a scientist would an amoeba. A middle aged man who looked vaguely military, an older woman built like an oak stump, and a younger woman who moved as gracefully as dancer. For a moment he held his breath as he watched her in particular. Even from this distance she was peculiarly enthralling to him.

The front door of the farmhouse was opened by the not-so-simple farmhand. He could see the man was still wearing his boots and coat. The three visitors were soon out of his sight, swallowed up by the chimney smoke and stone facade.

Who were they, he wondered? Friends? Acquaintances? Enemies of his? Whoever they were, they were becoming increasingly likely to be collateral damage.

He let out a long sigh, releasing the tension of the day and clearing his head. He cracked each of his knuckles, slowly and methodically. Although he regretted killing bystanders, some things were unavoidable.

21

SUPERINTENDENT PETTERS

WOODSTOCK, ENGLAND

The afternoon sun was waning, as a candle nearing its end, flickering its still brilliant bursts shorter and shorter as the impeding dusk crept. The small market town of Woodstock was glowing, its limestone facades soft against the winter landscape, paying homage to the coziness of village life.

Petters parked his small car about a block away from the pub and started walking along the sidewalk. As he walked he noticed two things. The first was that he appeared to be being followed by a woman in a dark emerald coat. The second was a small tree sparrow on the road, attempting to hop out of the way of oncoming traffic. Petters was not one to leave an injured bird to fare for himself, so he darted into the road and scooped him up. The little bird had a crooked wing, which was obviously hindering its ability to fly, so Petters decided to head back to his car to retrieve a small crate he had in the boot that he often used for carrying extra clothing. He noticed the woman following him was now pretending to browse in a store window across the street.

Placing the bird atop an old wool sweater, he decided it

would be better to keep the animal with him rather than leave him in a cold car, so he covered the crate with an extra piece of clothing and made his way towards the pub. Perhaps he could trouble the bartender for a bit of water and some grain.

The woman also resumed her position, approximately forty feet behind him. A classic tail. Superintendent Felix Petters carefully shifted the small box he carried under his arm and felt a soft flutter come from inside.

He had driven to Woodstock after arriving home in Chipping Norton that afternoon, frustrated and exhausted after his visit to London. He hadn't felt like making the drive to Woodstock but Professor Hargreaves had requested he meet him at the Blenheim Public House. He said he had the information Petters had requested on the executions approved by the Summerdyne Committee. His objective in London had been simple: to try and find the ringleader of the whole damn circus. He had hoped meeting Basil Wilkinson would give some clarity to the mess surrounding him but all his visit did was complicate things. Wilkinson's absence during the time of the murders in North Oxfordshire muddied the waters.

Glancing behind him one last time he entered the pub, its warm air smelling of hops and vinegar—or was it dirty feet? He couldn't tell. Professor Hargreaves was already there, sequestered at a small table for two, away from the pub's regulars. Petters took a seat from a neighbouring table to place the crate on, then sat down facing the Professor. His tail didn't enter the pub but instead cruised past the front door, glancing in a little too interestedly, and then carrying on. Petters wondered if he had somehow ruffled a few feathers in London.

Hargreaves raised his eyebrows at the crate and Petters nodded at him.

"Injured bird. He'll be all right. What have you got?"

The Professor leaned in so he wouldn't be overheard. "A list of the eleven executions between November 1914 and April 1916."

He pushed a folded list of paper towards Petters.

"What will you have?" The bartender was standing before them, wiping his hands on an apron that had seen better days.

"A pint please. And some bread and water if you can."

"Butter?"

"No thanks."

The bartender retreated and came back a few minutes later with the order.

Petters took a long hard sip of his beer, then broke pieces off the bread and put them inside the crate along with a spoonful of water. He unfolded the paper and read through the list of names and dates:

Lody 1914
Muller 1915
Otway 1915
Janssen 1915
Weber 1915
Roggin 1915
Buschman 1915
Fischer 1915
Ries 1915
Meyer 1915
Zender 1916.

Taking another sip of beer, he looked hard at the Professor. "Pretty much all but two were in 1915. Speaks more to public hysteria than truth, don't you think?"

The Professor nodded grimly.

"Is it possible that any of the eleven were not German spies?"

"Yes, very possible."

"Can you tell me which cases were not cut and dried? Cases

where the evidence of spying for the Germans was... circumstantial, let's say, or even better, inconclusive?"

Professor Hargreaves let out a long sigh, thinking about it for a moment before answering. "I would certainly ask both Rumple and Florence their opinions on that, especially Florence, as she was the most critical of the program. There was a considerable amount of tension at the time, even between Florence and the five of us on the inside. But certainly the first was problematic—Carl Lody. Although I *am* convinced he was spying for the Germans, it was more of a legal conundrum. D.O.R.A. at that point didn't have the authority to execute anyone. Apprehend, yes, imprison yes, but not kill. So Lody was tried and executed illegally, really. But he was made an example of, a cog in the wartime propaganda machine. Eventually D.O.R.A. was amended so subsequent executions were legally permitted under the act. But I suppose there could be aggrieved relatives of Lody's out there, or some rogue protester angry with the wartime actions of our committee."

"Anyone else?"

"Muller and Otway posed as cigar importers, but there was some evidence to support their affiliation with the German Secret Service, albeit, as you say, possibly inconclusive— although I still believe we were in the right with prosecuting them. Weber was absolutely a spy, no doubt about it, so nothing of interest there. Janssen was followed long enough throughout 1915 to ascertain that he too was spying for the Germans. Buschman's Achilles heel was his constant need for money, and his correspondence was traced all the way back to the German military attache Colonel Osterdat. He was a musician, sadly, and a very good one. His last request was for his violin and he played pieces from La Boheme in his cell the night before his execution. That one, in particular, haunts me, but I suppose his talent for the arts was what I find such a waste..." The Professor paused, clearly having difficulty reliving it all.

"Which leaves the last four."

"Hm." The Professor seemed miles away. "Yes. Georg Fischer was an interesting case. He partnered with a German woman living in England at the time and the two of them were followed extensively by one of our counter-espionage teams. They used to ride horses through the city as a cover, seemingly in love." The Professor smirked at the memory. "Eventually he was discovered passing information to the Germans via invisible ink on a newspaper about artillery movements near Swanage, and we had him. The woman was also tried, but only got ten years."

"So she is still incarcerated. It can't then be her."

The Professor nodded his agreement. "Unless she hired someone to do it for her." He drained his beer, and signalled for another. Petters took the opportunity to peek in at the sparrow and was relieved to find it pecking away at the bits of bread he had given it.

"Probably the easiest trial was that of Irving Guy Ries. Didn't grab any headlines, was pretty straightforward. American born, was found forging a passport on his way to Copenhagen or something or other. We thought initially the Americans would try to extradite him, but they didn't seem to want to touch him. Turns out Ries was an alias but he refused to reveal his real name to us, citing his connections at home in America. It was odd, granted, but I don't think he ever realized the grave danger he was in. He was communicating with a spy by the name of N.M. Cleton in Rotterdam, but I never really believed Ries himself was part of the German network. Spies can have many trades, and I believed this Cleton dabbled in all sorts of things. Ries could have been discussing things other than the German war effort with him. Anyway, that one does sit with me as, well...unsubstantiated."

Petters was making notes by each name on the paper as the

Professor spoke. He looked up at him pen poised. "And Meyer and Zender?"

"Meyer was guilty, with overwhelming evidence to support. Zender's case was less clear. He was a Peruvian and claimed to be a salesperson sent to buy sardines in England, handkerchiefs in Scotland, and steel from Sheffield. It was the wrong time of year for sardines so that seemed to be all the arresting authorities needed. I am not sure why we all agreed on that one. We needed a majority of the five to convict and we were unanimous on him." Professor Hargreaves shook his head as though trying to jog his memory.

Petters sat back and reviewed his notes. "So, that's Lody, Muller, Roos, Ries, and Zender. All inconclusive cases, all possible leads."

The Professor nodded. "I would omit Muller and Roos though, at least to start. The more I review their cases the more I think they were guilty."

"So, it's down to Lody, Ries and Zender then. Tell, me, did your path ever cross with Basil Wilkinson? I understand he played a key role in arresting many of your suspects."

The Professor shifted uneasily in his chair. "Yes. He was head of the Criminal Investigations Department throughout the war," he said, his face clouding over. "He was, oh how shall I put it...a self-aggrandizing, highly conservative anti-semite. Fashioned himself a *spy-catcher*, and wasn't quick to ever give anyone else credit for anything. He wanted all the glory for himself. Not an easy man to work with, I can tell you now."

Petters couldn't help but notice the Professor wasn't making eye contact.

"Mm. Thank you Professor. This has been helpful. Any word from Rumple or Lillie?"

"Not yet, no. They would be in Scotland by now though, and very likely Stirling." The Professor put some money down on the table. "This is on me."

Petters nodded his thanks and got up, carefully lifting the crate and putting it under his arm.

"I'll be in touch. In the meantime, you better stick close to Tynesmore. Until we know who we are looking for, I am fairly certain you are still in danger. Incidentally, should you even be travelling?" Petters noticed the Professor was having great difficulty getting up and he reached out to support his forearm while he struggled. No doubt his ribs were shattered.

"Probably not," he winced. "Good luck with your bird, Superintendent."

22

LILLIE

THE MILLICENT-MARKS FARM, SCOTLAND

Lillie thought that it was likely the type of house where one doesn't remove their boots—regardless of where they have last been. The wide planked floors, suffering through decades of dirt and hay and gravel, displayed the worn etchings of generations of Millicent-Marks feet scuffing across it.

The wood creaked now under the feet of the man who had opened the door, and who also, incidentally, happened to be pointing a rifle at them. He was strong, stout man who wasn't very old, and although his rifle was aimed perfectly at their heads, his eyes had an unsettling way of looking everywhere except directly at them.

It was freezing on the doorstep. The wind had picked up and it swirled bits of leftover, long-past autumn leaves around them in tight circles. Lillie couldn't feel her nose, she realized, nor her hands, and the thought of walking through that gun was a great deal more appealing than standing out here in the cold. She wondered how serious he was about shooting them should they move.

"Stuart!" A woman's voice called from somewhere in the

house, although Lillie couldn't see anyone from where they were standing. "For God's sake, put that goddamn rifle down."

She heard a rustling sound, a succession of quick footsteps, and then saw Rumple's face break into a smile. Despite being not more than six inches from the end of a rifle, she couldn't remember ever seeing him so pleased.

"Theodore? Oh! It is you." The voice was closer and louder now. It was the voice of a woman in complete control, surprised but self-assured and confident.

"Florence. How long has it been?" His voice was softer than it usually was. Perhaps his throat was frozen, Lillie thought miserably.

"Too long. What on earth are you doing here?" The woman was now in her sights and Lillie could see why Rumple would be so enamoured.

Florence Millicent-Marks was neither a short nor an overly tall woman. She was barely approaching middle age, had the kind of translucent ivory skin unassociated with years of farming, deep red hair which was pulled back into a neat but loose bun atop her head, and wide blue eyes which were framed by soft grey metal glasses.

"Please, please come in." She pushed Stuart's rifle to the side as she would a curtain and rushed forward to clasp Rumple's outstretched hand.

"May I introduce you to Lillie Mead and Mildred Green....my...companions." He made it sound as though he had a harem. Lillie chalked it up to nervousness on his part.

"Pleasure to meet you, Florence," Lillie said, stepping forward to shake her hand.

"Come in please, it's freezing out there. Stuart, would you *please* put that horrid thing away," she said, then smiled at Lillie and Mildred. "My charming brother is slightly edgy today, but never mind."

Florence led them through the small house, past a kitchen

that smelled of soup and baking, and into a medium sized sitting room that housed two black and white border collies snoozing in front of a roaring fireplace. It was the first time Lillie had been warm all day.

"I'll put the kettle on. Make yourselves at home."

Lillie looked around at the room as she removed her gloves. Two armchairs were situated close to the fireplace. Between them was a small side table with a lamp and on it lay a pile of books, marked and open, awaiting their absent reader. The walls were lined with low slung, overflowing bookshelves, and a large and inviting sofa clothed in worn olive tweed was situated under a row of leaded glass windows that looked out over frosted hills. An enormous herd of lumbering cows were but pinpricks on the dusty horizon. It was a pleasant room, not grand, but well appointed and comfortably used.

The three of them sat down and Florence was back in a few minutes with a tray of tea and some of the baking Lillie had smelled. Her gun wielding brother was nowhere to be seen.

She placed the tray on an ancient sideboard and began to pour, giving them a acerbic smile as she did so. "So....tell me, were you just in the neighbourhood and decided to pay me a visit? Milk, sugar?"

"Both, please," Lillie answered and Mildred also nodded.

She handed Lillie and Mildred each a cup and set pouring a third. "I remember how you like yours, Theodore."

When Florence was finished she placed a plate of steaming biscuits on the side table and sat down with her own tea. She was dressed in a simple but elegant navy blue pantsuit, a choice of dress that was quite at odds with farm life, and it hung from her slim figure as though it had been tailored for her exactly. She looked back and forth between them, obviously waiting for a reply.

"Hadn't you heard then?" Rumple was treading lightly.

"Heard what? I don't like the look on your face, Theodore. What is going on?"

"Patrick and Reginald have been murdered."

Her face fell. "Oh, no, they never were...."

"Just a few days apart. The police think it was the same murderer for both. But not only that, Professor Hargreaves was attacked in his home recently—we believe by the same man."

"Which would mean, of course..." Florence seemed to be going where Rumple wanted to lead her.

"That we are all targets, yes. All five of us."

"Well." Florence inhaled an enormous breath. "I am hardly surprised."

"Now..." Rumple began, but Florence firmly interrupted him.

"No. Theodore, you know my opinions better than anyone. Everything we were doing at Summerdyne—the fate we were bestowing on those souls. We had no right. No right at all. Playing God like that. It's no wonder. King and Country and all that rubbish, *really*, I ask you, what was it all for? Nothing changed, only that every single family I know lost a son, or a father. It was a vile disgrace, a waste."

"Which presumably was why you left early." Rumple's matter of fact statement surprised Lillie. Why had Florence left service before the others?

"I couldn't take it anymore. And let's face it—the establishment couldn't take me. They pushed me out as much as I decided to leave."

Lillie interjected. "So you didn't work with the Summerdyne committee through the end of the war?"

"No, I left in 1916. I had a number of issues that caused my early departure. My father died and I couldn't leave the running of the farm entirely to my brother. Stuart is—well, you met him—a little different in some ways. But the nature of the work wasn't what I had signed up for, or rather, it became of a nature that I didn't agree with. And, well, there were other reasons also. Personal reasons."

"Such as what was his name? In the PM's office?" Rumple asked gently.

"Yes, such as him."

"A boyfriend?" Lillie asked.

"Not quite. He wanted to be, but I never really thought of him that way, and the longer we worked together the worse it became."

"Meaning he was making life difficult for you?" Lillie prodded.

"Yes, that is a fair assessment. He had a lot of power at that time, and people didn't really say no to him. And, he was married, of course, as they so often are. It was an impossible situation, so when my father died, I took it as an opportunity to escape. In hindsight, I suppose I might have stuck it out, though, since Prime Minister Asquith and his personal staff were all gone by the end of that same year anyway."

"Do you know where he is now? Did he stay in government?"

"I really couldn't say. I never kept in touch, as you can well imagine. I will say this though—he was a nasty man, something that became increasingly clear the better I got to know him.. The Prime Minister had no idea of his treacherous personality, but I certainly saw it."

Lillie realized she was drumming her fingers on the side table, a nervous habit she had when she was thinking, and stopped.

Rumple placed his empty teacup on its saucer with a clink. "Have you noticed anything strange around the farm, or has there been anything out of the ordinary?"

"Not really. Although Stuart complained of some man who was posing as a French agricultural attache snooping around this afternoon, asking to speak to the owner of the farm.

Which, incidentally, is why he was so jumpy when he answered the door. But he tends to go off on tangents from time to time."

"Why 'posing,' did Stuart say?" Lillie was intrigued.

Florence seemed to think carefully about this. "He is so silly. He said his accent was fake. How he would know that I've no idea, but one thing about Stuart: he may appear uncomplicated, but he knows the most obscure bits of information. When he gets his teeth into something he is usually right." She took a sip of tea. "I suppose I shouldn't dismiss it out of hand—perhaps there is something in it."

The sun was making its departure outside the leaded glass windows and Scotland was beginning to take on the cold pinkish-blue glow of dusk. Lillie noticed with some alarm that snowflakes had begun to fall outside the window and wondered about the ability of Mildred's car to navigate what would surely now be a slippery road. That, coupled with her reckless driving, was enough to cause Lillie a great deal of concern. Mildred, Rumple and Lillie looked at each other across the room, their eyes speaking silent volumes.

None of them said out loud the question that was on all their minds as they processed what Florence had just said.

Was their killer already here?

23

THE HUNTER

THE MILLICENT-MARKS FARM, SCOTLAND

T he hunter was getting annoyed. He had been in the loft for the better part of two hours—his body pressed against dusty bales of hay, rodents scurrying around his feet, his eyes watering, his sneezes carefully aborted —while the three that had arrived in the car did God knows what inside the farmhouse. If he had a large explosive, he would just blow the whole house up and be done with it.

What were they there for? Were they local folks? They certainly didn't look it. Had they come to tell her of the murders? He shifted and got a strong whiff of manure. Of all the occupations the hunter could have ended up in, he was relieved dairy farming was not one of them. He disliked wearing rags for clothes, the permanent stench of dung ingrained into their rough fabric. He was cut out for much finer things.

The hunter decided he was safely hidden in the loft. Judging by the state of the barn downstairs, all the hay for the night had already been thrown down so no one should disturb him up here. He needed to urinate. He had been holding it all afternoon and decided to leave his watch post for a moment to find the furthest corner from where he stood now.

Zipping up his trousers, he heard voices outside and rushed back to the vents through which he had a view to the house. There was a woman he hadn't seen before standing on the front doorstep, saying something to the not-so-simpleton. The man was looking at his boots, nodding, a rifle slung loosely over his shoulder. He appeared to be agreeing with whatever it was she was saying. That must be his mark, the hunter thought, watching her.

Florence Millicent-Marks.

He carefully shifted his body. His back had begun to ache from standing and he longed for a chair and a drink. The hunter ran his hand over the handle of the knife in his pocket as he heard two dogs begin to bark. A couple of collies had escaped the house and were doing circles around the man's feet now. The hunter supposed it was time to bring the cows in.

It had started to snow, great fat flakes that descended from the skies like miniature zeppelins. The pink sky of moments ago had given way to a dark grey cloak. The hunter was grateful the dogs weren't German Shepherds or Rottweilers. Collies were entirely focused on cattle and wouldn't have the slightest concern with a man in a loft. They hadn't given any warning whatsoever when the other three had arrived.

He would wait here for now. If he was discovered by the farm hand, he would deal with that situation as it arose. The snow was falling more heavily now. He could hear the muffled sounds of the farm hand outside, his heavy boots trudging across the ground coupled with the incessant barking of the dogs and the great slow shuffling movements of the herd as it made its way towards the warmth of the barn.

What the hunter needed to do was to get closer to the house, and preferably inside it, if at all possible. He couldn't gather any intelligence sitting in this freezing loft. But for now, he would have to wait until the milking was done.

As soon as the cows were put to bed, the hunter decided he would make tracks.

24

SUPERINTENDENT FELIX PETTERS

CHIPPING NORTON, ENGLAND

Darkness had fallen some time ago, its creeping blackened shroud a welcome relief on what had been an exhausting day. Superintendent Petters walked wearily down the corridor to his office, carefully managing the crate under his arm as he did so. He was relieved to find his secretary in the filing room—she was so far the only living soul in the building. The two overnight patrol constables were already out on their rounds.

"Good evening, you are here late," he called to her. She gave him a little wave, files in hand, and raised her eyes to the heavens. He wondered if she too had no one waiting for her at home.

Petters carried on down the hall. Reaching his office he placed the crate on the side of his desk and sat down heavily in his chair, exhaling. He removed the cover on the box to allow the sparrow some light and retrieved Professor Hargreaves's list from his inside pocket.

His secretary had placed his mail on the credenza behind him. He leaned back to retrieve it and began flipping through the envelopes. There was a report on the staffing levels he had asked for, the (unsurprising) autopsy results for the murders of both Patrick and Reginald, a bill from the supply department that needed his authorization so his secretary could pay it, and a dark grey envelope addressed to him in a messy scrawl with no return address.

Petters held the grey envelope in his hand while he retrieved his messages from their usual slot under the desk top. It had taken him some time to train his secretary to put them there. She tended to leave them on his desk so he would see them right away, but this had the effect of destroying the order of the room. It jarred him to see them there, messing up an otherwise spotless desk, so he had repeatedly asked her to leave them in the slot he had so aptly labeled *Messages*. Finally she had succumbed to his ways, although it had taken the better part of a month to train her.

Jeremiah had come by to see if he had returned from London, good lad. He would pop by the orphanage in the morning to see if he couldn't take him out for some breakfast. There was another message from his mother asking him if he would like to come for dinner on the weekend. He was relieved to see a telephone message from Lillie. She had arrived in Stirling and was at the Millicent-Marks farm. She hadn't left a return number and this irritated him. It would have certainly made it a lot easier to find her if things went sideways.

Petters yawned and rubbed at his eyes. It was nearly nine o'clock and he had been awake since five that morning, with only sporadic sleep before that. His eyes felt like they had sand in them and he pulled at his eyelids in an attempt to clear them. It was time to go home.

Remembering the envelope in his hand, he used his forefinger to slice open the seal. From inside a small grainy photograph dropped onto his desk. He picked it up and stared at it, his mind a whirl of thoughts. It was picture of the boy, of Jeremiah, standing beside the long low stone wall outside the orphanage, his coat undone, holding a ball in one hand and stick in the other. His attention was focused on something outside the frame, another child perhaps, someone he was playing a game with. When was this taken? Today? Previously? He searched the photograph for clues—the trees were bare, the sky was overcast—it could have been any day this winter. Someone was watching Jeremiah, and letting Petters know it. The purpose was surely to intimidate him.

The Superintendent hurriedly pulled on his coat, glancing at the clock on the wall. It was late, certainly, but he didn't care. He rushed out of his office, his surprised secretary waving to him as he continued at speed out of the building and into his car.

The nuns wouldn't be happy to see him at that time of night but he needed to see the boy. To make sure he was all right. Because if anyone had laid even so much as a finger on him, Petters wouldn't hesitate to pulverize them.

The orphanage was dark when Petters pulled up in front. He cut the engine and glanced around him before getting out of the car. Noting the stone wall where the photo had been taken made Petters furious all over again and he marched up to the front door, knocking without hesitating. He was a policeman for Christ's sake, he shouldn't bother about not wanting to disturb.

It took some time but eventually the door creaked open no more than a couple of inches and the white and tired face of an old nun peeked out at him. Petters flashed his badge and without a word the nun opened the door wide so he could enter.

The hallway was lit only by a few small candles and Petters realized the entire household was asleep. The nun waited for him to speak.

"Sister, my name is Superintendent Felix Petters. I am here to check on the safety of one of your wards, Jeremiah Noble."

The nun nodded. "Yes, sir. He is sleeping now. Is something the matter?"

"I have reason to believe someone may be watching him, or wanting to harm him. Has there been anything odd today? Or yesterday? Or anytime really—that you have noticed, as pertaining to the boy?"

"No. But I am fairly new here so I really couldn't speak to past events. I've barely been here a week." She was looking at him strangely, in that calm, impassive manner that nuns sometimes had.

"I see. I would like to see him if I could. I won't wake him but I really should check in on him." He doubted she would say yes.

She appeared to be thinking about it and Petters prepared himself for resistance. "Of course you should," she said eventually. "Come this way."

Petters followed the nun down the dark hallway and up an old staircase that creaked under the weight of their feet, the aged floorboards nearing the end of their lives. The second floor of the orphanage smelled of sour potatoes and a damp mustiness. What little warmth the fireplaces gave on the main floor was all but absent upstairs. Petters wondered how any of the children managed to stay healthy.

Three doors down was Jeremiah's room and the nun opened the door quietly, holding her candle so Petters could peer inside. The room was small but had eight children on cots, side by side, with barely enough room between the beds to stand. He saw Jeremiah, three beds in, curled tightly in a small ball, a thin wool blanket pulled up to his chin. Petters nodded at the nun and she softly closed the door. They made their way back down the staircase to the main entrance, careful not to make a sound.

When they reached the front door Petters turned to the

nun. "I will be back before breakfast. What time do the boys wake?" He shivered against the draughtiness.

"Seven."

"Thank you. Oh, and would you please tell Sister Theresa I would like her to have adoption papers at the ready, first thing tomorrow morning."

"Oh?"

"Yes."

"For Jeremiah?"

Petters nodded.

"But he is...well, so *old*. The older ones rarely go to homes."

"I see. That is unfortunate, but it isn't the case this time."

She nodded at him silently, taking in his words.

"God bless you," she said softly.

Although Petters fashioned himself an agnostic, her words had a calming effect on him. As though peace would be found now, for all of them.

With that decided and executed, Petters pulled on his gloves. He didn't like to touch door handles without them. The darkness and cold outside was barely different from the atmosphere inside the orphanage. Petters reflected on this as he made his way through the cutting night air towards his car.

He smiled, feeling some relief and a dash of excitement. His life was about to become very different and he could hardly wait.

25

LILLIE

THE MILLICENT-MARKS FARM, SCOTLAND

"I think you all had better stay for dinner and possibly the night. I've never seen so much snow in such a short amount of time. It's almost biblical." Florence was peering out the window in the darkness. Bits of her red hair had escaped her bun and the wisps fell long against her elegant neck. She had pulled a yellow silk shawl over her shoulders and removed her glasses. She looked back at them all with her wide-set, intelligent eyes, now freed from their frames. "It isn't anything fancy—only a vegetable soup and some warm sandwiches, but there is plenty of food and I think it would be far more prudent than you attempting to drive in a snowstorm."

Rumple looked to Lillie, raising his eyebrows. She nodded a reluctant agreement to him but looked inquiringly towards Mildred. "It's your car, Mildred, what are your thoughts?"

The old woman got up from the chair by the fire and wandered over to the window. She studied the situation beyond the glass. "I agree, it is biblical, as Florence puts it. I'm not sure how the roads will be, so it may be best to sit tight until we have either some light or an end to the snowfall. But where will you put us all?"

"Oh, not to worry," Florence said, moving towards the kitchen. "We have a couple of spare rooms that can be made up, as long as you girls don't mind bunking in together. Rumple, pour everyone a drink, would you? There is some sherry in the sideboard, or something stronger if anyone prefers. I will just tend to dinner and we can eat when Stuart returns from the milking."

Rumple made his way in the direction of the liquor cabinet.

"Well, this is unexpected, isn't it." Lillie was relieved to be able to speak freely now Florence had left the room.

"I suppose we should have anticipated snow, what with the frigid weather we have been having." Mildred accepted a little glass of sherry from Rumple and tipped it back, swallowing the entire pour in one swift gulp. She held it back out to Rumple who, attempting to hide his surprise, refilled it.

"We haven't really got to the heart of things though, have we?" Lillie frowned.

"Meaning that we think someone is coming here to kill her and we think she should know about it?" Mildred was sipping her second sherry now, this time more slowly.

"I don't believe she thinks whoever the French man was is an imposter."

"Or," Rumple offered, "if she does, she doesn't believe our killer would masquerade as a Frenchman." He handed Lillie a glass.

"Well, who in their right mind would want to appear French?" Mildred said, entirely seriously. "I see her point."

"I'm not sure I do," Lillie confessed. "If that was him, what are the odds he is still here somewhere, on this farm?"

"Probably quite good," Rumple admitted, searching the cabinet for something stronger than sherry.

"So we just sit here, like ducks, having a civilized country dinner and reminiscing? I'm sorry, but I think we should get moving. I don't want to serve ourselves up like Christmas dinner for him."

"Fine by me," Mildred said, and hiccupped. "Excuse me. If you think we should attempt the roads, I'm in. Might be slippery but if we end up off the road there are enough of us to push the car out, that's for certain."

"So we aren't staying for dinner, then? At the risk of being murdered, that soup smells terribly tempting. I would hazard my life to have a bowl." Rumple had found the whiskey and had poured himself a large glass of it. "Besides which, we need to get Florence to believe that leaving with us is the surest way of keeping safe. We still have some work to do."

"As long as we are all in agreement that after dinner we need to get on the road. Preferably with Florence, since we came to assure her safety."

"Agreed." Rumple took a long pull of his drink.

Mildred nodded her assent.

The wind rattled at the windows, pushing and pulling at the mottled glass as it tossed the swirling snow around the house.

"It will be a hell of drive, mind." Aunt Mildred was watching the flakes pile up on the window sills as she spoke softly, hearing returning footsteps.

"Good, that's finished and we are ready to eat." Florence came back into the sitting room.

She was wearing a striped apron and drying her hands on its hem as she spoke. "Listen to that wind! Terrible weather. We don't stand on ceremony, so my apologies if you are all used to eating in a dining room—Stuart and I tend to favour the kitchen table and the fire in there is so much warmer."

The group followed her through to the kitchen and took their places around a large, weathered table with mismatched chairs. Florence ladled soup into earthenware bowls and placed plates of shaved beef sandwiches, cut into quarters, on the table. She opened a bottle of wine and poured each of them a small glass.

"Shouldn't we wait for Stuart then?" Rumple asked.

"Never mind. I had thought he would be here by now, but we may as well get started." Florence clasped her hands together and devoutly bowed her head. "O thou, in whom we live and move, who made the sea and shore; Thy goodness constantly we prove, And grateful would adore; And, if it please Thee, power above! Still grant us, with such store, the friend we trust, the fair we love, and we desire no more. Amen."

It was the longest grace Lillie had heard in some time.

"Amen," they repeated, in unison.

"Should we go find him?" Lillie had a fleeting thought that perhaps he had met their killer along the way. If he *were* here, was Stuart not in danger? Out there, alone.

"No, he'll come when he is ready."

Rumple took a few bites of soup and then, placing his spoon down, looked at Florence, long and hard. "My dear, I don't think we have been entirely urgent enough with you."

"Oh?"

"You are in danger. And I am in danger. You need to leave here with us, tonight. You aren't seeming to grasp the entirety of the situation."

"Don't be silly. This is my home. If someone is coming for me, I shall stay here and face him. I believe in vindication. Let him have it."

"But that is preposterous! You were doing your job! You don't deserve to be killed now for it."

"Perhaps I do. Which is about as much as I said to that horrible Mr. Wilkinson. Who, by the way, never sent a reply." Florence reached for a sandwich.

"What are you talking about?" Rumple asked.

"I wrote to him, Basil Wilkinson, a few months ago. I told him I needed forgiveness for everything the committee did and participated in. I have become a devout woman since my time in London. I need forgiveness, from God, from the families, from the public—for what I knowingly participated in. Not all those men who died were guilty. I am sure of that now and I told Wilkinson as much, for all the good it did. I told him I wanted to apologize. Publicly. I need this—" Florence stopped speaking, suddenly.

There was a rattling somewhere in the house, and she tilted her head to listen. They had all stopped eating now and Lillie felt herself freeze.

Silence ensued, Lillie hearing only the blankness of a house on edge, its suspended air, as they strained to listen for something that no longer seemed to be there. Eventually Mildred picked up her spoon again. "I expect it's just the wind and we are all a little on edge."

"Probably," Florence said, smiling and relaxing a little. "Can I get anyone more soup?"

Rumple nodded, handing over his bowl to her. "I would expect the last thing a man like Wilkinson would want is to draw any attention to himself and risk an inquiry."

"We were public servants, Theodore, and public servants need to be held accountable."

"My dear, it's over now. There isn't a thing we can do about the past."

"Perhaps not, but it doesn't mean it was right."

26

THE HUNTER

THE MILLICENT-MARKS FARM, SCOTLAND

The snow was falling hard and fast around the farmhouse. It fell into the hunter's boots, spilling over the top of them and freezing his calves through the thin wool of his trousers. Lamplight from the windows beamed outside, turning the snow an illuminated and flecked gold and causing the hunter to expand his arc to stay in the shadows.

He could hear noise from the barn, the faraway sound of cows and the clink of buckets and wheelbarrows, the impatient bark of the dogs. It amazed him that he had been able to sneak out of the loft unnoticed. The noise had helped muffle his climb down the ladder and he had chosen his moment well. The dogs were having their supper and the not-so-simpleton had been nowhere in sight. He had caught the eye of one of the collies as he hurried past, but the dog's food had tempted him far more than the stranger.

Having made his escape, the hunter peered now into the sitting room windows of the farmhouse. The light of the room caused the frosted glass to glitter as though it had been sprayed with diamond dust, while the warmth from inside smudged a diffused circle across its otherwise frozen surface. The room sat empty—a few dirty glasses were strewn across an antique sideboard telling him its occupants had moved on. He moved further along the outside of the house. Three more darkened windows. He rounded the corner. The smell of woodsmoke lingered on the thin air. There was a door here, and to the left a long narrow window revealing a dark hallway.

A few more feet along the side of the house was the kitchen window and he ducked below it, circling out further so he could have a look in without being seen. The four of them were at a long table, the redheaded woman was ladling soup and saying something while the other three watched and listened. He didn't really need to hear what was being said, although he couldn't stifle a creeping curiosity. He longed to be to a fly on the faded peeling wallpaper.

The woman serving them was his target, of that much he was sure. The other three remained a mystery to him and while he knew that killing number three on his list was his raison d'être, still he hesitated to storm into the house, the time passing, each minute threatening the return of the not-so-simpleton.

Something was causing him to stall and it bothered him. It was the scene inside the house perhaps, and the feeling in his stomach. A melancholy ache that he had felt before, years ago, so long ago he had nearly forgotten it. Now it reared its torturous head, taunting him. The woman who arrived in the car, the one with the auburn hair who was now sitting and listening, the one who moved like a dancer—she reminded him of a time he hadn't thought of since he was a boy.

He didn't like thinking of it now. He had been only eleven. His mother's dead body still in her bed while he sat there, on the filthy kitchen floor in their damp and derelict house. He had felt sick, and cold. He hadn't realized his shivering was causing his teeth to rattle, and nor had he realized that his shirt was wet from the tears that were streaming down his face.

And then she had come into the room and pulled him into her arms. She had been their neighbour, his mother's nurse maid in the last dismal months of her horrible life. The neighbour's presence that day had torn him back from a black abyss. She had pulled him to his feet and led him from the house, down the alley reeking of filth, and into the back door of a row house that was cleaner and softer than their own. The laundry hung on a line in her warm kitchen and she had small vases of flowers scattered around the room. Everything smelt of soap. She had fed him, and bathed him and given him a bed for the night. And one night turned into two and then three and then a few years passed. He had lived there, with her, never once returning home.

His home was gone. His home was with her.

She had also moved like a dancer, he remembered. She had long, beautiful chestnut hair and the lithe limbs that come with physical work and good genes. He loved her, like a sister he had never had and like the crush of a teenager. She had been good, and wholesome, and his whole world.

But for all her goodness, her rotten taste in men had gotten her to the bottom of a river one cold December day, her beautiful hair wrapped around her face and neck, her clothes torn, her spirit gone. He had just turned fifteen years old.

And so, years later, that man who had robbed his world of its light had been his first hit. He had found the man with relative ease—for he was as stupid as he was mean—and the not-yet-anointed hunter had waited outside the man's favourite watering hole and exacted revenge with the clumsy determination of an enthusiastic amateur. Her death had set his life on the trajectory that was to recreate him. A phoenix rising out of the ashes.

The snow had stopped falling now, allowing a slice of moon to peek through parting clouds. The scene inside the kitchen remained the same and he was relieved his reminiscing hadn't gone on long enough to jeopardize his mission. Pushing back the feeling in his gut, he moved towards the door and the darkened hallway. He would spare the one with the auburn hair, and if possible, the other two people with her. Not because he was discriminate, although of course he tried to be, but because he knew what it meant to love someone.

The door handle was rusted and it rattled as he worked on the lock. It was an easy one, but he silently cursed the racket it made as he entered the darkened hallway. The voices were to his left, around the corner, and he noticed they had abruptly stopped. Had they heard him? He waited, not moving, the quiet dripping of his coat on the worn floor filled his ears. They couldn't possibly hear that from the kitchen, could they?

A few minutes passed and he readied himself. Eventually he heard what he assumed to be the old woman say something he couldn't make out and their conversation resumed. There was a clink of dishes and the smell of celery root. And him in the hallway, slowly moving towards them, nothing but the soft squeak of his shoes, his rumbling stomach and a reluctance born out of a glimpse and a memory.

He moved slowly down the hallway, willing the floorboards not to creak. He could hear them clearly now, their words a swirl of nonsense against the pounding in his temples.

"You can't blame yourself." The man was talking. He had a commanding voice that matched his military appearance.

"Of course I can, and I do. We didn't realize the gravity of the situation—we were all caught up in it."

"Hysteria, you mean?" The woman with the auburn hair. He imagined her and found, quite startlingly, that he was projecting the long lost image of his neighbour onto her. He shook his head, as though doing so would stop the flood of memories that threatened to sink him.

There was a sound of cutlery being placed on a plate, the

clunk of a glass on the table, the scrape of chair legs along the wooden floorboards—all of it muffling the voices.

"...Spy hysteria. There should be an inquiry." His target again.

"That will open us all up to scrutiny and none more than Wilkinson himself."

The hunter froze at the mention of the name.

The man continued. "Which is exactly why he doesn't want anything to do with you, presumably. He was never one for self reflection, was he?"

"I don't care what he wants. That isn't important. The truth —*atonement*—that is what we need. What this whole country needs. We were wrong, probably more often than not and people died because of it. I don't know about you, but I need absolution, from those we hurt, from the Church, and ultimately—from God."

There was a pause in the conversation for a moment and what the woman said next caused a chill to run up his spine.

"And while the Lord may say, 'it is mine to avenge; I will repay' I will tell you this: there were a great many more people involved in wartime wrongdoing; department heads, underlings, staffers, the Prime Minister's office—they shall all pay."

It wasn't at all the conversation the hunter had expected to overhear, and he didn't like the unsure feeling it stirred inside him. Until now, his mission had been black and white—locate his targets and eliminate them. Simple. He hadn't anticipated remorse and regret coming into play, and nor had he anticipated that the Summerdyne Committee was just the tip of the iceberg. By the sounds of it, a great more ice lay beneath the surface and along with it, a huge population of people who were just innocently following orders.

From where he was now the hunter could see through the foyer window down the long drive towards the barn. It was black outside and the steady swinging of a lantern in the distance told him the not-so-simpleton was returning to the house. He retreated back the way he had come, quickly and silently, knowing he was leaving wet footprints as he did so.

With his hand again on the rusted handle of the door he paused, both needing to gather his thoughts and preparing himself for the blast of cold. With a heavy heart and the perplexity knowledge can often bring, he disappeared through the door and back into the darkness.

27

LILLIE

THE MILLICENT-MARKS FARM, SCOTLAND

T he sound of a door slamming startled them. There was a shuffling of boots and the sound of something heavy being dropped and then dragged across the wooden floor.

Stuart emerged into the kitchen, covered in snow, still wearing his coat and boots and his hair dripping onto the flagstones. His cheeks were red from the cold and his eyes darted around the room, taking in each of them without ever meeting an eye with his own. He hoisted the rifle he was still carrying onto his shoulder and Lillie wondered if he had served in the war. At that moment, he looked every bit the soldier. It almost didn't matter he couldn't make eye contact with his current underlings—he looked over their shoulders into the distance, as surely as an officer would, searching the horizon for the Hun. When he spoke, it was with the authority of a general, donning his battle call, rallying his troops to face the enemy.

"Someone's here," he said, "and he isn't French."

"How do you know someone is here?" Florence looked at her brother as she nervously fiddled with her napkin, twisting it around and around. She got up from the table with rapidity and closed the faded floral curtains over the kitchen sink.

"Footsteps, big ones, round and around the house." Stuart looked at Rumple's shoes pointedly. "Not his, not big enough, and he isn't wearing boots."

"Right, Florence, you are coming with us. And we are leaving, now." Rumple was out of his chair and making for their coats.

"But he will just follow us, don't you see? There isn't any point."

"The point is you will live. And from what I can see, or more to the point, what I *can't* see, is another car here. He has to be on foot, so we have an advantage. Stuart, are you are coming with us?" Rumple was looking back and forth between them.

"No. Have to look after the herd. You go." He was motioning to Florence to hurry up.

"I'm not leaving you behind. You will be in danger here."

"He's not here for me."

"He may not be that discerning."

"Then I will shoot him. Go." Stuart motioned with the butt of his rifle.

"No more death, Stuart. That is not the right path. I have to get some clothes..." Florence was rushing around the kitchen.

"Stuart, could you accompany your sister to get her things?" Rumple asked and then added, "Quickly."

The two departed and Rumple looked at Lillie. "I'll check the perimeter of the house."

"Or don't. What if we just blaze out that front door and get on our way? Do you really want a confrontation now, here? In the middle of nowhere, on a snowy night, with no one to back you up? And besides, we don't know a thing about this man except he is very capable of murder." She rubbed at her forehead. "No, I insist you stay here with us."

Rumple looked thoughtful as he pondered this, redirecting his gaze to Aunt Mildred. "All ready?"

"Ready as I'll ever be. I just hope the car starts."

That was all they needed. "Does it not usually?"

"Usually it does...but not always." Aunt Mildred winced and Lillie pushed back a sinking feeling.

"Let's assume it does and we get away from here. We had better get back to Tynesmore immediately. Is there a late train from Edinburgh?"

"We will have missed it by the time we get there. The next one will be first thing in the morning, so I will have to put you on that one."

Disappointed, they sat in silence for a while, listening to the sound of Florence upstairs opening and closing drawers, her shoes clacking across the floorboards above them. Quick and hurried. Nervous.

She reappeared a few minutes later with a bag in one hand, her eyes wide. "He has been here, inside the house." She was shivering involuntarily.

"How do you know?"

"There are wet footprints in the hallway, and by the back door."

"Right." Rumple was on his feet immediately. "Everyone get their coats. *Now*."

28

THE HUNTER

EN ROUTE TO EDINBURGH, SCOTLAND

T he night sky was luminous and arced with stars whiter than the fallen snow. They glinted by the thousands far above his insignificance as the hunter moved through the frozen wild. He had been walking for hours, the farm was at least fifteen miles from Stirling and the snow was slowing his usual efficient pace. Staying off the main road had made the going even tougher but he was a physically fit man and although he could no longer feel his feet, the rest of his body was unusually warm from the exertion.

He would retrieve his bag from the hotel and make for the train station. Or, even better, hire a car to get him from Stirling to Edinburgh. He could afford to be frivolous in order to be comfortable. Especially after this night. A sharp pointed boulder he didn't see slashed at his shin as he negotiated the underbrush and emerged at the crest of a hill overlooking Stirling. He realized how hungry he was, and wondered if he should stick around long enough to refuel before embarking on the next leg of his journey.

And this was what puzzled him now. Overhearing the conversation inside the farmhouse had caused him concern—

concern that he didn't have all the facts and might be operating under some false assumptions. No, not assumptions. He had been fed everything, bought everything, and assumed nothing. He had trusted his source which, in hindsight, might have been his first and most grave error. He didn't necessarily regret his first two hits, he reflected, although he conceded it was possible he might grow to regret them. What he needed now was clarification and he intended to get it.

He had heard their car pass him some time ago. Its engine whined against the spinning and crunching tires as it made its way from the farm. He could just make out the darkened profiles of four people as it passed, the man driving—his body hunched forward, and the three women staring ahead into a path the headlights sliced across the frozen countryside. It didn't matter that they were ahead of him, for he knew exactly where they would eventually end up. He could always find them later.

Reaching the hotel the hunter made his way through the dimly lit hallway to his room, thankful the front desk was empty and he wouldn't need to role-play the Frenchman any longer. He decided to run a bath and as he did so, he peeled the frozen clothes from his body, grateful for the warmth of the room. His feet tingled painfully as he lowered them into the water, allowing it slowly envelop his body. He had lost weight these last few weeks and it was no wonder. He had hardly stopped since he arrived in England. His stomach had the concave look of a prize fighter, his strong arms were even more defined, sinewy and long, his legs now red from the heat of the water. Sometimes when he looked down at his own body he was surprised it wasn't the body of that boy, the one crying on the kitchen floor. Because even though he had morphed into this man, and no matter how hard he tried, he wondered if that boy had ever really left him.

He felt dreadfully tired and fought the urge to doze in the

tub. He needed sleep, food and a new plan—one that he was now methodically formulating. He hung his feet outside the tub and gave a long stretch. He couldn't help yawning and decided he would dry off and get an hour of sleep before daylight.

Once dawn broke he would need three things: breakfast, some new boots and a ticket south.

His plans were about to take a little detour.

29

SUPERINTENDENT PETTERS

CHIPPING NORTON, OXFORDSHIRE

"Superintendent Petters?"

The line had a fuzzy sound to it.

"You've got him, how can I help?" Petters adjusted the telephone earpiece so it sat flush against his ear, as he was having trouble hearing the man on the other end.

He watched as Jeremiah carefully lifted the sparrow out of its crate and put him on the desk in front of a small dish of bird seed. The morning sun was streaming through the window, illuminating the boy's pale face and picking up the gold flecks in his eyes.

"My name is Jack Abbott, I am a friend of Lillie Mead's... and also Harry Green's, incidentally. I have just spoken to Harry and he hasn't heard from Lillie. Neither has the newspaper. I wondered if you have?"

That was better, he could hear everything now.

The voice was nervous, Petters could tell. The anxiety was layered over with a naturally professional tone, but the man was concerned, that much was very obvious. Jeremiah pushed the seed closer to the bird and smiled as he began to peck at it.

The boy looked up to see if Petters was watching and the super-intendent nodded at him encouragingly.

"Mr. Abbott, yes, Harry mentioned you when I saw him a few days ago." A thought occurred to Petters as he remembered what the man did for a living. He would certainly be able to move about in government circles easier than Petters ever could. Being a country policeman, he might as well have been wearing a bullseye on the back of his uniform. He either raised alarm or elicited gross indifference wherever he went.

"And Lillie?"

"Oh, sorry, yes, Lillie. I had a message last night that she had reached the Millicent-Marks farm in Stirling."

"But nothing else? Not when they would be back or if they found anything there?"

"No, afraid not. I wasn't here when the call came in and she didn't leave a return number."

"Oh." His disappointment was almost palpable.

"Listen Mr. Abbott, I wonder if you might be able to...er... help me out."

"If I can...certainly."

"Could you meet?" Petters had never trusted the telephone. One never knew who was listening.

"Yes, when?"

"I could come down to London later today? Or tomorrow?" The train took just under two hours so it wasn't a huge imposition.

"I'll come to you. I'm due a few days off anyway and I want to get back to Oxford. I'll leave this afternoon. Can you come to Tynesmore this evening? I'll stay with Harry, I think."

"Of course, why don't we say eight o'clock? I don't want to interrupt dinner." Which wasn't true, of course. Petters couldn't think of anything he would like better than to be invited back to Tynesmore for a meal.

"Eight is fine. I'll see you then."

The line clicked, leaving Petters to his thoughts. He needed someone in government. Someone in London. Someone with contacts and the ability to slink in and out without being noticed. Who better than an intelligence agent?

Jack Abbott had called at just the right time.

LILLIE

OXFORD, OXFORDSHIRE

The smell of cigarette smoke, stale coffee and moist paper wafted out to Cornmarket Street as Lillie pushed through the glass front door of the Oxford Daily Press. She had come straight from the train station and still wore the clothes she had traveled in. Her skirt was wrinkled from the train, her coat smelled of the dining car, and her shoes were still damp from last night's Scottish snow. She had attempted to smooth her hair into a large clasp at the nape of her neck but she had the distinct feeling it was slowly, piece by piece, escaping its intended confines—she reached up hastily to re-clip it as she hurried past the unfamiliar secretary at the front desk. Jeremy Winston, her boss, was an excellent newspaper man, but he did tend to go through staff with alarming regularity.

"Good afternoon, I am Lillie Mead, head of the crime desk." Not wanting to get bogged down with the usual pleasantries, Lillie gave her a wave that she hoped was friendly while hardly slackening her pace.

"Yes, good morning, Ms. Mead..."

The voice faded as Lillie put considerable distance between

herself and the reception desk. Jeremy wasn't at his desk, so she carried on towards the lunch room. She nodded to various colleagues as she moved through the line of metal work tables, all lined up side by side and housing various brands of typewriters, stacks of papers and overflowing ashtrays. The hallmarks of factory journalism.

The lunchroom was empty so she continued towards the rear staircase and up to the second floor which hummed with the monotonous drone of the printing presses. It was a sound she loved and she paused, listening, as her eyes searched the cavernous room for any sign of her boss.

She spotted him giving instructions to one of the operators, his dingy grey suit too large for his diminutive figure—it hung from his slight shoulders and puddled around his shoes making him look like a disheveled schoolboy. Spotting her he gave a little wave, adjusted his spectacles, and started across the floor towards her.

"Come, it's so dreadfully loud in here, let's talk downstairs. I can't hear myself think." Jeremy pushed past her and led the way back down the metal staircase, step by step as she watched his trousers drag on the floor over the heel of his shoe. He steered her back to the lunch room, where he pulled out a couple of chairs around a small, chipped table and poured them both a cup of coffee before closing the door.

"So...tell me, how did you get on in Scotland?"

"It certainly was interesting." She took a long sip of coffee, thankful for its warmth. "I'll get you something quickly for this week's column, although I daresay I will be omitting a great many details. At least for now."

"Mm," Jeremy nodded. "Quick turnaround, though? I didn't expect you back so soon."

"We managed to locate Florence Millicent-Marks. She is with Rumple at Tynesmore now, which is a relief, I don't mind telling you. There was some evidence of our murderer being there at her farm and, although I didn't see him personally, everything points to the fact that he was indeed watching her."

"Which begs the question: why didn't he just kill her like he did the other two and tried to do with the Professor?" Jeremy looked puzzled.

"Perhaps because he didn't get the chance. There were four of us there, after all. Five including her brother."

Jeremy rubbed his bristly chin. Lillie rarely saw him with stubble. Today, in conjunction with his overly large suit, it had the effect of making him look like a boy playing dress up. Lillie waited for him to say something else but he appeared lost in his thoughts. Eventually he looked up at her. "You are a credit to the press, Lillie. This newspaper is very lucky to have a reporter who has as much grit as you do. Not many would hop on a train to Scotland in the middle of the night for a story."

Lillie thought about this. Jack was always so critical of how she conducted herself professionally—she took too many risks, he said, or she didn't heed his warnings or concerns. If she were honest, it was all becoming a little tiresome. It was nice to hear another point of view for a change.

A young staffer pushed through the lunch room door but Jeremy abruptly waved him away with a jerk of his head.

"Out!"

The young man nodded, embarrassed and confused, and exited the way he came.

Lillie frowned at him. "You really can be rude, you know."

"Mm."

"Listen," Lillie continued. "Florence regrets her role in the wartime executions the Summerdyne Committee sanctioned at the behest of the Crime Committee's recommendations."

Jeremy watched her with his hawklike eyes. "Go on."

"She apparently tried to get in touch with the then assistant Commissioner of Crime—a Mr. Basil Wilkinson—rather recently. Florence believes, you see, that there should be a public inquiry into the executions. It is her belief that some of the people executed weren't actually guilty of espionage."

"That would be...well, a colossal admission of failure on the part of a major wartime government agency. What did this Mr. Wilkinson say?"

"Nothing. She had sent him a message to that effect but he never responded. He has been promoted since the war, to Director of Intelligence." Lillie stared hard at her boss. She wanted to make sure he understood the gravity of who they were possibly dealing with.

"Oh, Lord. You have got to be kidding me."

"I assure you I am not. And apparently he is an arrogant, prejudiced, and ultra-conservative man who isn't very amenable to criticism. He despises Jews and suffragettes and Bolsheviks—he deplores free speech. Am I painting a clear picture?"

Jeremy nodded. "And you want to go after him."

"Well..." Lillie knew she was being coy, but she wasn't sure how to convince Jeremy it would be a good idea. She needed to draw him a road map. "Essentially, there are two stories here. The first is obviously the two murders and the attempted murder of the Professor. This is something the crime section of the paper needs to cover, no doubt about it. But there is something else going on here. And that something else is political, and it's headline news. I'd like to write a story on how the British Government dealt with 'suspected' spies during the war and how, after recent reflection, perhaps their policies were flawed."

Jeremy didn't look as though he needed any convincing. He nodded as he replied. "There is a bigger picture," he confirmed his understanding. "And that bigger picture goes all the way up the political decision-making ladder. You want to call out the whole government apparatus, is that what you are saying?"

Lillie began to feel emboldened. Jeremy was smart man, and connecting the dots was something he could do faster than anyone she had ever met. "Look," she started, "with no due process whatsoever, England institutionalized the killing of foreigners during the war. They labelled them, for whatever reason—maybe it was fear, perhaps they thought it would whip up public hysteria—but they said they were *spies*. According to Florence, many of them were no such thing! They were just men doing who knows what: buying sardines, traveling in and out of the country, conversing—unbeknownst to them—with the wrong people. At the very least, discussing this in the newspaper creates some accountability, doesn't it? Perhaps I am being naive, but presumably it might affect the way England deals with foreigners in the future. Heck it might even cause them to pause for thought—perhaps putting a prejudiced and unbalanced man in charge of a major government department such as intelligence is a mistake! Wilkinson is, at the very least, a pirate—and he is in charge of this country's secret service! It's absurd." She was getting her blood up and she willed herself to calm down.

"As written by an American." Jeremy gave her a sarcastic smile. "But I love your enthusiasm."

"I suppose it is easier for an outsider to criticize, granted."

It took Jeremy a moment to make his next statement. It was an enormous leap, to be sure, but Lillie had already arrived there herself. Her faith in him was validated when he finally, and somewhat reluctantly, said, "Are you suggesting that Basil Wilkinson has been systematically trying to kill off members of the Summerdyne Committee because he doesn't want to be exposed?"

Lillie stared at him, hard. "Would that be so far fetched?"

"Accusations like that can ruin careers," he stated matter-of-factly. Lillie wasn't sure if he meant Wilkinson's or theirs.

"Yes," she agreed.

Neither of them spoke for a time. The both weighed the gravity of what they were considering.

Eventually she added, "These are just threads floating around, and to be honest, I may be way off target. Maybe Wilkinson has nothing whatsoever to do with this, and obviously I can't draw conclusions I can't support yet."

"Calling out an official at Wilkinson's level could be like lighting a cigarette with a firebomb."

Lillie leaned back in her chair and gave a long, exhausted sigh. "I suggest we start by connecting the murders to one another. I'll write a little bit about the Summerdyne Committee —but only that the victims knew each other and worked together. We won't go into too much detail about it. It gives us more time to flush out the rest. After all, it's just a theory, and how often are theories correct?"

"That depends on who formulates them," Jeremy replied with a smile. "I'll put a teaser in tomorrow's paper. Why don't you try to have the full story to me by next week?"

"I doubt I'll have all the threads tied by then."

"No but we can do a series, over say...the next four weeks? Of course, I am hoping things become clearer as time goes on."

"Oh, I expect they will. Especially once Wilkinson realizes someone is looking into his past."

"And you think he will want to protect all those skeletons he has in his wardrobe?"

"I'm counting on it."

31

SUPERINTENDENT PETTERS

CHIPPING NORTON, OXFORDSHIRE

A thick fog had rolled in with the departure of the afternoon light and what little Superintendent Felix Petters could see of the road from behind his windshield was now wet and slippery. He leaned out of his driver's side window, thinking his lack of sight must be partially because of the car's dirty glass. It wasn't, and the biting cold made his eyes water and his cheeks burn. He ducked his head back into the car and dried his eyes with his handkerchief, fighting back the suffocating feeling of claustrophobia which he always got when there was fog.

The orphanage wasn't far from the police station, but the poor visibility had caused their journey to take nearly double the time as they finally pulled up in front of the building near a long, low, crumbling stone wall. A small lantern glowed by the front door, lighting the path with the bare minimum of illumination. Petters wondered if he shouldn't walk the boy inside to explain his tardiness for dinner. He smiled to himself. Jeremiah wouldn't have to have many more dinners in this dismal building. Once the adoption papers were approved, the two of them could dine wherever and for however long they pleased.

Something fluttered just outside his line of vision as he halted the car. Jeremiah had his hand on the handle of the door and Petters wordlessly held up a hand. The car's headlights shone into the fog, giving it the illusion of being thicker than it actually was. Unmistakably, Petters saw the flash of an emerald green coat he had seen before and he realized he was still being followed by a woman not astute enough to realize that a tail needs to change clothes in order to not be detected. Why would London send such an amateur? Was it Basil Wilkinson who had hired her? Or that perfectly dressed gentleman who disliked gruesome crime scene photos?

"Stay here a minute, would you?" Petters was out of the car in a shot and moving quickly towards the spot along the wall where he had last seen the coat. She was gone, as was expected, but he made a quick jog of the block anyway to see if he could catch up with her. A clear night would have make the task easier, he thought, as he hurried back to the car with the sound of his shoes on the pavers echoing against the mist.

"What was that all about?" Jeremiah looked at him, perplexed, still sitting in his seat.

"Nothing. I thought I saw someone I, uh, knew. Must have been mistaken."

The boy stared out over the dash. "Or not telling the truth."

He was too astute, this kid.

"I better get going, the nuns don't like late arrivals for dinner...usually means the strap," the boy said, pushing his door open and getting out with some reluctance.

Petters winced at the thought. "Right—I'll walk you in, shall I?"

Jeremiah put his head back into the car. "Or perhaps I could come to Tynesmore with you tonight?" He raised his two perfect little brown eyebrows.

Petters hadn't yet told him of the adoption, he wanted all

the paper work tidied up before he broke the news, just in case there were any holdups.

"I would like nothing more son, but I don't want to give the nuns any cause for dissatisfaction with me. If I bring you all that way, you won't be home before midnight." Before Jeremiah could protest, Petters was out of the car and making long strides towards the front door.

He certainly didn't want to leave him here, but until he was living under his roof they had to abide by the orphanage's rules.

"They never make anything good for supper, all watery potatoes and meat with tube things sticking out of it..." the boy said, trudging behind him slowly.

Petters turned to look at him. "I am too late for dinner at Tynesmore anyway, so it isn't likely you would be fed there regardless."

"Yes, but Mr. Green has such good cakes, after supper cakes I mean...different from the tea ones..." He looked up at Petters with this last, desperate plea.

"You will be exhausted. It's a long way." Why was he even considering it?

"I'll sleep in the car on the way home. I promise." He held his hand over his chest as though he were taking an oath rather than making a promise.

Petters looked out into the fog. The woman with the emerald coat was nowhere to be seen, but it didn't mean she wouldn't be back. He sighed and stared hard at the menacing front door of the orphanage. It was imposingly tall and made of un-oiled oak that had cracked in long ribbons with years of weather. Black wrought iron hinges stretched like fingers across its surface, giving it an eerie quality, especially in the fading light.

His mind was made up, mostly because he despised this place. "Don't be expecting dinner there, young man."

"I won't."

"All right, wait in the car. I will have a little talk with the Sisters. Let's see what we can do about it."

The boy's smile reached straight across his face and into Petters's heart. Who was he to say no?

32

LILLIE

OXFORD, OXFORDSHIRE

"Try this one," Harry said, shoving a large piece of something with a pinkish hue towards to her. She caught a sudden whiff of smoked fish. She opened her mouth just in time, supposing it was easier than protesting.

Nodding her approval and then swallowing she said, "Mm yes, very good. Salty, though."

"Precisely what I thought. Here..." He reached over and grabbed a plate of assorted canapés from the side table. "This is more what I was thinking instead." He handed her something dark and shiny on a water biscuit.

Lillie looked around the room and found Professor Hargreaves smiling at her. No doubt he had had to put up with Harry's wedding food tests for the past couple of days.

"Jack?" She held out the unknown piece of food to him in the hopes he would take it off her hands.

"I don't want to ruin my dinner."

"We have already had dinner."

Honestly! The last thing she wanted to do was ingest any more food. She stifled a yawn and glanced at the clock. Five past eight. Superintendent Petters should be arriving any moment. Perhaps he could play the food critic when he arrived and give her a break.

Sighing, she popped the canapé in her mouth, disliking the texture immediately. She looked inquiringly at Harry as she held it suspended on her tongue.

"Eel," he informed her.

She spat it into her napkin. "That's it then, Harry. I'm finished. No one wants to eat cold eel at a wedding, I can assure you. Shouldn't you wait until Primrose comes home? Surely her choice in food will differ greatly from yours, at least I hope that's the case. I still can hardly believe she has left this undertaking to you." She wiped her mouth with the napkin again, hoping to take the taste away.

The door to the drawing room opened and Rumple came in carrying a large tray of tea and dessert, followed by Superintendent Petters.

"Good evening, everyone." Petters smiled at the four of them and Harry got up to shake his hand.

"Sit, sit, here by the fire. Thank you Rumple, but please, sit down now. We can serve ourselves."

Harry retrieved the canapé platter and bowed in front of Petters. "Please, won't you try some of these...here, take one of each. Actually just take them all, would you? I need some input on my wedding menu and it seems the rest of the room won't oblige me." He went on to describe each piece as he loaded up a small plate for Petters and handed him a napkin. "I personally like the smoked halibut...oh and the asparagus tart...here, this one is some mousse something-or-other, not cheese exactly but sort of creamy all the same, this is salmon— also smoked, and here is a lobster terrine...not my favourite I admit, rather dirty tasting, probably not the right time of year for it..."

"Harry! Stop pestering the poor man," Lillie scolded.

He pointedly ignored her. "Where is your sergeant tonight?

Young chap, not a day over ten and appetite like a lion? I bet he could help me out here."

"I did actually bring him. I hope you don't mind too terribly...."

Rumple interjected before Petters finished. "I have taken the lad down to the kitchen. Seems Rose has some leftover dinner and she didn't want it to go to waste."

"Last time I saw him he was knee deep in roast chicken and caramelized parsnip mousse. You do spoil him here. It's no wonder he won't let me come alone." Petters looked apologetic.

Harry laughed, startling the superintendent. "I wouldn't have it any other way. Nice to have a young man in the house for a change."

Jack rose from his chair and moved closer to the fire.

"Tell me, Superintendent, how can I be of assistance to your investigation?"

"Yes, I..." Petters glanced around the room, then settled his gaze on the Professor, hesitating. "You know, I wonder if it isn't something perhaps we should be discussing later. I hadn't expected Ms. Mead to be here and I wouldn't mind hearing about what happened in Scotland in more detail. Rumple has kindly filled me in on the majority of it—incidentally, where is Ms. Millicent-Marks? I thought she would be here tonight."

"She is, but she has gone up to bed. None of us slept very well overnight and I think the stress of the situation has made her very tired. It was a long journey home and we were all constantly looking over our shoulders."

Lillie exhaled, stifling the urge to fall asleep herself.

It was nice to feel safe again and she longed to crawl onto the rug by the fire with the Irish wolfhound and bury her face in her fur.

"But he never revealed himself to you?"

"Our elusive murderer? No, I'm afraid not. But I do believe he was there, and in her house, so I suppose leaving was all we could do under the circumstances." Lillie turned her head so the rest of the room didn't witness her enormous yawn. "I do plan to do something more, however. Help flush him out."

"Meaning?" Petters had a look of intrigue mixed with trepidation painted on his face.

"An expose of sorts. In the newspaper. Presumably Rumple told you of Florence's state of mind and how it might affect England's very own new Director of Intelligence, Mr. Basil Wilkinson? He could be the key to this whole thing. If Florence wanted to atone for the sins of war, Wilkinson would be directly in the line of fire. He practically handed each and every one of those so-called spies to the Summerdyne Committee. He oversaw every investigation. In fact, he made the initial decisions on who the Committee should investigate. He was their supervisor. The public would lynch him."

Professor Hargreaves had moved from his chair and was standing to one side of the fireplace. Although tall in stature, he looked oddly effeminate in the light. Lillie noticed he had the oddest look on his face, but before she could press him, she was interrupted.

"I think you better tread carefully," Petters warned. "You know what happens when one pokes the hornet's nest."

"I do. And that is precisely what I am hoping for."

The door to the room opened once again, this time by a footman who stood to one side and admitted young Jeremiah into the room.

Jeremiah stood on the threshold of the room, looking nervous under the gaze of the grownup eyes, all of which had now turned their focus onto him.

"Finally!" Harry exclaimed jumping up. "I have been waiting for you all evening. Now...just over here is a sampling of desserts I want you to try. They are for my wedding in a few weeks time and I need you to tell me which ones I should choose."

Jeremiah nodded, his eyes round as he spotted the desserts on a sideboard. Harry looked enormously pleased and Lillie wondered how long it would be before he filled the house with children of his own. He was at his best in the presence of the next generation.

"Would you excuse me a minute," Petters said, getting up and giving a short nod to Jack, who followed him from the room.

"Very secretive," the Professor said, watching them go.

"Hm, yes. I am sure it is just Jack's way of getting me off this case. I'll bet he figures the best way to convince me of that is to do it through someone else," Lillie said.

The Professor didn't look particularly convinced. And, to be honest, neither was she. Why *were* they sneaking off?

"When do expect your story to be in the papers?" The Professor had a sudden uneasiness in his manner.

"Oh, about a week or so, I would think. I have some more research to do, but you shouldn't worry—I don't plan to reveal much about the Committee itself. I respect that the work you undertook was highly secretive. I do, however, plan to make our readers aware that the victims knew each other and that they worked together during the war. I also want to allude to the way that the police and crime units systematically attempted to hunt spies, specifically in 1915. What I am hoping is that this might urge Basil Wilkinson to either respond with some kind of explanation or elaboration, or, alternatively, try to shut down our story. Either way, I want him to make his way out of the woodwork."

"I see. Of course it will put us all in a rather harsh light, I would think—regardless of whether that is the intended consequence or not."

Lillie looked at Professor Hargreaves. Was it nervousness she was reading on him? Surely, as an educated man, he would understand the need for government transparency?

"I hardly think *I* would be shining the harsh light when the woman asleep upstairs—your colleague—has no compunction about telling the world about the way you all unjustly treated accused spies!" Lillie immediately regretted her outburst. She was irritated, to be sure, but much of her irritation also came from a frustration that Jack worked for the very same department Basil Wilkinson now headed. It was all so horribly intertwined. "I'm sorry, Professor. Please forgive me, it's been a very long few days."

"Yes, of course." The Professor neatly brushed away her comments, and set about pouring himself a whiskey from the sideboard. The next few minutes passed with a heavy silence between them.

Jack and Superintendent Petters re-entered the room, still discussing whatever they had started with hushed voices. Lillie tried to shake the troubled feeling that her lapsed conversation with the Professor had rooted. As she watched the flames of the fire flicker, she tried to pinpoint where her anxiousness was coming from. Was she really just overtired? Was she concerned about the reaction her article might garner? Was she irritated by Jack's secret conversation with Petters?

Harry was whispering something to Jeremiah about having a morning coat fitted for him, and she smiled as she listened in, happy for the diversion. *Won't it be terribly grand?* the boy was saying. Harry replied, *I should certainly hope so—you will have a very important job. The ring needs some safekeeping...can you meet at the tailor then? Never mind, I will pick you up, that's better.* Then Jeremiah again, *The nuns are so stuffy about us leaving...* Harry, *Nonsense! They just haven't met me yet, I can be very charming.* Jeremiah was laughing now. *I've never been to a wedding before.*

She liked the boy very much, but wished everyone would leave. It was time to sleep. Clarity eluded her, and this alone threatened to overwhelm her.

33

THE HUNTER

LONDON, ENGLAND

The hunter lay in a small, sagging bed somewhere in a tucked away Mayfair mews with views of a crumbling cobblestone street and a limestone house opposite with painted yellow windows that looked as though they had been put in crooked.

It was very early. Somewhere he could hear a rooster crowing, and he wouldn't be the least bit surprised if it was on this very street. It was a haphazard neighbourhood of tightly clustered buildings leaning on one another, as though for support. Some had horses below, others had goats, and the smell of manure wafted up through the thin curtains of the bedroom window as the morning muckers got to work.

He looked down at the woman sleeping beside him. She had long pale hair and the kind of face one would expect a secretary to have. Pasty from spending much of her time indoors, the odd pimple from too much tea and sugar and not enough fruit and vegetables, and the softly sagging jawline that came with always carrying a moderate amount of excess weight. He wasn't the least bit attracted to her.

She stirred, prompting him to reach under the bed to

retrieve his glasses. He was an American banker after all, or so she thought, and bankers wore spectacles.

"Good morning..." she said, reaching up and stretching. This caused her breasts to flop to the side, and he averted his eyes in disgust. She really wasn't his type.

"Yes, good morning. I didn't want to wake you, but I need to get going. I have an early meeting."

"I need to be in early as well. Mr. Wilkinson comes back today and he expects everything to be just as he left it and me at his beck and call."

The hunter remained silent, absently stroking her arm as a lover would.

"You haven't told me exactly what you do."

He knew, of course. Why else would he be here? It had taken him the better part of a week to get her into bed. She fashioned herself one of the bright young things. Young, perhaps...but hardly bright.

"I'm an assistant to a very important man."

He made a suitably surprised and impressed face. "And who might that be?"

"The Director of Intelligence."

"That is quite something. And is he an nice man to work for?"

"Not particularly, no. He's demanding, short tempered and intolerant. But the pay is decent." She didn't elaborate, seeming to want the focus back on them and not on her work. She placed his hand on her flaccid breast.

He reluctantly obliged her. "Perhaps we could have dinner later?"

He needed a few things before he pushed off and she seemed naive enough to comply.

"I should like that." She gave him a coy look that suggested dinner was a just an appetizer to something else and moved his hand lower on her body. He hid his revulsion.

"Good. Why don't I come and collect you from the office around 6." He painted on a falsely seductive smile as he adeptly removed his hand.

"I'll have to meet you downstairs. They don't allow visitors on our floor unless I obtain a special pass for you."

"Of course. I can imagine it would be very secure." He wondered exactly how secure, but all that would be revealed in time. "It's a shame, really, for I should so like to see your desk and where you work. Is it terribly difficult to obtain a pass?" He rubbed her leg beneath the quilt for good measure.

"It takes a bit of doing, but since it's you who is doing the asking..." She leaned in and kissed him. "I might have a little more time before I have to go to work..." she whispered, letting her clichéd sentence linger on the stale bedroom air. "And then maybe I could secure a floor pass for you after all."

At least he was getting what he came for. The hunter sighed inwardly. The sooner he started, the sooner he would finish.

34

LILLIE

LONDON, ENGLAND

L ondon was its usual teeming self. Lillie hadn't been back to the city since she had been sick with a debilitating radiation poisoning—a dangerous result of the last case she covered—and she consciously pushed away the memory. Oxford was so quiet by comparison, and she noted she missed hearing the sounds of birds and the steady breeze as it blew through the trees and whispered across the fields. She was rapidly becoming a country dweller, she mused. She missed her little cottage.

She sat at a small cafe watching as Londoners moved en masse, great throngs of them crossing streets, going into office buildings, or having lunch. They moved as a flock of birds would, in a group, changing direction, the odd straggler here and there moving against the grain, only to be gathered up again as the crowd adjusted, moved, and swallowed everything in its path.

Across the cafe table sat the man she reluctantly loved. Jack was wearing an astonishingly beautiful navy blue suit which set off his athletic figure to perfection. His crisp white shirt had a flawlessly pressed collar and a sky blue tie that perfectly set off his ivory skin and almost made it look as though it had been kissed by a winter Mediterranean sun. While they had had the odd sunny day, it was something sorely lacking here and his glow seemed at odds with the rest of the cafe patrons. Jack just had good colouring, she noted, which contributed greatly to his overall attractiveness.

"I'll come with you of, course," he was saying. "Petters insisted I do. We really don't know what to expect with this man." He was looking at her in a serious way that didn't suit his handsome face. "Lillie?"

"If you insist." She sighed. "Although I don't know the good it will do. I am much less menacing on my own."

"I hardly think a reporter is not menacing to a man like Basil Wilkinson. Quite the opposite, in fact."

"Won't it be odd that I am there with an intelligence officer? And you told me you've met him before, he knows you."

"Yes, but only in passing, and there are so many of us in differing departments that I doubt he would even remember. After all, my department isn't his department, so we are quite separate entities."

"And so your role in all of this would be?"

"Well obviously, if I come, it will get his back up even quicker, which presumably is what you want."

"Yes, but what will you tell him?"

"Only that we are acquaintances and I am facilitating your inquiries."

"Won't your department be angry with you, for enabling a reporter?"

"Spies are a different breed, I don't mind telling you. We don't worry as much about our reputations as about the work we do. A high profile civil servant like Basil Wilkinson, however, is a different kettle of fish altogether. I should think he will be very concerned indeed."

"It still sounds odd to me." Jack said nothing, so she continued. "We have the last meeting of the day. 5:30 at his office. His secretary said he likes to leave by 6."

"Good."

"In the meantime I am going to head over to the War Offices and see if I can't find out a little more about his work during the war. I'm meeting with an old colleague of his and then I am hoping to get into some of the records."

"Tread carefully."

She nodded and winked at him. "Always."

35

SUPERINTENDENT PETTERS

CHIPPING NORTON, OXFORDSHIRE

I t was the third time in as many weeks Superintendent Petters had seen the woman in the green coat.

He had spotted her at the market that morning while he was buying some vegetables for his supper. He had been paying for an unusually large bunch of carrots and thinking of how he could possibly use them all when he caught sight of her lingering outside the stalls. Again the green coat. Again the quick stare and the pretending to look through him. Was she being deliberately obtuse, still wearing that coat that screamed 'here I am' to any subject remotely aware of their surroundings?

Which raised the infuriating question again. *Who was she?* He was beginning to have doubts she was a professional, unless she was the absolute worst trained tail in the business. He had given the merchant his money in haste, quickly bagged the carrots, and had set off to follow her. She had slipped away through the crowd and in all likelihood out the back of a neighbouring store, for he had rapidly lost sight of her.

He had mused that while she might be the world's worst tail, he was probably the world's worst detective for not catching her. He had retrieved his bicycle and put his groceries into the basket on the back. As he had pedalled down the road, he had reflected on their small reprieve from winter. Late January often brought with it a hint of spring—the days were longer and the sun a little higher in the sky.

It was Thursday and he should have been in the office, but he had taken the morning to discuss the matter of his living arrangement with the adoption board. A sour faced woman and a needle of a man had come to his house that morning to ascertain whether or not he would be a suitable guardian for Jeremiah. They certainly knew how to string it out, he thought. While they tiddled about making themselves feel important, rooting through the cupboards and sizing up his extra bedroom, the boy had sat in that draughty orphanage eating gruel and wishing for a better life.

In the end, they had reluctantly agreed that even with his less than desirable situation of not having a wife, he could possibly still provide a suitable home for Jeremiah. Petters had snorted in reply, looking around his home and trying to see it through their eyes. It was immaculate, for one. Scrubbed clean each morning by his own hand before he left for work. The stone floors were covered in cozy rugs that were shook out weekly, his dishes were cleaned and put away—each cup and plate lined up perfectly. The laundry was folded, his bed linens were fresh and fluffy, and his books spoke to a healthy diversity of interests. He had even placed fresh flowers, kindly donated from the Tynesmore hothouse, around the house to welcome his guests. A nice touch, he had thought, although those two dimwits probably hadn't noticed.

It would go now to a final review, they had said as they left, along with their recommendations that Superintendent Petters could provide an adequate home for one of the state's wards. As long as no relative came forward, the woman had said in her pinched voice, the approval could come in as little as two weeks time.

"I don't suppose that is likely now that he has been in an orphanage the better part of ten years, do you?" He had attempted to keep the annoyance out of his voice.

"It has been known to happen," the woman had said, buttoning up her coat and adjusting her dismal hat. "We did have a case of a grandmother stepping in at one point and sinking the whole adoption process in the final hour. So, you just never know."

"I see." Petters was irritated with the whole business. Surely any relative who had left a boy for ten years in those conditions shouldn't be allowed to take him now, regardless of the blood that flowed through their veins. It was ludicrous.

"Good day." The woman had said and she and the pin prick of a man had started down the path while Petters leaned against the door frame, watching them disappear around the ivy cloaked hedge.

He couldn't stand bureaucratic red tape but he supposed it wouldn't be long now.

Now, having a third cup of coffee and lamenting his unusual lack of self control as he bit into an iced cinnamon roll he had bought at the market, he wondered how Lillie was getting on in London. The fact that it had been weeks since the first two victims had been found and still he didn't have any concrete leads bothered him. But he supposed these things took time.

Unfortunately, he wasn't a very patient man.

36

THE HUNTER

LONDON, ENGLAND

The building smelled of tobacco and floor polish. And coffee, the hunter realized after a moment, craving a cup. He was early, but that had been his plan. He wanted to have to linger, to wait. It was the perfect subterfuge to suss out the man at the head of it all.

He obtained the floor pass Basil Wilkinson's secretary had left for him at the reception desk and started up the staircase to the third floor. There was a small elevator but he didn't want to chance being stuck in a space the size of a mouse box breathing someone else's second hand air. He adjusted his glasses, smoothed down his hair, and practiced his smile.

Reaching the third floor, he followed the directions given to him at reception. After a few minutes of navigation, he found himself looking at the woman he had spent the night with in Mayfair.

Her hair was pulled back in a low bun, which made her face look slimmer and she was sitting down, so she almost looked an attractive weight.

"There you are!" Her face looked so genuinely happy the hunter almost regretted his part in the whole thing.

She got up from her chair and came around the desk, ruining the effect of her initial appearance. She breathed something he didn't care to hear into his ear and gave his arm a little squeeze. The remnants of her lunch lingered on the air between them.

"I'm early, I know…"

"Yes, and he is still with someone so I can't leave quite yet. Would you like to have a seat and wait? Or there is a lunch room down the hall, you could have some tea? I could walk you down there, if you like?"

No doubt she wanted to parade him in front of her colleagues. This, of course, would be antithetical to his whole operation. The very last thing he wanted was to be seen and then remembered later on. "I don't mind waiting," he replied. There were a couple of chairs lined up against a far wall. "If that's okay with you?" he added.

"Of course, I like looking at you."

He fought the urge to grimace.

The hunter could hear voices coming from inside the closed office, one of which he assumed to be Basil Wilkinson's. There was a mottled glass sidelight to the left of the door and he could make out that there were three people in the room. From their shadows he deduced two men and one woman. Their voices were low and he couldn't make out what they were saying. He tapped his fingers on the armrest of the chair impatiently and picked up a newspaper, flicking through it without reading.

There were no guards here in this reception area, which surprised him. Once past the main floor, there was no difficulty. Basil Wilkinson wouldn't recognize him. The entirety of their correspondence had been through letters and coded telegrams.

He frowned, his own incompetence annoying him—he should have checked into Wilkinson's wartime role before he took the information fed to him at face value. Of course

Wilkinson left out the bit about him overseeing the Summer-dyne Committee himself.

He had been played.

The secretary was filing something in the drawer underneath the desk. He could hear the click of the lock as she pushed the drawer shut and began tidying up her desk for the night. She turned and placed the key in a small cabinet behind her. He took note. The clock on the wall said ten minutes past six.

"I'm sure it won't be much longer," she assured him. "Where are you taking me for dinner?" She seemed nervous.

He hadn't really thought about it and threw out the name of somewhere in the West End, knowing she would like that. She fashioned herself a flapper. He had arranged their first meeting in a smokey club in Soho after he had tracked her there one night after work. On it's cocktail drenched dance floor, he had observed her in her glittering, sequinned dress, her fleshy arms bobbing up and down to the beat of the jazz band, her dance partner stumbling around in a drug induced frenzy. He had escorted her quietly away from him, and through the drink and haze she had hardly noticed the Hunter's irritated disdain for the place. That night he had easily began his false courtship with her.

He thought about dinner again. He hadn't made a reservation but it didn't matter. He had plenty of money in his pocket.

The door to the office finally opened and there stood a man he assumed to be Wilkinson. He had the seasoned look of a police officer, his short cropped hair and thick moustache trimmed to perfection. He had hooded eyes and a chiseled mouth that looked as though it rarely found humour in anything. Beside him, to the hunter's astonishment, was the young woman he had seen at the farmhouse in Scotland.

His head began to swim and he realized he was holding his breath. Her hair was longer than he'd thought it was. It was a deep auburn and pulled back with a tortoiseshell clip. Up close he could see now she had round, intelligent green eyes and a large but delicate mouth that stretched across her face. She was even smaller than he had realized that night in Scotland, and although slim, she looked to be physically capable of even the most arduous task. There was a man with her who looked vaguely familiar, although the hunter couldn't place from where. He was tall and dark with impeccable clothing and a demeanour that suggested he belonged here, somewhere in these corridors. He seemed intelligent—more so than Wilkinson, who, despite the title, was little more than a narrow minded thug.

She was thanking the thug for his time with a cool shaking of hands and the heaviness of dissatisfaction. The hunter caught a whiff of citrus from her perfume. She met his eyes for the briefest moment as she and the well-dressed man moved towards the corridor. It was a mistake to let his linger for as long as he did. And then in an instant, she was gone.

Wilkinson spun on his heel and returned to his office, hollering for his secretary as he went.

37

LILLIE

CHIPPING NORTON, OXFORDSHIRE

"Careful with him now, he obviously has an injured paw and won't be comfortable being put down on a hard surface. Why don't you use this?"

Lillie watched from her chair in the police officer's office as Petters reached up and pulled his wool sweater over his head, handing it to the boy. Jeremiah lay the sweater down and carefully placed the most enormous ginger cat Lillie had ever seen on the sweater. She wondered if he wasn't part mountain lion.

"Better," the boy agreed, attempting to examine the pads on the cat's paw. Lillie was surprised he could even get close to the animal. "It looks like there is a thorn in it...why don't I hold him and you can see if you can't pull it out," Jeremiah said, looking up at them. Lillie nodded her agreement and readied herself for battle.

"I'll have to find the tweezers," Petters answered.

"Here." Jeremiah was a step ahead of him. The boy carefully gathered the cat up, its enormous head nearly the size of his own, and held him so he wouldn't squirm while Petters searched around for his glasses.

Lillie reached over and took the tweezers. "I have better

eyesight," she concluded while wondering if Petters wasn't stalling for time, and set to work on finding the source of the angst burrowed somewhere deep in the midst of pink toes and orange fur. Finding it, she gave a little tug. With a hiss and a swipe it was quickly removed, and only the slightest amount of blood was drawn. Unfortunately it was from Lillie's hand.

"Done. He really isn't the most grateful creature," she said, mopping at her palm with a handkerchief which Petters had swiftly provided.

The cat, now on the ground, set to licking its wound, intermittently starting up at them with a look of disdain.

"You're welcome," Lillie said, glaring at him.

Jeremiah crouched on the floor and began stroking the cat between the ears. A incongruous purring filled the room. The animal got up, stretched, and began weaving in and out of Lillie's legs.

This amused her. "He hardly holds a grudge, does he?"

"Fickle creature. How was London?"

"Oh, you know, things are probably more muddled now than when I left." She raised her eyebrows in the direction of Jeremiah.

Petters took the hint. "Son, why don't you head down to reception and see if you can't get Rosamunde to bring us a few sandwiches and some coffee?"

"Yes, sir."

With him gone Petters looked back at Lillie and motioned for her to sit down. The lion jumped directly into her lap and promptly began to doze off.

"Feel free to dump him on the floor."

"I'm fine. He's quite sweet really," she said, laying her hand on his fur.

"I can think of some other words for him. So, did you see Wilkinson?"

"I did, although he wasn't too happy to meet me. And bringing Jack just annoyed him, as I suspected it would."

"They don't work directly together, though..."

"No, but I'm sure Wilkinson considers him a traitor to the service—aiding a reporter, and all that. I treated it as I would any other story; asked questions, probed a bit, generally unsettled him. I told him we had it on good authority from a committee member that there was a possibility that some of the executions were unjust."

"Did he seem nervous about your story?"

"Irritated more than nervous. He is a man who doesn't seem to fathom that he could even be humiliated, let alone unseated or tried. He wouldn't admit to receiving any correspondence from Florence and treated us both as insignificant annoyances. He is arrogant, I'll say that."

"But she is certain he received it?"

"Fairly certain, she wrote on a number of occasions, and the last letter she sent went by registered mail. His secretary signed for it, so he can hardly pretend he didn't get it. His lack of response can only be interpreted one way. It's irrelevant now anyway. I am writing the story and he won't feature well in it. I have Florence's testimony. And Rumple's."

"And the Professor's, of course."

"That one is less certain," she said, hesitation in her voice. "I don't think he is as willing to expose the department as flawed."

"I didn't get that impression when he gave me the list of executions. He even pointed me in the direction of ones which might be our trouble spots. Which incidentally, I am following up on now."

"Any suggestion where our killer might be from? Assuming it isn't Wilkinson."

"I am narrowing it down, or trying to. I have one in particular that doesn't sit right with me. Irving Guy Ries. An American, on his way to Copenhagen and was picked up here, in..."

he consulted his notes. "Manchester it looks like, doing something or other, it doesn't really say. Anyway, he was supposedly communicating with a known German spy in Rotterdam so they figured it was a cut and dried case of him also being a spy."

"Go on," Lillie said, leaning forward with interest. "I assume there is more."

"Yes. I got the majority of that story from the Professor, but I've found out more since. Turns out, the spy he was communicating with in Germany had a couple of occupations, one of which was drug smuggling."

"Probably more lucrative than spying for the German government."

"Exactly. Somewhere in the correspondence on Ries's incarceration it was said that although they suspected he was using an alias, he wouldn't give his real name. One of his guards said that he once alluded briefly to being from New York City. They were discussing food and Ries was lamenting not being able to have his usual fare."

Lillie was nodding. "New York has good restaurants, I'll say that for it."

"I can imagine. I have a friend on the police force in Manhattan so I got in touch with him to see if he had ever come across Ries's name. Apparently there is a fair amount of gang warfare going on in your home city—the five corners or something or other."

"Five Points."

"Right, that's it. Five Points. An Italian-American gang, which has been warring with a Jewish-American gang headed by a Guy Reidel—sometimes known by the alias Irving Guy Ries. Now, I don't think the Summerdyne Committee ever had that information, at least not according to the Professor." Petters sat back, triumphant. "The thing is, I don't think Ries ever wanted to give his real name because he didn't want to be picked up on drug running charges. I don't believe he ever really thought he would be executed. Apparently he had legal counsel while he was in prison and probably figured he would get off. Lack of evidence. Why would an American Jew be spying for the Germans? It was ludicrous."

"Which of course it was, but Wilkinson needed to get his number of arrests up, presumably. And who knows, maybe he salted the evidence against Ries, at least enough to get the committee members to agree to his execution. It would follow that the head of a criminal organization might certainly have people who would avenge his death."

"Oh yes. Apparently Ries's gang was formidable. A real tough bunch, with plenty of resources both with financial means and able-bodied killers. Some of them were even recruited by the military for special operations during the latter half of the war. They needed men like them."

"It seems...strange somehow. To be executed for something you had no part in. And yet, he should have been in jail, obviously. That was where he belonged."

"Jail, yes. Shot by firing squad—probably not."

"What about the other executions? The other ones that the Professor suggested might not have been guilty."

"Certainly problematic, but I can't find anything to suggest they would have people who would go to quite these lengths for revenge. I mean, we have someone here willing to systematically *murder* those responsible. It's got to be criminal."

Lillie shifted uncomfortably under the weight of the cat, trying not to wake it. "How do you think Basil Wilkinson fits?"

"That I don't know. Not yet. But I am working on it."

The door to the office re-opened and Jeremiah scuttled in, balancing a paper bag in one hand and couple of mugs of coffee in the other.

"Here you go," the boy said, placing the bag on the desk and handing Lillie a cup with drips of coffee down one side. "Sorry, a bit tricky to carry without spilling." He wiped his hand on his pants.

"Thank you very much. You are very helpful, aren't you?"

"I try to be."

"He is," Petters agreed, digging into the paper bag for a sandwich. "He most certainly is."

38

LILLIE

OXFORD, OXFORDSHIRE

The gravel courtyard in front of Tynesmore, usually witness to the leisurely arrival of dinner guests and the odd wine delivery, was wet from the melting snow and now a staging ground to an astonishing amount of activity. There was a florist truck, a wagonette filled with caged doves who were squawking and flapping about, a quartet of musicians unloading their instruments, a caterer, a bakery truck and the most enormous red and white hot air balloon. Directing the lot of them was a man dressed in a midnight blue suit that looked as though it had been borrowed from a theatrical wardrobe.

"I said *red collared doves*! Not mourning doves you imbecile! It isn't a bloody funeral, it's a wedding for Christ's sake." The blue suit was jumping up and down and waving his hands this way and that. "And move that balloon! I need to get the carriage through there and it's a team of six." Somebody called something to him that Lillie couldn't make out and the suit threw his hands up in frustration. "What do you mean lame? So now it's five? Forget it, forget it. Harness the four then...the black ones instead...yes, yes, hurry up. I said *move it...move it...*" The suit grumbled something else and went to inspect the bakery truck.

Lillie took the opportunity to sneak in the open front door unnoticed.

She found Harry wandering around the hall aimlessly scratching the top of his head. Rumple was up a ladder attempting to fasten an enormous bunch of white hydrangeas to the outside of the staircase bannister.

"I thought the wedding wasn't for another week."

"Rehearsal day. Although I admit it is rather more involved than I expected." Harry winced as there was a clattering of something sounding like glass falling off a tray in the foyer.

"What with that general you have out there marching people around and giving orders like it was the battle of the Somme?"

"He is a bit over the top isn't he?"

"And all this without the bride?"

"She should be here by this afternoon. They are making their way back from the country today and then she is finished with that dreadful family forever and ready to be my wife."

"You know Harry, all this could be a bit overwhelming for Primrose," she said gently as she motioned to all the commotion.

"I had thought of that."

"She isn't one for the limelight and you don't want to scare her away. All this is..." Lillie motioned to chaos around them, "well, it's a bit excessive, don't you think? Couldn't you keep it a little simpler?"

"Of course not, one only gets married once—usually. And anyway, this pandemonium should have calmed down by the time she gets here. At least I hope..."

The blue suited man was inside the house now and barking orders up Rumple's ladder. Rumple stared down at him with a look that could silence a steam engine and the suit wisely hurried away.

Lillie stifled a laugh. "I'm going home. I'll see you tomorrow."

"Tonight, not tomorrow. It's the rehearsal dinner!"

"Oh, must I be at that?"

What she really wanted was sleep and a bath. And her cottage.

"Yes! And you are supposed to be staying here. I told Jack you would be here. This is where the security is."

"They aren't after me, whoever 'they' are. It's Rumple, the Professor and Florence you need to secure. I am just a nobody."

"Jack won't be happy with you."

"It won't be the first time, nor the last," she called over her shoulder. "Goodbye then, I'll be back for dinner."

"Eight o'clock. Don't be late."

"I wouldn't dare, not with that general running around."

39

THE HUNTER

WILTSHIRE, ENGLAND

The early morning train ride to Salisbury was long and tedious. The hunter had lost sight of Basil Wilkinson as he boarded the train in London, but he knew he was on it somewhere, rattling along the same track in a first class carriage similar to the one the hunter was travelling in now. The golden velvet bench on which he sat smelled like an unused attic.

He sighed and stretched, pondering whether or not he should try to find some breakfast in the dining car. It had been a long night. Dinner with Wilkinson's secretary had been as dull as a prairie winter and just as protracted. Citing a headache, he had escaped her clutches shortly before midnight and made his way back to Wilkinson's office directly from the restaurant.

Having stolen her keys from her purse when she had gone to the ladies room (an annoyance she would have realized by now), the entrance to the darkened building gave him no difficulty, nor did the door to Wilkinson's private office. He'd found what he was looking for immediately—a diary of appointments, past and future, and a stack of correspondence labeled

For Immediate Action. This he had flipped through quickly, but none of the papers had anything to do with the war or contained his previous correspondence with Wilkinson regarding the Summerdyne Committee.

He was about to give up when his eyes had settled on a letter from the Royal Engineers Experimental Station. It was regarding the suspected theft of a shipment of phosgene which was catalogued as entering the facility on the first of December the previous year but which was now missing. It hadn't been signed out or used for research and, by the looks of the letter, its absence was now being considered a matter of national security. Along with the letter was an updated inventory list, which Wilkinson had scribbled comments across in red ink. The hunter made a note of the name of the substance as well as the facility's location in Wiltshire and carefully placed the letter back into the pile of papers. As he did so he noted a yellow message slip, written in the secretary's careful hand and dated that day, which was clipped to the back of the letter and the inventory list. *Porton Down, missing chemical gas, immediate reply requested, investigation required.* It could have been something or nothing, but it was a big enough concern to be in Wilkinson's diary for the following morning. *Train to Salisbury, o-six-hundred,* read his careless hand.

The hunter had decided on a whim to nick some of Wilkinson's letterhead, a few sheets along with envelopes. He had also helped himself to his signature stamp, which he quickly used on each sheet of paper, its distinctive green ink bleeding into the thick ivory stock. One never knew when it would come in handy.

The train lurched, jolting him from the memory. It slowed for a few minutes as it passed through a small ivy clad town and then resumed speed. The hunter decided it was time to eat and stood up to retrieve his wallet from his overhead bag. The train lurched again, this time suddenly, throwing the hunter forward and causing him lose his balance. It immediately slowed, quicker than he thought a train could. The little town and its brick station were behind them now so whatever was happening was unscheduled. Perhaps a mechanical issue, the hunter thought irritably as the train came to a standstill. This setback would just make the journey even longer.

He reached up and pushed down the window so he could peer out onto the track. Passengers up and down the train were all doing the same thing, their palpable confusion doing little to subdue the hunter's own. Three cars ahead he caught the blur of a dark overcoat and hat as a man quickly exited the train. He stumbled across the tracks, tripping from time to time as he hurried. The man looked back at the train when he was about thirty feet away from it, scanning the cars quickly, his eyes settling on the surprised face of the hunter. He then set off at a jog towards the station they had just passed.

He was familiar, this man—his coat flapping, briefcase dangling from his left arm. It took but a snippet of a moment for the hunter to realize that Basil Wilkinson had just ordered the train stopped so he could get off. *He was on to him.* He had probably recognized him from the day before in the waiting room of his office and knew this morning he was being followed to Porton Down by the very same man. No sooner had the hunter recognized Wilkinson did the train begin to move again, gathering speed and blowing its lonely whistle. The hunter angrily punched at the empty seat beside him as the train hurtled on towards Salisbury.

He had just seriously underestimated his mark.

40

LILLIE

OXFORD, OXFORDSHIRE

T he cottage was exactly how Lillie had left it a few days previous. The remnants of Jack's broken dishes were still swept into a neat little pile in the corner of the kitchen. Cupboards had been left open to the process of putting things away, much of which still remained in boxes scattered around the kitchen. The absence of a fire in the cooker or the hearth meant the stone walls and floors of the cottage were positively glacial. But even so, the space was beginning to feel like home.

Once she had finished lighting the fires and sweeping the kitchen floor Lillie unpacked a few more boxes of dishes, finally closing the now full buttercream cabinets. She cleared away the clutter on the countertops and the bleached pine table, wiped down the kitchen furniture with warm water and lemon soap, and put a kettle on for tea while she set out to tackle the sitting room.

The fire was roaring now and the smell of wood smoke lingered on the rapidly warming air. There were a few more boxes of books she wanted to get put away, so she started filling the bookcases underneath the leaded glass windows which faced her garden. It had turned into the most glorious day, she noted as she worked, watching the plumed heads and yellow tipped tails of a flock of waxwings having words with each other atop the bare lilac in her delicately overgrown garden. She was looking forward to taming it once the weather turned warmer.

She straightened up, hearing the whistle of the kettle, and went back into the kitchen to make the tea and search for something to hold her over until dinner at Harry's. There wasn't much in her bare pantry so she settled for some tinned cookies she still had left over from Christmas and drank her tea black. She took her cup and saucer into the sitting room and curled up on her chesterfield, pulling a wool blanket over legs as she sipped her tea, watched the fire, and planned which room to tackle next. Deciding on the spare bedroom, she yawned and thought about closing her eyes for a few minutes first.

A ringing sound startled her and she realized it was the telephone Jack had insisted she install in her boot room. She had forgotten she had one.

"Hello?"

"Lillie!" A voice she recognized well breathed crossly down the line.

"Jack!" she imitated back.

"What are you doing? I thought we agreed you would stay at Harry's?"

"I just came home to straighten up a bit. If you saw the circus going on at Tynesmore, you would hardly blame me for leaving."

"It did sound rather chaotic when I rung there earlier today. Listen, I am just about to leave London on the train for Oxford. I won't make it in time for dinner so I will eat on the train but I will see you there later?"

"If I last the evening. I really am rather tired."

"I expect you will be staying at Harry's tonight, though..."
He was pushing her.

"I hadn't planned on it. I really want to spend some time at home and I am not in any danger here. It's the Professor and Rumple who need to be looking over their shoulders."

"Except now you've gone and revealed the angle of your article to Basil Wilkinson, so who knows what is on his mind. Speaking of which, I have something to tell you, something I have discovered through some correspondence that inadvertently came my way. I'll fill you in when I get to Harry's."

Lillie nodded as though he could see her. "See you tonight."

"You will. And don't forget to pack an overnight bag."

"Goodbye Jack." She knew by being noncommittal, she would irritate him further.

With her tea now cold she wandered back into the kitchen and placed it in the sink. It was nearly five o'clock and the sun was setting over her garden. She watched as the colours of the sky turned clementine, magenta, and then the deepest indigo.

She would have a bath instead of sorting the guest room, she decided, and made her way through the sitting room and down the narrow hallway to the bathroom to run the tub. As it filled, she swished the water around with her hands and added some salts. When it was nearly full she switched off the water and began to remove her stockings.

A creak outside the bathroom door caused her to stop. She strained her ears but didn't hear anything else. *An old house makes noises*, she told herself and continued with the stockings. With her back to the door she leaned over the tub to test the water and then began to unbutton her dress. As she did so she reflected on how she would approach her article for the paper. Should she have Florence on record? In an interview perhaps? Or Rumple? It would give it the weight it needed, to be sure.

Another creak interrupted her thoughts. Surely she was alone, wasn't she? She fought the urge to go back into the hallway and check. No, she was being silly. The house was warming up with the fires and this would cause wood to expand and make noise. She removed her dress and stood in her slip, dangling her toe over the water to make sure it wasn't too hot.

It what seemed like a split second, she heard the door behind her being flung open. It hit the wall with such force that bits of plaster exploded and rained to the floor. Someone was covering her mouth with something, a towel or a cloth, and she fought back against him, kicking and elbowing into his ribcage, desperately gasping. She was suffocating, she couldn't breathe, she couldn't see, and then there was nothing but darkness as she felt the cold tiles of the floor meet her face.

41

SUPERINTENDENT PETTERS

Chipping Norton, Oxfordshire

Superintendent Felix Petters had just sat down to a late supper when his telephone rang. He thought about ignoring it, and probably would have, had Jeremiah been with him. As it was, he was already assuming the role of a worried father and didn't want to miss a call if something was wrong with the boy. Petters had an ingrained tendency to worry and so he reluctantly pushed back his chair, wistfully eyed his steaming lamb chop, and made his way back into his kitchen.

"Superintendent Petters here, how can I help?"

"Superintendent...it's Jack Abbott calling. Something has happened...to Lillie..."

Petters could hear the man trying to catch his breath. He had been running, obviously, and sounded frantic.

"Go on," Petters urged. "What exactly has happened?"

"She's missing. She was supposed to turn up at Tynesmore for Harry's wedding rehearsal dinner this evening but she never showed. I didn't get there until about half past eight and I tried ringing her but there wasn't any answer."

"Did you go to her house?"

"Of course!" The voice was exasperated. "I'm here now, and she isn't! She has been taken. Her door has been pried open, the lock damaged, and it looks as though she has been dragged out of her bathroom...her clothes were still on the floor and the tub was full..." Petters could tell he was choking back tears.

"I'm leaving immediately. I'll meet you at the cottage. What is the address?"

"Orchard Cottage...I can't remember the street name. Come directly to the center of town, it's north of the village green, first right, last cottage before the fields. Please hurry. In the meantime I am going to do a sweep of the village. Harry is out there now, with Rumple, knocking on every door."

"Good, I won't be long."

Petters grabbed his coat at a run and headed for the police car, his lamb chop cold and forgotten on the table.

42

THE HUNTER

OXFORD, OXFORDSHIRE

I t was nearly midnight when the hunter finally arrived in Oxford. After losing Basil Wilkinson, he had no choice but to remain on the train to Salisbury—frustratingly, it was an express route. There hadn't been any point going to Porton Down without Wilkinson being there; he wouldn't know what to look for or where, and so he had simply crossed the track and gotten onto the next train to Reading. Once there he transferred trains and headed north to Oxford.

It was a gamble, not heading back to London to track Wilkinson, but it was one the hunter was willing to wager on. He figured resuming his watch of the remaining three on the Summerdyne Committee would probably reveal more to him than chasing a more astute than previously imagined head of intelligence across the country. He was making an assumption that the three remaining committee members were either together, or at least in close contact with one another now they had the Scottish woman in their possession. His late night foray into Wilkinson's office hadn't revealed as much as he would have liked. But of course, why would he write down his actual plans in a diary where anyone could see it?

And so, here he was, exhausted and weary from a day of trains, attempting to check in at the Raven Inn on the Oxford high street.

He rung the brass bell to the left of the check-in desk as he heard in the distance a police car siren wailing into the night. A young man came out from a room behind the desk.

"I'm sorry to be so late, I hope I didn't wake you." The hunter always liked to start off on the right foot.

"No sir, it's been quite a hop and chop night actually...seems there has been a kidnapping tonight and the town is crawling with police," the young man said. He rubbed at his eyes with one hand as he pushed the registration papers across the counter. "How many nights would you like?"

The hunter pushed back a sinking feeling. "Two, and I may extend."

Although he wondered now if he shouldn't leave right away.

"Room 307." The man turned to retrieve a key from the cubbies behind him. He swivelled back around and handed it to him.

The hunter nodded his thanks. "Incidentally, who was kidnapped?"

"Oh." The man reached under the desk and produced a leaflet with a woman's picture. "They are handing these out all over town. Some reporter for the newspaper, which presumably is how they got all these leaflets printed in record time. Contact number is on the bottom if you see anything during your stay."

The hunter stared at a grainy photograph of a smiling woman staring back at him. She had the same hair and the same eyes he had run over in his mind again and again since that night in Scotland. The same type of face that reminded him he had once been a vulnerable boy with no prospects. A face and body so similar to the one they had pulled out of that dark, icy river all those years ago. He shuddered.

"Thanks," he said hesitantly, carefully folding the paper and putting inside his breast pocket. "I will."

He climbed the stairs to the third floor and put his bag in his room. Although it was the middle of the night, he didn't plan on sleeping now. Listening to the sirens in the distance caused a tightness in his chest that surprised him. He wondered why he cared what happened to a woman he had never met. She just reminded him of someone he had loved a very long time ago. She was nothing to him and he was hardly the type of man who should care after everything he had done in his life—the people he had killed, the business he was in. It was laughable.

Two things niggled at him. In his line of work, most of the time people didn't see him coming. The first two names on his list this time hadn't the slightest idea they were about to die. They had gone about their middle class lives without a worry in the world. And then, one day, he had shown up.

The Professor, however, had seemed to know exactly what was going to happen—and he was prepared for it. At the time the hunter hadn't given this thought enough weight, and perhaps he shouldn't do so now, but it did strike him as strange.

Basil Wilkinson also saw him coming. Perhaps it was because he was trained well. Perhaps, the hunter reluctantly admitted to himself, Wilkinson might even be somewhat lucky at times. But the thing was...Wilkinson wasn't particularly *good* at anything. He firmly believed Wilkinson was as all thugs are, generally ignorant and dim-witted. Yet, Wilkinson knew enough to wait until he was on the train to make his escape even though he must have already known back in London that he was being followed. He actually led the hunter away from the city intentionally. He too, seemed to expect he was going to be followed, as though...as though they knew his every move.

As though they were one step ahead of him, as though they were playing him.

He shook the thoughts from his head. Did either of these men have anything to do with the disappearance of the reporter? Possibly. Maybe.

Either way, he thought as he locked the door behind him, it was time to go hunting.

HARRY

Oxford, Oxfordshire

Tynesmore was bathed in the soft glow that can only come from the flames of three hundred and ninety-nine hurricane lamps. Harry's wedding coordinator had counted them, irritated that one had arrived broken. The remains of a dinner that had been so lavishly served, each course precisely timed with the one proceeding it, each plate coupled with a speech lasting no more than four to six minutes, now sat cold on the monolithic dining room table Harry had purchased for the occasion. The guests had been ushered out by Rumple, one by one following the main course, as Harry and Primrose had sprinted from their own rehearsal dinner on the news that Lillie had been kidnapped. It was now midnight and the two of them stood huddled around the telephone in the great hall while Harry cradled the receiver against his ear.

"Winston? Is that you?" Harry raised his voice so it would carry over the noise of an exceptional number of wait staff that were now scurrying through the corridor with the remains of the uneaten pheasant. Harry's orders had been given to him by Jack: telephone the newspaper and find out if Jeremy Winston had any information on what Lillie might have been doing when she disappeared. Perhaps there was something they didn't know about? Some additional information on the murders that had come up and she was conceivably following—a thread, a lead—-something. Harry wondered if Petters wouldn't be a better source of information on the ins and outs of the case than the head of the newspaper. But he had his marching orders and he obeyed them. Jack was in a state of frenzy, and it was no wonder—it would hardly be prudent to question the logic at this late hour.

He had woken Winston on the advice of the answering service at the newspaper. Apparently he always left instructions with the night operator to connect emergency calls to his home telephone.

His voice was hoarse from sleep when he picked up the call, but it only took a split second for Jeremy Winston to become sharply alert. "What have you got? What's happened?"

"Lillie is missing, she was taken right out of her cottage tonight, signs of forced entry."

"Oh God..." Winston groaned. "What is being done?"

Harry could hear something muffled on the other end, clothing being pulled on in haste, he assumed.

"The police have search parties going all over town. Jack and Petters are at her home now, using it as a sort of makeshift base to coordinate the village volunteers. As far as I can ascertain, it's just door to door searching, beginning at the centre of town and fanning out."

There was another groan from Winston. "I'll get over there immediately."

"Wait, before you go—was there anything new Lillie might

have found out? Had she any leads that might have taken her somewhere new, uncharted territory?"

"Look, Harry, she's got a big fish on her line and she was getting ready to reel him in. If you're asking me if there's more than one fish—or more than the one I know about, then I am just as in the dark as you are. But that in itself wouldn't be unusual for Lillie, she often works with her cards close to her chest. I don't check in with her on a daily basis. When she has something, she sends it to me."

"I see." Harry felt the disappointment wash over him. They had nothing. No leads. No suspects. Nothing on the whereabouts of his best friend.

"I'm sorry Harry but I really should get over to the volunteer centre. I've got to go."

"Right. Yes, thanks Jeremy, I'll see you there. Oh and Jeremy —" It was an afterthought but Harry thought he had better be forewarned. "Tread lightly, Jack is like a caged animal ready to pounce. You know how he feels about her work at the newspaper—you won't be seeing him at his best tonight."

Harry hung up the telephone and took a worried Primrose into his arms. She smelled of strawberries and he hugged her close, inhaling her scent.

"We'll find her," he said, wondering if he believed it himself.

The sound of a door closing startled him and looked up to see the Professor standing before them. He was wearing his Wellington boots and Harry wondered if he had been outside.

"Professor, you startled me. I thought you weren't feeling well so I hadn't expected to see you downstairs. You missed quite a rehearsal dinner."

"I've just heard," the Professor said, not addressing the state of his health. He had begged off the evening on account of a migraine headache. "Rumple filled me in. Please, tell me what I can do to help," he urged.

"Yes, terrible, terrible night. There is search force being

organized at her cottage—Jack and Superintendent Petters are there now. I'm sure whatever help you can give in the way of manpower would be appreciated. I'm heading over there now and could give you a lift if you are well enough to go."

"I'll get my coat and hat." The Professor had already started from the room and Harry looked down at Primrose.

"Stay here my love..." he said softly. "In case she comes looking for us."

Primrose nodded and gave his cheek a quick kiss. "Find her Harry, please find her."

"I will. And one more thing my sweet—who turned down the beds in the second floor guest bedrooms tonight?"

"Missy, but she would have left ages ago now. Why?"

Harry thought about this. Was he being overly paranoid? "It's nothing to worry about now, never mind."

Harry retrieved his coat and hat from the closet and made his way quickly towards the door.

LILLIE

SOMEWHERE IN OXFORDSHIRE

The room had an odour of damp, something akin to what a basement or warehouse might have. The ceiling was at least twenty feet high and there were small windows at the top of one wall through which she could see a clear night sky, the stars flecked with silvers and blues. The only light came from a sliver of a moon, unseen but imagined. And it was cold. The floor was stone, mottled and rough as though it had been laid hundreds of years previously, with a slick layer of something living and slippery on its surface—moss, perhaps, or algae. The entire place had a cold that seeped into your bones and threatened death.

Beside her lay a blanket smelling of horse hair and must. It was thick burlap lined with a moth-eaten grey wool and she pulled it around her shoulders as she got up. She wasn't wearing anything other than her slip but there were shoes on her feet now, short, thick gardening boots someone must have put on while she was unconscious. Why? Were they expecting she walk? She had the sense she was completely alone and didn't have to look around to confirm it. There wasn't another breathing soul in the vicinity, of that she was sure. The air hung undisturbed, its weighty silence creating the unnatural ringing that comes with isolation. Water gurgled somewhere outside, its faint but constant rushing telling her she was near a stream.

There was one door in the room and while she moved towards it now, she wasn't hopeful. It was made of a thickly planked, oiled wood, and was locked from the outside. Boarded, possibly, for it didn't give at all as she pushed her shoulder into it.

Lillie didn't know how long she had been unconscious for. She rattled at the door again, pushing and pulling and kicking at it in vain. And then, frustrated, she let loose a long, high pitched howl that, for all she knew, not another living soul would ever hear.

45

SUPERINTENDENT PETTERS

OXFORD, OXFORDSHIRE

Orchard Cottage had become the makeshift headquarters for Superintendent Petters's search party. It buzzed with a palpable urgency.

Although he was an officer of the Oxford Constabulary, Petters's usual geographical beat of Chipping Norton effectively rendered him an outsider when it came to administrative authority in the town of Oxford proper. The politics in a police department was just as insidiously nauseating as anything in the legislature, he reflected miserably. As such, Petters was encountering the usual territorial resistance law enforcement was infamous for. He wasn't getting the officers he had requested, nor were the search parties being organized in the manner he thought most effective.

He was barking down the telephone line now at a lowly constable on the night shift. "How can you possibly think it is the best use of our man power to have such large groups going house to house?" There was some excuse being made on the other end, but Petters was so distracted and annoyed he was barely listening. "She isn't likely next door having supper, now is she? Not since her cottage was forcibly entered and she was dragged out of it against her will. You ninny! Put your super-visor on the line."

As he waited Petters motioned to one of his crew to put some coffee on. He pointed at Lillie's stove and the percolator that sat idle beside it.

Finally, after what seemed an eternity, the flat voice of Chief Constable Heatherington came on the line. "What can I do for you Petters? Not like I haven't enough to do around here. Inci-dentally, this isn't your show, it's mine, so how about you quit ordering my staff around?"

Petters ignored him. "I need a larger volunteer base. We have to expand our arc outwards, into the surrounding areas. I have a few good people here but I need more. And maps—all the unused buildings within a ten mile radius to start. And then get started on the twenty mile arc. Also eyes on cars coming and going, cordon off the main roads...."

Heatherington interrupted him. "I have a system Petters, just as you would if you actually spent any time in your own district instead of coming here all the time and butting your nose into mine."

"How much time are we going to spend on this?" Petters voice rose dangerously. "I am in the middle of a murder investi-gation, and I can tell you as sure as the sun rises that this missing person is related to that very investigation, so I suggest you get your head out of your backside and give me what I need! Immediately!" He slammed down the phone with such force it shook the table.

He looked around the room at the shocked faces. Harry, Jack, the Professor, and a smattering of village volunteers stared back at him.

"Sorry about that..." he said, attempting to apologize. "But it was necessary."

Jack came over to the table with a large piece of paper and a pencil. On it he had drawn a rudimentary sketch of the village and its outlying areas. It appeared to depict his suggested plan for the search groups.

Petters nodded at it. "Good. Have we enough volunteers here, though?"

"Almost, and I will find more, whatever it takes."

Petters looked around the room. "Divide into groups of two —no more than two. I need fifteen groups in total, but more would be beneficial." He consulted the map again for confirmation, recounting.

There was murmuring and the shuffle of feet as the volunteers organized themselves.

"Good," Petters said. "Now, everyone listen up. Form a line and talk to Jack here about your assignments. The sooner we get started the better. Have we got enough torches?" A volunteer nodded in agreement.

He sighed and received a cup of coffee from a volunteer. He carefully inspected the cleanliness of the cup and, deeming it acceptable, took a long sip. "Thanks," he said, cupping it in his hands for warmth. "And Professor?" Petters's eyes scanned the room, not finding him. Wasn't he just there a moment ago? Perhaps he had gone out for a cigarette. "Has anyone seen the Professor?"

A couple of head shakes and no's came back to him. For an instant, Petters imagined an emerald green coat, a dead body in the churchyard, and Jeremiah's translucent skin.

A volunteer scraping his chair across the floor jolted his attention back to the present. He noticed the front door had been left slightly ajar. A rush of night air breathed in through the space, but the Professor was nowhere to be seen.

46

THE HUNTER

OXFORD, OXFORDSHIRE

I f he were to hide someone in the middle of the night, someone he knew would be searched for furiously by police and friends and townspeople, he would take them as far from the centre of town he could reasonably get in a short amount of time. He would pick somewhere remote and unused, somewhere that didn't have houses around it, or stores or farms. Somewhere that he could get back from quickly so as not to arouse suspicion.

He shuddered at his next thought, disgusted in himself that he knew the next steps in a killer's mind—remove the victim from his or her familiar surroundings, extract whatever information necessary, dispose of a life. Problem solved. Whoever had kidnapped Lillie Mead likely intended to kill her, which meant he didn't have much time.

He knew her name now from the leaflet folded in his breast coat pocket. Lillie Mead, reporter for the Oxford Daily Press. Lead Crime Reporter. Obviously she'd been covering his two murders in North Oxfordshire. He felt a sharp pang of regret.

The hunter had studied maps from the lobby of the hotel.

He had asked a few questions of the inn keeper before he had started out. Were there any abandoned storage facilities outside of town? Any old barns, now unused? Any mothballed factories? The inn keeper had looked at him as though he was mad, asking about buildings in the middle of the night.

"I'm from America," the hunter had told him—truthfully. "I just arrived and my clock is off by about six hours. I'm looking at potential sites to relocate a clothing factory...from Chicago," he'd added for good measure.

The inn keeper had nodded as though he understood but the hunter wasn't entirely sure he wouldn't call the police the minute he stepped outside.

He had a map of the area in his hand now with all the sites the inn keeper had given him marked. There was a bicycle shed behind the hotel and the hunter handily picked the lock. He chose one closest to the door and set out on his way.

There was activity in the town, teams of people made up of two or three, sometimes with officers and sometimes plain clothes volunteers. They were going door to door down the darkened streets. He checked his watch, it was just past one a.m. It was madness for him to be out here, but he had his cover and he forged ahead. It didn't surprise him that the officers would be searching within town for her although anyone with an ounce of intelligence would realize the last place anyone would stash a kidnap victim would be here. As far as he was concerned all these people were doing was wasting precious time and resources.

The hunter steered the bike away from the centre of town and started the trek into the countryside. The fine gravel crunching under his wheels as a rush of wind ran its fingers through his short hair, freezing his scalp. He had four potential stops on his itinerary. The first was an old munitions factory about three miles to the north of town. It hadn't been in use

since 1917 and, according to the inn keeper, was on the demolishing block.

The hunter arrived at it quietly and out of breath. He
dismounted and pushed the bike up the shoulder of the gravel
drive staying on the grass to muffle the sound of his footsteps.
He couldn't see any sign of life, but decided to check the
building anyway. He found an entry door with a rusted lock
and crushed it with the remnant of a brick he found near it.

Once inside he shone his torch around the cavernous interior, a few bats flew up narrowly missing his face and startling
him. There were tall windows covered in wire mesh and, with
the exception of a thick layer of dust, the assembly line area
looked as though it had been abandoned mid-shift. There were
bound pieces of copper wiring and tubed metal canisters still
lined up as though they were expecting the next crop of
workers to swoon in and finish them off. Large pulley systems
overhead hadn't been dismantled and the hunter wondered at
the sheer size of the place.

There were offices located to the rear and sides of the
assembly line room and he checked each one carefully, not
finding her. Frustrated, he returned to fetch his bicycle and
started towards the water mill, the second location on his map.

It took the better part of an hour to reach it and he
wondered if at this rate he would ever find her. A car would
have been so much more expeditious. After taking a few wrong
turns he eventually gave up and followed a stream until,
rounding a particularly sharp bend, he saw it in the distance.

He was lucky the night was clear or he might have missed it
altogether. Its smokestack had all but disappeared and its darkened stone facade faded into the night. If it hadn't been for the
reflection off a few high windows on the stream side of the
building, he wouldn't have known it was there. As he got closer
to the mill he thought he heard a woman's voice, but it stopped
so suddenly he figured he must have imagined it. He walked

around the perimeter and located an entry door that had been boarded up, relatively recently by the looks of it.

The hunter gave the door a solid knock, knowing full well if the kidnapper was inside he would now have removed his advantage of surprise. There was sound inside and he put his ear to the door to hear it.

He knocked louder, this time shouting. "Hello? Is there anyone there? Hello!"

"Please..." The voice was on the verge of a whimper. "Please help me."

"Hang on, I'll get the door open, hang on!" The hunter stood back and took a good look at it. It was crisscrossed with newly nailed boards; he would need a saw or a hammer to either cut them or break them off. He doubted he could kick it open, but it was worth a shot.

"Just stand aside," he called to her through the door. Then he stood back, turned his body sideways for maximum power, and kicked it with every ounce of strength he had. It didn't move. He kicked it again, and again, and again. Nothing. He ran back to the bicycle and began to dismantle it. He would use one end of the handlebars to pry at the wood and loosen the nails. Returning to the door, he spoke to her through it.

"It's going to be all right. I am finding something to get the door open with."

"Thank you..." Her voice was quieter now, calmer.

He attempted to insert one of the ends between the door and the board. It was too thick so he set to work removing the hand grips to make the ends narrower. Then he tried again. He was able to get one end of the bar inserted enough that he could put some torque onto the other end of the metal bar and pry the nails out. With some effort he had the first board off within minutes and started on the next three. Whoever had put her here hadn't much intention of coming to get her, he thought with disgust. What a horrid way to die—slowly and torturously. Surely a coward had done this.

With the last board giving away he wrenched open the door, flinging it back against the building with such force that he heard it splinter.

There stood a tired and shivering Lillie Mead.

47

LILLIE

OXFORDSHIRE

"Thank God," Lillie whispered to the man in the doorway, taking a step closer to him. "I can't thank you enough..." The man backed away hesitantly and her brain registered this as odd. Was it possible that this man was the one who had knocked her unconscious and was now coming back to kill her? She studied him guardedly in what little light they had. He stood a few feet away from her and made no attempt to come any closer. She read his body language as careful and cautious, but also strangely reassuring. He was showing her he wasn't a threat. She relaxed slightly, but not entirely. There was so much else to think about.

Her saviour looked to be easily over six feet tall and had the long leanness of a distance runner. He wasn't yet middle aged, but neither was he young, and his face had the etched and intense look of someone who knew their business. What that was, or what he was doing out here in the middle of the night, she neither knew nor cared. What she did know was that he looked familiar somehow, although she couldn't place from where.

"I take it you are the missing person the entire town is

looking for at the moment." His voice was light and kind, although underneath there was a hint of something else.

"I believe I am, though how I got here or by whose hand I really couldn't say. Are you with the police?"

Aware she was wearing only her slip, Lillie pulled the blanket around herself more tightly. She peered down at the boots on her bare feet and legs. There was a scrape she hadn't noticed along her leg and she felt the burn of open skin.

He ignored her question. "Whoever it was is a nasty piece of work. That door wasn't easy to open and I don't believe he had much intention of coming back."

"I shudder to think what would have become of me had you not shown up." Why was he deliberately sidestepping her inquiries?

The man nodded his head at her, encouragingly. "I think we should go in case I am wrong and he does return. It's a long walk back, can you make it?"

"I can make it anywhere that takes me away from here."

"Good, stay close. We will take the path by the river in order to stay off the main roads. Once we get into town you had better get into the police station, there is quite a search party going on."

The walk along the water's path was thankfully easy although the night was cold and Lillie struggled to keep the blanket on as she walked, pushing away the very real fear that this man was leading her deeper into the wilderness to facilitate his killing her.

"You're an American," she said as she watched the man duck the branches of the trees.

"Chicago," he said, not looking back. "And you?"

"New York originally, although I live here now." She was beginning to get the feeling that they were, in fact, heading in the correct direction. She let her guard fall a little more and exhaled an enormous breath.

"Any idea why you ended up locked in the old water mill?" He looked back at her for a moment and, apparently satisfied she was keeping up, continued at the same steady pace.

"Probably. I am a reporter and sometimes people don't like what I write." She didn't want to say much more and thankfully he didn't pry.

They continued on in silence, dodging the water and the rocks, for what seemed like an eternity. The boots she wore weren't hers and they rubbed at her heels every step she took. She had half a mind to stop, but fought through the pain in order to put as much distance between them and the site of her incarceration as possible.

"May I ask what you were doing out here in the middle of the night? Not that it's any of my business, of course." She was attempting to make conversation.

"I couldn't sleep, still in the wrong time zone. I'm out here for work and I needed to see a few old factory sites, so I thought why not go for a little bike ride and explore them before tomorrow."

"Really?" She didn't mean to sound so incredulous, but it did sound like a cover story if she had ever heard one. "Most people would just read or toss and turn."

"I like the exercise," he answered, still not looking back.

"You look familiar to me," she continued, watching his back stiffen. "Have we met?"

"I don't think so." His shoulders relaxed in perfect unison, as though with intention. "I just got here yesterday."

The sky was beginning to lighten with the dawn and she could see him better now. He was staying a good distance ahead of her but he matched his pace to hers. If she got too close, he would pull away again and then readjust his speed. If she slowed, he would as well. He clearly didn't want her too close to him and she began to feel uneasy again.

In the distance she could see a faint outline of Oxford and

she was relieved they hadn't far to go. At least he was taking her in the right direction, so regardless of who he was, he wasn't here to harm her.

He too must have realized they wouldn't have much longer together, and so he asked the question he had apparently wanted to ask earlier. "What is the story you are working on, or can't you say?"

She thought about this a moment. Should she say, she wondered? How much did this man already know? He wasn't just a man out for a bike ride in the middle of the night. There was much more to him than that, but she reluctantly decided being honest was her only real option.

"It's a piece about a couple of murders in North Oxford-shire. There appears to be a connection between both victims and a committee they served on during the war."

The man kept walking and didn't turn around. "What type of committee?"

"I really shouldn't say until the story is released. There are three other committee members who would likely be in danger."

He appeared to be thinking about this. "I hope they are somewhere safe," he said.

"They are all together and under supervision."

"Perhaps you shouldn't write the story. It doesn't seem to be in your best interest."

Although this statement had the overtone of friendly concern, Lillie felt that underneath there was a warning. Not a threat, exactly, but something.

They met a road and the man stopped abruptly. He appeared to be considering whether or not they should take it or continue through the fields and brush, which would take them on a more direct and unseen route into town. For the first time that hour he turned and looked directly at her. His eyes were a deep gray and harboured something she couldn't place

—perhaps loneliness, or melancholy—but they didn't match the rest of his uncompromisingly competent face. He might have even been considered handsome by some, but there was too much of the unknown simmering beneath the facade for her to think so. There was a brutal honesty about him and she, perhaps mistakenly, believed she could speak freely with him.

She blurted it out before she had time to think. "Who are you really?"

The man's face didn't move a twitch. Nor was he surprised. He continued to stare at her and his eyes looked almost amused, as much as that was possible in a face carved from granite.

After what seemed like a very long moment he replied. "Does it really matter?"

"To me it does."

"Hm." He appeared to be thinking about this and a small smile crossed his lips. "This way..." He turned and started across the road to the brush, apparently satisfied with the current untraveled route they were already on.

"You aren't very forthcoming."

"No, I suppose not," he replied quietly. "The truth is I am nobody. I came here for a job and it wasn't what I expected. I've had to reconsider things and it is almost time for me to return home."

"Almost?"

"I have a few more things to do."

"Such as?"

"Has anyone ever told you that you are a bit...pushy?" He had his back to her again but she could tell by his voice he was smiling.

"I *am* a reporter," she replied, swatting at large blackberry bramble that had caught her leg, tearing even more skin off. "Well...whoever you are, I thank you."

The man ahead of her nodded and continued down a low

sloping hill into the village, his stride long and measured, his back straight and strong. As he moved away from her, Lillie watched him for a moment—his mysteriousness unsettling her, the darkness around him a weighty shroud—then she hurried to catch up.

48

JACK

OXFORD, OXFORDSHIRE

I t was 3:30 a.m and they still didn't have any concrete leads on Lillie's whereabouts.

The cottage was a veritable revolving door for people of all walks of life: young, old, official, unofficial—all exhausted and surviving on copious amounts of tea and coffee. A plump, old woman who lived in the neighbouring cottage and had heard the commotion had come over to see what she could do to help. Finding herself at home in Lillie's kitchen, she kept the kettle full and the percolator bubbling. Without any fuss, she had also efficiently commandeered the neighbouring kitchens on the street in order to secure additional bread, cheese, and meat to make sandwiches for the volunteers. A stack of them now sat on the central kitchen table, wrapped in brown paper and tied with string, awaiting the next change of shift.

Jack was seated on one of the kitchen chairs speaking with a wan-faced man wearing an old fisherman's sweater. "Forgive me, could you give me the name of the inn again?" Jack was making notes on a pad in his lap. His head ached from the sheer pace of the entire day—a full day in the office, a train ride from Oxford, the panic of arriving and not being able to find his fiancé, the horror of finding her cottage door violated, the bathtub full, and then the resulting organization of a full-scale search. He looked up at the man's bleary eyes and sincerely hoped he wasn't wasting his precious time.

"The Raven. He arrived just before midnight, which isn't all that odd in terms of guests, but he asked for maps of the area. I figured he wanted them for the next day, but then he headed straight back out into the night. Strange, really. What tourist does that? In the middle of the night—I ask you."

Jack really didn't think it had a thing to do with Lillie's disappearance but had they had the extra manpower he might have it investigated. As it was, they were burning both ends and there wasn't an officer to spare. The very last thing he was willing to do was to pull them off the search because some inn owner had a strange guest.

Jack sighed and handed the pad of paper over to the man. "Tell you what, write down the specifics here, if you wouldn't mind. Name, description, any bits of conversation that you remember. It all helps. I'll see if I can't get someone over there in the morning to investigate the fellow."

"Not tonight then?"

"I'm afraid not, I just can't possibly spare anyone at the moment."

Petters came into the kitchen trailed by Harry. "Jack," he commanded, reaching for another mug of coffee. "We might have something." He took a long sip and headed to the logistical map he had hung on the wall opposite the sink. Jack got up to join him. The inn keeper was scribbling down his notes, head cocked to one side, eavesdropping. Petters ignored him.

"We've got a possible sighting about a mile and a half from the old water mill—here..." He used a pointer to indicate. "A woman and man travelling south along the river on foot."

"Towards town?" Jack felt a surge of optimism.

"Possibly. They were spotted by one of our teams at the

intersection of the road about an hour ago but they lost sight of them again almost immediately. The brush here..." he indicated an area on the map, "is tremendously thick. It'll be slow going if they are moving that way entirely and not using the roads."

"It's got to be the kidnapper moving her. Why else would they choose not to travel by road? And just where the hell do you think they are going?" He was about to reach a boiling point and he could feel himself losing control.

Petters adopted a tone which was probably meant to calm him. It had a negligible effect. "I've sent all our incoming teams directly there. We will have at least twenty people on that route within the hour."

"It's not quick enough!" Jack exploded. "I'm going, now —Harry?"

His friend was already at the door. "Car is ready, old sport."

49

THE HUNTER

OXFORD, OXFORDSHIRE

The road into town, coloured chalky pink with the dawn, was devoid of human life. They had passed a few small farmsteads, smouldering chimneys and twitching curtains their only sign of the living as the road wound its way past bare willow trees and honeyed cottages into the centre of town.

He listened to her footsteps as he walked—quick drops, more like a rabbit than a human, he mused. He negotiated the road while keeping an eye out for the search parties. He didn't want to cross paths with them and have to explain who he was or what he was doing with their missing person.

"You know," she said from behind him as they rounded a bend in the road and crossed over a trickling stream. It was soft and melodic. "I never asked your name."

He didn't answer right away, thinking about her question instead of answering it. He thought about all the roads that had led him here, the trajectory of his life and what his future held. The remorse that threatened to engulf him, and the loss he had left in his wake. He wasn't unlike Florence Millicent-Marks, he thought ironically. He too, needed to atone for his actions. But, once taken, a life could never be put back.

"Didn't you?" He hadn't slowed his pace at all and now he increased his stride, his footfalls further and further apart, as though this would somehow distance himself from his own thoughts. "It's Daniel," he called back over his shoulder. The first truth he had ever told her.

They were on the high street now and he could sense behind him that she had stopped walking.

"It's this way..." she called out.

He stopped suddenly and turned to face her. "What's this way?"

"My cottage. And the police station. Should I perhaps go home and get some clothes before I go to the station?" She was looking down at her ensemble: a filthy blanket and a nightdress as thin as paper.

"No, police first." He was definite with her, but more acutely, he didn't want her to go back into an unknown situation.

"I'm just so tired."

"Of course you are," he said, walking towards her, "but you are very likely in danger. How do you know this...this person, isn't there, watching your house?" Illogically, the very thought incensed him.

She nodded firmly. "Yes, police, of course." He fought the urge to grab her waist and draw her close to him. He had never wanted to kiss someone as much as he did her at that very moment. What was wrong with him?

"But the cottage is en route—it's just there," she said, pointing to a lane a few blocks up and to the right of where they stood now. "I have no doubt that my friends will be there, after all this time, and with my not showing up for Harry and Primrose's rehearsal dinner..." He didn't have a clue what she was talking about. "And if they aren't, well...if you are with me, then...shouldn't it be alright to just get *something* to wear."

"If you insist on going home first then yes, of course I will accompany you."

He wasn't happy about it, but he didn't want to argue out here on the street. He fought back the prickle of warmth she had stirred in him.

"Good, it's just this way."

She led him up the road past small cottages and darkened shops, past a dewy common green, and to an intersection. Turning right she proceeded down a smaller lane for a few minutes until the road dead ended and rolling fields stretched out before them. There was activity in the cottage that bordered the vast grasslands beyond. Its windows lit up the road in front of them, the front door was ajar, and the murmur of voices complete with the redolent of coffee and smoke told him not only was this her home but it was full of police.

He stopped walking immediately. The very last thing he needed was to be surrounded by police.

By now she was through the front gate and standing on the little pathway.

"Are you not coming inside?" She had a perplexed look on her face and he noticed how small she was, still wrapped in the blanket, old boots on her feet, her sinewy legs scratched and bleeding.

"I, uh...no, it looks like you are in good hands."

He could see a few officers through the window, their black uniforms like a caucus of crows organizing a hunt. He was backing away before he even realized it.

She didn't move from where she stood and he felt her eyes on him, searing through him, as though she could see every muscle, every bone and ligament, all his thoughts and fears, everything.

He held up a hand and waved goodbye. Then he turned and hurried back down the street. He could hear her behind him, faintly, as though in a dream.

"Thank you..."

He didn't dare turn back.

By the time the hunter reached his hotel on the other side of town it was seven thirty and coffee was being served in the dining room. He gulped down a few cups and set about organizing his day. He would now not only have to understand why Basil Wilkinson had discovered he was following him and where he was now, but why someone had kidnapped Lillie as well. It *was* possible Wilkinson had had the time to get from the train he had neatly abandoned, make his way to Oxford before the hunter arrived, kidnap the reporter to stop her story being written, and then disappear again.

The other thing niggling at the hunter was the disappearance of chemical weapons from Porton Down. Wilkinson had been going there when he had jumped off the train, and while one thing might not have to do with another, it did make the hunter wonder.

He pushed away his cup and saucer and thought about getting some breakfast and a bath. Sleep would be elusive, this much he knew.

As he opened the neatly ironed pages of the Oxford Daily Press, he told himself he wasn't searching for her column—but of course he was. He flicked through the pages and finally found a teaser pertaining to a future article about the Summerdyne Committee and the role of the police in apprehending suspected German spies during the war. There was a picture of her, and he stared it for a long time. He then turned to the local news section and was relieved not to find anything pertaining to the two murders in the North.

There was some village news: a flooded cottage and road that the neighbours were riling about, the annual art show's call for watercolours and then there, in black and white, the announcement of Harry Green's marriage to Primrose Hyssop. At first it looked as all marriage announcements do, contrived and uninteresting, but her name caught his eye—maid of honour to be Miss Hyssop's university flatmate, now Oxford reporter Lillie Mead. Best man Jack Abbott. The wedding, to be held at the *magnificent*—he rolled his eyes—Tynesmore, the article read, was expected to be exceedingly well attended by local and London friends of the Green family, and government department dignitaries.

A pin dropped. No doubt all three of the remaining Summerdyne Committee heads would be at the wedding. They all seemed to be intimate enough with Lillie and her case to be considered part of the group. And the hunter knew very well that Theodore Rumple lived at Tynesmore. This information was in his initial correspondence. Everyone would be in the same place at the same time.

He waved the waiter over and pointed to the announcement in the paper.

"Any idea who might be catering this splendid affair?" he asked him, using language he normally never would to appear a genuinely interested outsider. "I need to have a little party myself and I figure whoever is doing the food for this wedding would be a good fit for my corporate dinner. Obviously they are very good or the Green family wouldn't be using them."

"I couldn't really say for sure, sir, but I would wager a guess it's Whitman and Sons. Best in the village, so I hear."

"Thank you."

The hunter neatly folded the paper and placed it to the left of his cutlery. After breakfast he would pay them a visit.

50

SUPERINTENDENT PETTERS

Chipping Norton, Oxfordshire

Superintendent Felix Petters steered his police cruiser carefully into Chipping Norton along Burford Road and headed north into the centre of town. He rubbed his eyes with the front of his sleeved arm—who knew what germs his hands had picked up—and let out a huge yawn. He hadn't slept a wink and would pay for it today.

Lillie's return a few hours previous had been a blessed relief. They had had the local doctor examine her and with the exception of a few cuts and bruises, she had seemed to be relatively unscathed. Jack's response had been interesting, he reflected. He had still been out with Harry when she came in, which gave Petters some time to get the details of her capture and return, and it was a good thing—by the time Jack had returned the place was turned upside down. He had embraced her and sharply scolded her simultaneously. Jeremy Winston had been there at the time, and Jack had unleashed such a furious tirade of abuse upon him that the newspaper man had scurried out of the house faster than a cat in pursuit of a mouse. None of which sat particularly well with an exhausted Lillie who had simply turned to Harry and asked him to remove Jack from the room, which he did expeditiously. Petters imagined the two of them married and living under the same roof. He deduced it wouldn't be for the faint of heart.

The high street shops were open and clear skies promised their shoppers a dry day. It was a market town after all, and he felt the same enjoyable bustle he always did when he returned home.

The face of his watch reflected the sunshine as he rested his hands on the steering wheel. He decided it was as good a time as any to visit the orphanage. He hadn't heard a thing since his initial meeting with the two dreary officials who had done the home visit—things could probably use a little prodding along. Petters disliked the institutional lolly gagging that often came with large organizations—church or government it didn't matter, they were all the same.

The police cruiser turned into the orphanage parking area and Petters switched off the engine. He stared out at the formidable building while he gathered his thoughts, its stone facade imparting the most melancholy feeling in him. He was probably just fatigued. A few of the boys were outside attempting to play some sort of game involving a ball and a stick, cricket perhaps, or tennis. He didn't see Jeremiah among them.

It was a mild day, he reflected as he got out of the car, waving at the boys who stood up straight, one by one, as he passed them. He was pleased a uniform still garnered some respect amongst England's youth. Or perhaps they were doing something they shouldn't be doing and were covering it up, he mused, smiling to himself.

The inside of the orphanage had its characteristic damp

smell as though in complete defiance of the sunshine outside its walls. He stood in the reception area as his eyes adjusted to the dark interior and looked around for Sister Theresa.

"She's in a meeting."

A nun had emerged from the breakfast room and he hadn't heard her behind him. They did tend to move with complete silence. Petters thought they would make terrific spies. She repeated herself.

"Sister Theresa is in a meeting—if that is who you are looking for?"

"Yes, thanks. I'll wait for her."

Petters sat down on a long pew like bench and marvelled at how uncomfortable it was, its legs squeaking like a pack of mice in a bell tower. A few boys wandered out of the breakfast room and headed up the stairs to the second floor while two nuns dressed in aprons swept and mopped the floor around him. Missing spots, he noted, as a pile of dust bunnies moved this way and that but never got picked up. He fought the urge to commandeer the broom from the nun and do it himself.

Five minutes passed, then ten, then twenty, and finally he heard voices in the hallway. Sister Theresa emerged with Jeremiah and, to Petters's astonishment, the woman in the emerald green coat. She was carrying it now, slung over her arm, and up close Petters could see she was barely approaching middle age. She had wide-set dark eyes and the same clear alabaster skin as Jeremiah. He felt his heart sink.

"Superintendent Petters," Sister Theresa said, looking surprised at his presence. "Please, let me introduce you to Calista Hemny, Jeremiah's aunt."

Aunt? Aunt. How was this possible? The same woman who had been following him for the better part of three weeks, whom he had thought a rookie intelligence officer, was here, in this very orphanage, claiming to be Jeremiah's aunt. Although it wasn't just claiming—he knew very well just by looking at her that she was, in fact, who she said she was. His stomach turned and he fought a sudden rush of nausea. He surely had no claim on the boy now that a family member had turned up.

He hadn't responded and was in no hurry to do so. Jeremiah's eyes were downcast and he was scuffing the toe of his shoe along the floorboards. Each bump and scrape pulled at his heart, the pit in his stomach widening.

The woman with the green coat stepped forward and held out her hand to him. "Pleased to meet you, Superintendent."

He let her hand hang there for a moment, then reluctantly shook it while staring coldly into her eyes. He didn't want to talk in front of the boy.

"Son, how about you give us adults a minute, to talk a bit."

"Yes, sir," Jeremiah said, and reluctantly took himself off outside, glancing back at them hesitantly before he exited the building into the sunshine.

Petters watched him go and then returned his attention to the aunt.

"Just what the hell are you playing at?" he hissed at her, startling the two nuns who were sweeping. Their brooms stopped in unison and they scurried out of the foyer.

"Now, Superintendent," Sister Theresa cut in, "I don't think that is language befitting our surroundings. We are in the house of the Lord...."

He cut her off angrily. "I don't give a damn if we are in Westminster Abbey, this....this...imposter is an opportunist, a cheat!" He was reaching and he knew it. "She has been stalking me for weeks, spying on us. I have a good mind to arrest you for harassment."

Calista's dark eyes widened and she took a step back as though he might hit her. If he was honest, he felt like putting his fist through the wall beside her, so she wasn't far off.

"I'm sorry—obviously I've upset you but I assure you, I only have Jeremiah's best interest at heart..." She stayed well out of his immediate reach.

"What a crock!" He was aware his voice had risen and that he was dangerously close to losing control. "You show up here, now, after all these years, just when he is about to be adopted? Shame on you! Shame on you for not letting him have any sort of life. And to send me that picture of him! A threat!"

"What picture? I don't know about any picture—I haven't sent you a thing. I think if you calm down and listen for a minute, you will feel differently." She shifted her coat to the other arm. "Please just sit down and let me explain." She pointed to the bench as though it was an order, not a request. He reluctantly complied.

Once they were seated, she continued, her voice calm and measured. "I didn't know about Jeremiah until a year ago. My sister, his mother, died shortly after he was born. At the time she was living in Yorkshire, with a...not very nice man, whom she had run away to be with. None of our family knew where she was or that she had even had a baby. A friend of hers from Ripon only just got in touch with me. She sent a letter saying there had been a baby that my sister had given up—that the father had left her shortly after he was born. He didn't want anything to do with Jeremiah and my sister had tried, unsuccessfully, on her own for a few years—before she got sick and gave him to the orphanage."

Petters listened with his head down. She was here to take him home with her, surely. She looked competent enough. She had decent clothes and a correct, suitably educated, London accent. He felt completely deflated.

"Why didn't your sister leave the baby with you? Or your parents?"

A darkness clouded her eyes. "My parents never approved of her, and they all but disowned her when she ran away. I...

well, I'm ashamed to admit I let her slip out of our lives too. I suppose she didn't feel she had a family anymore..."

She looked so forlorn Petters thought she might start to weep and he regretted asking.

"Anyway," she continued, "this friend didn't know the name of the orphanage, only that it wasn't in Yorkshire. I have been searching for him for the better part of a year. When I finally found him here and found out that he was in the process of being adopted, I wanted to see him, and to see who loved him enough to take him on. This is why I followed you. I just wanted to know more about you."

"You are aware that tailing a police officer isn't really an advisable course of action, aren't you?" He looked at her sternly, but hearing her story had dissipated most of his anger.

She stared straight back at him, her eyes shining, and to his surprise, she started to laugh.

"Yes, I am aware," she said. "Listen, Superintendent, I just want to know my nephew. I don't have children of my own. I manage a small dress shop in London and there isn't any family left now. Just Jeremiah. If he came to live with me, it would be in a tiny flat without a bedroom of his own and he would have to adjust to city life. I'm not sure he would like that very much. Why don't we give him the choice? Or even better, why don't we just not make any choices and get to know one another? As friends with a mutual interest? I don't want to battle anyone. Not anymore."

He didn't know why he said what he did next—perhaps nervousness, or a desire deep down for Jeremiah to have a sense of family. Or, perhaps it was that her eyes and skin and gentleness reminded him of the boy so completely that it disarmed him.

"I have to go to a wedding Saturday," he blurted out. "After the night I just had I didn't think there would actually be a wedding, but that's all solved now."

She looked confused at the course the conversation was taking.

"Jeremiah is the ring bearer. It's in Oxford," he continued, aware he sounded like a discombobulated fool incapable of having a coherent conversation.

"Oh yes..." Her eyes told him she was still unsure of where he was going with this all but she seemed to be trying to follow along.

"Well?"

"Well what, Superintendent?"

"Would you like to accompany us?"

51

THE HUNTER

Porton Down, Wiltshire

The white-washed administrative building had a blue tinged glow against the darkening Wiltshire sky. Set amongst fields of nothingness, Porton Down was a ominous figurehead rendered nearly insignificant by its setting, its stone facade diminutive against the canvas of mother nature. But for all who knew its true purpose as the premier research centre for chemical weapons, its very existence was enough to send chills along the spine of returning soldiers. For it was they who were to witness the wasteful death and destruction at the breath of bromide, chlorine and mustard gas in the trenches abroad.

The British government, however, wasn't about to repeat the mistakes of the past—allowing their soldiers to go into war unprepared for what might be thrown their way—and this building, this entire complex, was its very own beast. Its scientists buzzed around like bees in a hive, its military personnel carefully guarded their work. Test tubes and labs and microscopes hid behind locked doors. Each and every person was logged in and logged out. Masks and suits were worn. There were clearances given and taken, the hierarchy willfully maintained, the public kept out.

It was a good bloody thing the hunter had an ace in his pocket. It wasn't the first time a piece of letterhead and a signature had gained him admittance somewhere he wasn't welcome, and he patted himself on the back for remembering that little trick the night he had crept into Basil Wilkinson's office.

Today he was Markus Weinstein, assistant to the Director of Intelligence, and at the moment he was holed up in a little alcove poring over the rosters of ins and outs for the past three months.

He was acutely aware he might be on a wild goose chase. The missing phosgene might have nothing to do with the Summerdyne Committee or Basil Wilkinson or Ms. Mead. It could just be some random theft that had Wilkinson's office on high alert, which obviously it would be with a chemical weapon floating around God knows where.

A dowdy looking lab assistant put her head around the corner.

"Need anything else Mr. Weinstein? I'm just about to go on my tea break."

"No, thank you, I think I have everything I need here. I am trying to cross reference who was here at the facility at the time of the disappearance of the compound in December. I suppose, however, it could have disappeared earlier than that and was only noticed in December of last year?"

"It would have been noticed fairly quickly. At the week's end we compile a lab inventory of the entire facility. A week previous to its disappearance would be as far back as you would need to look."

"I see," the hunter said, and adjusted his spectacles. "Well, there is one other thing perhaps, and forgive my ignorance— I've only just started with the Director, before that I was in an entirely different department—how does phosgene present itself, as a weapon, that is?"

"Initially it's quite innocuous, actually—it's colourless and smells like musty hay. Which, I suppose, was why it was so effective as a killing agent. Soldiers didn't see it coming, but it was responsible for about eighty-five percent of the deaths from chemical weapons during the war."

"A formidable foe it seems."

"Oh yes."

"I see, thank you."

He was politely dismissive.

The assistant left him and he continued to pore over the records from the end of November. Most of the names were becoming routine to him. Scientists, lab assistants, office staff, military personnel. The same names signing in at the same time each and every day. It was possible that one of the staff had stolen it and were keeping it for use or ransom at a later date. It didn't matter how many references or interviews were given, people could always hide their true intentions behind a cloak of gentility.

He flipped back to the beginning of December and started cross referencing names with the roster of staff, ticking off names as he found them in the employee directory. He would focus on outsiders coming in as visitors first and then get in to researching staff members if need be. There were always government officials from London coming and going, which complicated the search. He scrolled up and down the lists, his eyes searching.

And then there it was, staring him in the face like a lighthouse beacon. A name he knew well, its scroll in deep blue across the line marked *December the seventh*. He blinked twice at it to make sure he wasn't seeing things, closed the book and got up.

There was no doubt in his mind about what to do next.

52

LILLIE

OXFORD, OXFORDSHIRE

"Good morning, may I speak with Basil Wilkinson please. It's Lillie Mead calling, from the Oxford Daily Press."

"I'm sorry Ms. Mead, Mr. Wilkinson isn't in the office."

Lillie frowned into the receiver. "I realize it's Saturday, but we had a time set for today. When do you expect him back?"

"He is away on government business until next week."

"I see."

"Shall I leave him a message that you called?"

"I don't suppose there is any other way to get in touch with him? Perhaps he forgot about our interview today? It's for an article I am writing. Mr. Wilkinson set this time himself."

"I am sorry, I don't believe so."

"I see. Thank you."

Lillie hung up the receiver with frustration. She exited the small alcove in the Tynesmore foyer that housed the telephone, narrowly missing a flood of caterers as they whisked by her with carts of dishes and glasses.

Mr. Wilkinson was proving to be a difficult man to track down and while it seemed almost unfathomable that the

Director of Intelligence could be a kidnapper, or worse, a murderer, she wasn't ruling out anything.

The Professor was outside the large front windows directing a steady stream of behind the scenes wedding traffic. Flowers, balloons, birds and food were being unloaded while he pointed and gestured this way and that, calmly nodding and streamlining the whole circus. Guests would start to arrive in a few hours and still they weren't nearly set up but presumably someone was in charge and the seemingly complex event would be miraculously pulled off.

The Professor was now talking to someone, a short, squat man dressed in dirty overalls and a faded coat. Their heads were close together as though whatever was being said wasn't to be overheard. The Professor shook his head violently at something the man said and pulled away, turning on his heel and leaving the poor man staring after him. It was uncharacteristic of Professor Hargreaves to be so rude.

"What a bustle of activity," a voice behind her marvelled.

Florence Millicent-Marks was dressed for the wedding in an oyster gray dress that just skimmed the tops of her ankles. Her red hair was wound into a bun at the nape of her neck and she wore nothing but pearls in her ears for jewelry. She looked simple, tailored, and attractive.

"Ah yes, it is quite a...." Lillie searched for a word to describe the scene unfolding before them. "A dog and pony show."

"And is the bride ready?" Florence raised an eyebrow.

"Almost, finishing touches now. I really should be up there with her but she has maids whirling about the room like the Russian ballet and they seem to have everything under control. To tell you the truth, I don't have the beside manner to calm nervous brides."

Florence's laugh had a tinny sound and Lillie wondered if she weren't humouring her.

"And what is the schedule of events, exactly? I have yet to hear where they want us and when."

Lillie recited what she had been told ad nauseam. "For you and the Professor, the cars are leaving for the church at one-thirty. For the wedding party, there are pictures at noon in front of the drawing room window as long as the weather holds. Carriages have been ordered for one o'clock sharp. A drive through the village with the groom and groomsmen. The bride to follow in her own carriage. Ceremony at the cathedral at two. Back here for the cocktail reception at four. Some speeches and general merriment. Dinner is served early at seven, to be followed by the band and dancing. Oh, and the cake will be cut just before midnight."

"Oh? I thought the ceremony would be held at the Tynesmore chapel? Wasn't that the original suggestion?"

"Yes, it was but the wedding planner didn't think it sufficiently grand so he changed venues at the last minute..."

Lillie trailed off, noticing Florence's attention was elsewhere. She was staring out the window at the Professor who was directing yet another catering cart, and began walking towards the front door. Seeming to remember she had been in a conversation, she turned to give Lillie an absent wave as she disappeared outside the house.

How odd. Lillie's bemused thoughts were interrupted by the ringing of the phone. As she moved towards it, she was surprised to see the ridiculous wedding planner hurtling towards her at great speed. He waved his fat little hands in the air, his voice a crescendo of hysteria.

"Ms. Mead! I haven't a minute to lose—please, please help me! The cook is refusing to give us an oven for our tarts and they must be started now if we are to have them for the reception! Mon dieu! To think that stupid cow supposes her refreshments are superior to the caterers! It's ludicrous. Please come at once!"

The telephone was still ringing and Lillie took another step towards it but was reprimanded in a manner she normally would not have dreamed of heeding had it not been Harry's wedding day.

"Tout de suite!" the little man said with emphasis. Lillie felt his spittle land on her cheek.

She reached up slowly and wiped it away with the back of her hand.

The telephone kept up its incessant ringing, but she decided it wasn't worth the effort. It was probably just another family well wisher anyway. There had been hordes of calls all day and she might as well deal with the latest crisis at hand.

Reluctantly she followed the Frenchman through the foyer and then through a small door leading downstairs to the kitchen. As she did she couldn't help but wonder where all the English wedding planners had gone?

SUPERINTENDENT PETTERS

Chipping Norton, Oxfordshire

H e was going to be late for the wedding, of that there was no doubt. Superintendent Petters thoroughly disliked being late for anything.

After a host of police matters ranging from a domestic argument where a wife had clubbed her husband with a bottle to a particularly disconcerting case of a missing goat, Petters suggested Jeremiah and his aunt make their way to Oxford in the car Harry had provided without him. Jeremiah was the ring bearer after all, and it wouldn't do for him to also be late. Petters would catch up with them later.

He strode back into Police Headquarters and made his way to his office. He needed to file a report on the status of the clubbed husband, having just sent him to hospital.

"Gwen!" he hollered once he reached his office, realizing too late that he perhaps should have taken the time to find her. No one liked being bellowed at, he reflected.

"Sir?" His receptionist poked her head around the door and Petters realized she really was once of the best staffers he had ever employed.

"I'm terribly sorry for yelling, been a bit of a hectic day. Could you see if you can find Constable Barrow so I can hand off this missing goat case to him? I'm not even supposed to be here today and I really need to get down to Oxford."

"Yes, of course," she said, turning to leave. "Oh, I almost forgot, there's been a man calling for you all morning. Refuses to leave a name and insists it's urgent. I tried to get him on with someone else but he wants you. I expect he will call back shortly."

"Thanks, I'll be here for a little while anyway, filling out this blasted report."

Petters got down to it as she left the room, scribbling furiously and wondering if it would be too much to ask his receptionist to fetch him a cup of coffee. He could feel himself waning. In the end he decided he should get one himself. He had read somewhere recently that coffee could increase productivity in a person by twenty-five percent. He could certainly use the boost.

The sound of the telephone ringing at reception caused him to stall. Perhaps this was his mystery man trying again. He waited straining to hear the telephone operator and whether or not it was for him. The call was put through to his office and he grabbed it on the first ring.

"Superintendent Petters here."

There was a short pause before he heard the voice. It was deep and smooth, American, or possibly Canadian.

"I have some information on the supply of phosgene that is missing from Porton Down."

"I don't know anything about that. Why would you call me about it and not the proper authorities? Being a chemical weapon I would certainly think this is a national matter and something for the security services?"

The voice was silent for a moment.

"Because I think the person who took it has something to do with a couple of murders you are investigating, that's why."

Petters wondered briefly if the author of the smooth voice was in fact his murderer.

"I see. Are you planning on telling me who took it and what they plan to do with it?"

"Of course," the voice said carefully, "but I am going to need something in return."

LILLIE

Oxford, Oxfordshire

February always brought with it a deliriously stunning change of light—beiges and browns were banished in favour of violets and blues, their pastel hues scattering the optimism of an early spring across all of England. Crocuses were threatening an end to the cold and bitterness, their purpled and white plumes a testament to the changing of the guard. The days stretched out just the smallest amount, leaving the cloak of winter gloriously vulnerable.

Harry was in his dressing room, fiddling with his tie in front of an enormous gilded mirror. Rumple dashed around gathering up pieces of his wedding attire, trying not to soil his own impeccable costume, which appeared to be more Renaissance than 1920; his wine coloured vest, laced tightly over a billowing white blouse, bordered on the absurd. He stood behind his master now, miming the movements of tying a tie while Harry frowned, pulling the entire thing apart and starting again.

"Shall I sir?"

"No," Harry said firmly, "I need to know how to do this. How can I possibly go on a honeymoon without you otherwise? While I enjoy your company, I hardly think it fitting you accompany Primrose and me to the south of France." Harry eyed Rumple's reflection in the mirror. "Are you really going to wear that?"

Rumple ignored him. "We really should have practiced this on a day when you weren't getting married," he murmured under his breath.

Lillie was watching the scene with amusement from the doorway, not daring to interrupt. They had quite a relationship, servant and master, and although it was unorthodox Lillie supposed that was what precisely made it work. She doubted neither Harry nor Rumple had the patience to hold up the norms of the previous generation. Not with everything that had happened during the war—the importance of Rumple's work in wartime intelligence, the endless slaughter of young men, the tragic ruination of entire families. No, the world had indeed seen the folly of blindly trusting authority and tradition and it would never again be as it was before 1914.

"You look handsome," she said softly, startling them.

"I feel like I am playing dress up. I can't believe I am getting married! I thought you would have been with Primrose, is everything all right?" Harry had the look of a groom who imagined he might be left at the altar.

"Everything is fine, and Jeremiah has just arrived with the rings. I settled him in the drawing room with a board game and some sandwiches. We have loads of time still. Although there was a little mishap between the caterer and your cook, but I think I've solved it. Anyway, I wanted to see how you were getting on."

"Recovered from your ordeal, have you?" Harry looked back

to the mirror and attempted his tie again keeping his eyes on her.

It had been a week, and she had only been missing for a few hours, but Lillie wouldn't deny the whole incident had shaken her confidence. She didn't have any recollection of who had attacked her or how she had ended up at the old mill. She thought briefly of the man who had happened upon her and gotten her back home safely. He wasn't just an American businessman in search of a location for his factory, of that she was sure. That was about the only thing she *was* sure of.

She could hear the faint ringing of the telephone downstairs and wondered if anyone would pick it up.

"Where is your best man? I should have thought he would be here plying you with drink and warming your cold feet."

"Hardly. He left a few minutes ago in search of you. Oh blast and dammit, Rumple, could you?"

Harry's tie lay in a mess around his neck and Rumple stepped in to take control.

"I'll leave you. See you downstairs for pictures."

Neither responded, the tie proving a serious distraction. She quietly left them to it and headed back down the elaborately dressed stairs in search of Jack.

She found him in the kitchen, holed up on one corner wolfing down a sandwich as sparks erupted again between the catering manager and Harry's cook.

"I can't give you all my silver platters, then what would I use! Surely a fancy company like yours would have their own? Honestly..." Harry's cook busied herself with a line of devilled eggs, filling them with such force that surely half of them wouldn't ever see a server's tray.

"I'm not asking for *all* your silver platters, only *one*. Ours are in transit and haven't arrived and I need to get this terrine out first. We are setting up a small sampling for the wedding party," the catering manager said, rubbing his head in frustration.

Jack was watching the exchange with amusement.

Harry's cook threw her spoon down with a clatter. "*You* are setting up a sampling? I thought that was what *I* was meant to be doing!"

"Apparently not."

"Now you listen here..." She picked the spoon up again and pointed it menacingly at the catering manager.

Lillie couldn't take much more of it. "Stop this, please. It's Harry's wedding day and I should think we could all try to be a little more tolerant. Please, lend the poor man a silver tray. I can see very well that we have more than enough. There has to be at least fifty of them in the silver room. He has been hired to do a job and I suggest we let him do it, for all of our sakes."

Lillie nodded at Jack who reluctantly got up from his ring side seat and followed her into the hallway.

"You look very nice," he said, his eyes taking in her brides-maid gown. Lillie had to agree that the water blue silk Primrose had chosen hastily upon her return was most complementary to her complexion.

"Is it just me or have you also noticed Florence and the Professor are acting strangely?"

"If you ask me everyone is acting strangely. You just witnessed that uprising in the kitchen, and that has been going on all morning. To say nothing of Rumple's choice of dress..."

"No," she said, cutting him off. "I mean really odd behaviour. I've never seen the Professor so agitated and Florence seems as though she is out with the fairies—I could barely have a conversation with her. She left me mid-sentence and wandered outside. Which leads to me to wonder. How well does Rumple really know her?"

"Meaning what exactly?"

"Just that she seems...oh I don't know, different from the woman he describes."

"In what way?"

She thought about this for a moment and realized it wasn't something she could put into words.

"Never mind, I am probably imagining something that isn't there."

"Are you perhaps a little sensitive, with what you have been through the past few days? It is a wedding after all and weddings drive people batty at the best of times."

"Hm, I suppose."

She could hear the telephone ringing again.

"I suppose I should try to get that."

"Leave it. It'll just be something else that needs be done or checked on."

"Probably."

"I see Jeremiah is here, but no Superintendent Petters?"

"I think he is on his way. Incidentally, the night I was kidnapped—you told me on the phone you had some new information, something you wanted to talk to me about."

"Right, yes. Well, it isn't important now—we can talk about it after the wedding."

"Nothing about the case or my article?"

"No, nothing about that. A promotion came up at work and I wanted to tell you about it."

Why did this irritate her? It shouldn't, she reflected.

"Oh, well yes, I would like to hear about it."

Jack gave her an elaborate wink, oblivious of her thoughts. "Later, there's too much going on now."

Nodding, Lillie gave him a quick peck on the cheek and left him to the sparring match in the kitchen as she headed back up the stairs.

SUPERINTENDENT PETTERS

Chipping Norton, Oxfordshire

W here in the hell was everyone and why was no one picking up the telephone?

Superintendent Petters held the receiver to his ear for what felt like the millionth time, listening to the tin-like ringing, imagining the hallway at Tynesmore, full of caterers and the wedding party, yet none of them bothering to pick up the phone. Unless of course something had happened and there was no one there to pick it up.

His heart sunk. What if he was too late?

He slammed the receiver down, scribbled the number of Tynesmore on a piece of paper for his receptionist and grabbed his coat from its hook.

As he raced down the hallway and past the reception desk he flung the piece of paper at the telephone operator.

"Please, keep trying this number every minute until you get someone. Tell them I'm on my way and under no circumstances to gather the wedding guests in one place, do you understand? Talk to Lillie, or Jack, or even Harry but explain in no uncertain terms that the entire wedding party is in grave danger. In the meantime, call the Oxford Police Station and have them go to the house, tell them there is a stolen chemical compound, weapons grade, that is going to be deployed against Harry Green's wedding party."

The woman was furiously scribbling the instructions as Petters rushed through the front doors of the station and down into his car.

There wasn't a minute to lose.

56

THE HUNTER

Oxford, Oxfordshire

His tie was perfect. His livery was a little loose around the waist. His short hair was combed to perfection.

The hunter looked every bit the part as he walked up the long gravel road towards Tynesmore. *Into the lion's den*, he reflected, rubbing his hands together to combat the chill in the air.

The road stretched out before him and in the distance he could see the soft chalky stone facade of the house, awash with the morning light. From where he stood the wedding staff appeared like a swarm of flies, buzzing around their territory in black and white, dwarfed by an enormous red and white hot air balloon hovering like a dragon above the lawn.

His stomach flipped. He couldn't remember the last time he had felt nervous. He knew who he was looking for, after all, but whether or not he would get there in time was another matter altogether.

It took him the better part of ten minutes to finally reach the front courtyard. He was passed on the driveway by carts of flowers, wine trucks and a bakery delivery. The flies were now people, although the buzz hadn't diminished, and he passed them quickly as he walked up the shallow stone steps and into the front hallway of the house.

It was a bold move, but time wasn't something he had much of.

The house was full of people, whirling away in their own worlds, reminding him of a Russian ballet. Not one gave him a second glance.

He strode through them as though he owned the place.

The drawing room was full of photographers, fiddling with their equipment, the dining room he avoided after seeing the catering manager holding a staff meeting with his servers, the library held an impeccably dressed boy playing a card game with a middle aged woman wearing a deep yellow dress. The boy looked up at him as he entered, his dark eyes intensely aware of the hunter's presence.

"Oh, excuse me," the hunter said as he backed out of the room.

The boy got up from his chair. "Who are you looking for?"

"No one in particular, just trying to sort out where they are wanting the serving staff."

The boy held his gaze. "I am pretty sure you should check in downstairs in the kitchens."

The hunter nodded and turned to leave. A steady stream of photographers were now emerging from drawing room and heading outside the house. He watched their backs as they exited, their camera equipment slung over their shoulders, tripods held in outstretched arms. The man the hunter assumed to be the groom came down the flowered staircase a moment later. The groom didn't give him a glance, but turned to say something to a man who stood behind him. As he did the hunter realized that he recognized the man from the house in Scotland. Same military style cropped hair. Same stance. Same voice.

He neatly avoided them by heading down the hallway in the opposite direction of the front door while trying to quiet his mounting anxiety.

It was here somewhere. In a bedroom perhaps, or an outbuilding, somewhere hidden but easy to get to. He couldn't very well check the upstairs bedrooms while the bride and groom were still here. No, he would focus outside first, he thought, and he made his way with hurried steps towards the back of the house and out a pair of French doors.

Time was of the essence.

57

OXFORD POLICE HEADQUARTERS

Oxford, Oxfordshire

"I t's your deal."

Constable Meyers handed a tattered deck of cards to the junior officer sitting to the right of him.

"I thought it was Deeken's turn?"

"No, he went two times ago, it's yours. Pay attention would you?"

Meyers slapped the makeshift card table with an open hand to make his point. Deeken laughed and reached for his cigarettes.

"Doesn't matter if the kid deals or not," he said, lighting his cigarette. "Can't seem to win a game to save his life."

Meyers motioned for a cigarette and Deeken handed the case to him. He extracted one, lit it, and handed the case back to Deeken. Neither of them offered one to their underling who was now dealing the cards with the speed of molasses leaving a jar.

"Christ man, sometime before Christmas would be nice," Meyers added. This was the last time they would ask this nitwit to play with them.

In the reception area a telephone began ringing.

"You getting that?" Deeken raised an eyebrow, taking a long inhale from his cigarette and making no move to get up. He exhaled. "You better if you want this card game to continue. Otherwise we are going to have to get junior here to start dealing all over again—don't think I could take it."

Meyers pushed his chair back with reluctance and placed his cigarette, still lit, in the ashtray on the table.

"Would be nice if we had a secretary on the odd Saturday wouldn't it? Not really getting paid enough to be doing two jobs in a day."

Meyers trudged out to the reception desk, hoping the caller would hang up before he reached it. He paused for a few more rings before he committed to answering it.

"Oxford Police."

"I am calling from Chipping Norton detachment at Superintendent Petters request. He urgently needs a team of officers dispatched to the Green wedding at Tynesmore. In addition, he will need another team stationed at Saint Mary Magdalen for the ceremony which is to begin at two."

Meyers chewed thoughtfully on the inside of his cheek. He was in no hurry to bow and scrape to another detachment, especially not to the Superintendent who had done nothing but interrupt their fine investigation into that missing persons report a week ago. He had shown up here, in a village not his own, and started throwing his weight around.

"Is that right?" he eventually drawled. "And just why is that now?"

He could hear Deeken arguing over something with junior in the back room.

"The Superintendent has it on good authority that a stolen

chemical weapon is going to be deployed either at the ceremony or the reception, by someone who is wishing harm on a
handful of people but who won't be discerning about collateral
damage."

"I see..." The sound of the woman's voice was beginning to
annoy him. A chemical weapon, really? Was he on set at the
theatre? Was this a novel she was writing? Ridiculous. He
couldn't be responsible for chasing up every cracked lead that
some wildly hallucinogenic Superintendent thought to
dream up.

"You must hurry!"

And now she was telling him what to do and how quickly to
do it.

"Will do," he said with as much indifference as he could
muster.

Putting down the telephone he headed back to the card
table and took his seat. He reached for his cigarette which had
gone out.

"Bloody hell, hand me another would you?"

Deeken passed the cigarette case to him. "What was that all
about?"

"Some nutty woman wanting us to check out the Green
wedding."

"Why?"

"I've no idea, nothing of what she said made any sense
to me."

"Cards first, wedding later?"

"You bet. I see junior here is finally finished dealing."

58

LILLIE

Oxford, Oxfordshire

"Are we ready for photographs?" Harry stood at the threshold of the front door, the light forming a halo around his outline. Lillie squinted towards him.

His tie was perfect.

"I think you've done this backwards, haven't you? Photographs before you see the bride in the church? It seems a little non-traditional, even for you," Lillie admonished.

"I was hoping to catch the light but I see the issue."

"They are here all day, are they not? The photographers?"

"Yes, what do you suggest?"

"Have the groom and groomsmen get their photos now and then you all leave for the church. We can have the bridal party done once you depart. And then you can have your together photographs done in front of the church after the ceremony. Isn't that a better idea?"

"Splendid. What would I do without you?"

"I do wonder. I'll go and find Jack, shall I?"

"Please. Rumple and I will wait here for you."

Lillie walked back through the foyer to the staircase leading down to the kitchen. The rooms on the main floor had all been decorated with the most arresting displays of flowers, all in whites and pinks and dripping with glossy green leaves. She glanced out the window as she walked—the hot air balloon was a magnificent sight, and whether or not anyone even rode in it, it did create a superb festival feeling in the wintery garden.

A quick blur of olive coloured fabric caught her eye just beyond the dining room window and she paused to see the Professor dashing through the garden. The photographers were just setting up and he passed them without a word heading at speed down a gravel pathway that disappeared behind a hedgerow. What was down there that he needed to get to so urgently? Only a smattering of small sheds and outbuildings, as far as Lillie knew.

"Miss Mead?"

She turned to see a maid standing behind her, wringing her hands.

"Yes?" Lillie recognized her as one of the ladies helping Primrose dress.

"The bride is asking for you," the maid said, raising her eyebrows in silent communication, glancing nervously over her shoulder as she did so. Everything was far from all right, apparently.

"Certainly, I'll go now. Could you go downstairs to the kitchen and ask Mr. Abbott to join the groom outside for photographs?"

The maid nodded and Lillie, sighing, made her way up to Primrose's dressing room.

She could hear voices coming from inside the room before she even knocked. A quiet anxiousness in Primrose's voice and soothing shushing from whichever maid was still in there with her. She gave a quick knock and entered.

Primrose was dressed in a delicate ivory silk gown that draped her curvy figure to perfection. The bodice was layered with pearls. In her ears and around her neck she wore the palest aquamarine and diamond set. Her dark hair was piled at the nape of her neck and pinned with ivory combs that matched her gown.

She looked up when Lillie entered, her eyes full of unshed tears.

"I can't do this."

Lillie raised her eyebrows in question. "Get married?"

"Yes. I can't get married. It's too rushed, too fast really. I knew we should have waited to get to know one another better. I don't even know anything about Harry!" She looked wildly about the room.

Lillie turned to the maid. "Would you please get Ms. Hyssop a glass of brandy to calm her nerves."

"Trust me Lillie, brandy isn't going to help."

"Come sit. Take a deep breath," Lillie said, motioning to a settee near the window and then immediately regretting it as she noticed it was the perfect vantage point to see the photographers now focusing their cameras on Harry and his groomsmen.

She situated Primrose so her back faced the window.

"Now, what is all this rubbish? Of course you know Harry. You have known him for years. You know him as well as I do."

"Yes but not in this context. I am going to be his *wife*! He is terrific to pal around with, but to marry? Remember how he treated his last fiancée?"

"According to Harry, Beatrice wasn't actually his fiancée. He never intended to marry her, you know that. It was just some idea cooked up by their parents."

"Which brings me to my second point. His parents—well

his mother to be exact. I don't want to spend a minute with her. She is controlling and cold and downright spiteful. She will despise me. I'm not from his class, his world. How could we possibly be happy?" She choked back a sob and it caught in her throat.

"Those things matter much less now than they used to, and to Harry they don't matter at all. His mother will grow to love you, how could she not? And you won't need to spend time with her, for goodness' sake, Harry won't even spend time with her. Why do you think he rarely travels to London to visit them?"

Primrose sniffed, wiping her eyes, and nodded. At least Lillie was getting somewhere. Nerves were a formidable foe to wrestle with a few hours before a wedding.

"Now, feeling better?"

"Yes, somewhat. I don't know what has gotten into me."

"Just wedding jitters, happens to almost everyone. Don't give them another thought."

Lillie pulled Primrose to her feet. "Now, finish getting ready, your carriage will be here shortly."

Lillie watched as the groomsmen arranged and then rearranged themselves outside the window. There were still many of the wedding staff lingering around where the pictures were being taken and the head photographer was angrily waving them away if they got too close to the frame.

No wonder Primrose's nerves were shot, it was a veritable zoo outside.

One of the catering staff stood taller than the rest of the crowd, his back to the window. He was familiar somehow, but she couldn't make out his face. Harry was taking warm drinks off a sideboard someone had set up on the gravel under the drawing room window for refreshments. The sun had chased away the morning frost and everyone looked beautifully extravagant in their wedding clothes. She reminded herself to ask the photographers to take some less formal shots of the guests when they arrived.

The wedding party was beginning to take their leave and make their way to the church. The groom's carriage had arrived and the horses looked just as smart as the wedding party. She watched Jack whisper something to Harry and they both laughed, their handsome faces kissed by the sun, as they loaded into the carriage and drove away.

It was then the tall man dressed in the catering livery turned towards the house. Lillie caught her breath. It was the same man who had found her at the mill, the same man who had returned her home.

"I...I have to go, I will be back," she managed, hurrying from the room and taking the stairs two at a time with as large a stride as she could muster. Her dress threatened to tear as she did.

When she reached the garden, he was gone.

59

SUPERINTENDENT PETTERS

Somewhere En route to Oxford, Oxfordshire

T he road was littered with round rocks the size of his fist. Superintendent Petters carefully negotiated his car around them, not wanting to suffer a flat. The sun glinted off his windshield and he held up a hand to shade his eyes, glancing at the face of his watch as he did so. He was making good time, or had been until he had met this mess on the road. He hoped it didn't go on for much longer.

A horse and cart were ahead of him, taking up the majority of the narrow road and Petters had to slow again to remain behind them until he could safely pass. He wondered if his receptionist had managed to make contact with anyone at Tynesmore yet.

He was regretting sending Jeremiah and his aunt on ahead. Now they were there, like sitting ducks awaiting slaughter.

Seeing the road widen slightly, he took the opportunity to accelerate and overtake the horse and cart, giving the driver a wave of thanks as he did so. The road was smoother now and he was able to open up the throttle. Hearing the car whine made him feel that at least he was doing something to stop this madness.

He wondered, not for the first time since the telephone call, if the voice on the end of the telephone was toying with him, sending him hurtling into a situation that might not even exist. But why—was it for some other reason, some other aim? And if so, what was it? Petters couldn't shake the feeling that the voice likely belonged to the man who had killed Reginald Blackwater and Patrick Donvegan. Perhaps he was having regrets now? It wouldn't be the first time Petters had a murderer with a conscience on his hands.

He had the car at a dangerous speed now. It was taking the corners with a reluctance borne from tires too narrow for the job required of them. Up ahead he could make out the village of Woodstock, its haphazard rows of houses piled on top of one another, this way and that, lining the crooked streets. He would find a telephone and then get back on the road.

He accelerated dangerously towards the centre of town.

60

LILLIE

OXFORD, OXFORDSHIRE

W hat was going on?

Lillie stood out in the open, rubbing her bare arms, searching for the man masquerading as a caterer.

Jack and Harry's carriage was down the driveway now and she could see it far in distance, a moving speck of black framed by a vast robin's egg sky. It was followed by a stream of cars, snaking along the road behind. The bride's carriage had been pulled up in front of the house and a team of four greys stood impatiently, snorting and stamping out their excitement as their driver attempted, with increasing futility, to appease them.

Primrose had made her way outside with the help of two maids, and she stood on the threshold of the house while an assertive photographer gave her instructions on where she needed to stand to best take advantage of the light.

"Lillie?" she called to her as the group moved around the corner of the house. "Are you coming?"

"Be right there!"

Consciously hiding any concern on her face, she painted a false smile and hurried to join the bridal party. Through the bulb flashes and incessant changing of positions, she let her eyes search for the man.

"Miss Mead, this way please, follow my lens, everyone... and...smile now..." A large flash caused her to see spots. "And here..." Another flash. How much longer could this go on?

She grasped Primrose's hand between takes. "I will meet you at the church. I won't be far behind. I just need to make certain the house is ready for the reception upon our return."

"Oh, you won't be in the carriage?"

"No, but you will be fine. I'll send both of your maids and meet you in the staging area of the foyer. Your father will be there to meet you."

"But how will you get there in time?"

"I'll have someone on staff drive me to the village in one of the cars. Not to worry."

"Thanks Lillie. And I am sorry about before."

"You seem better now. I'm sure most brides get cold feet, I know I would." Lillie smiled at her friend and gave her hand a squeeze while the knot in her stomach tightened. She wished the wedding party would get on the road.

"One last shot in front of the laurel hedge please, ladies, bride in the centre, that's it...I've got everything I need now. Please make your way to the carriage and I will just shoot a few more of you leaving for the church..."

WITH THE CARRIAGE thankfully on its way to the chapel and the facade of cool and calm dropped, Lillie resumed her anxious search for the man in the garden. The only people left at the house were servers and cooks and with the wedding party gone so went their veneer of civility. Accents that would cut leather were being thrown around like leaves on the wind. This, coupled with cuss words rarely heard off the docks, provided a raucous scene in the dining room.

One particularly prolific young man looked as though he had swallowed his tongue when he realized Lillie was standing behind him.

"Terribly sorry, ma'am," he said, attempting a discreet bow that looked ridiculous after the words she had just heard leave his lips.

"Never mind," she said, rushed, "I am looking for one of your staff, a man, quite tall and slim, with short hair—very short hair."

"Ma'am? Is there something I can help you with?"

"No, there isn't. I need this man particularly."

"I don't know to who you are referring."

"Whom," she corrected, immediately regretting it. "Forget it, I'll keep looking."

After fifteen minutes of searching the entire house and finding no sign of him, she grabbed her coat out of a closet by the front door and made her way outside. With the departure of the wedding parties, the garden had an eerie calm. A couple of male service workers were folding up the drinks table from the photography area but all the equipment had already been packed up and was en route to the church.

She didn't bother asking anyone else about the man and chose instead to head down the gravel pathway she had seen the Professor on earlier in the hopes she might find someone around the stables.

The livery yard was cluster of low slung stone stalls, each fanning out from a central building that housed a common area for tack and hay on the main floor and grooms quarters above. With the departure of two teams of horses, one for each the bride and the groom, only a handful of riding horses were left quietly masticating their hay in the dusty dimness of the stable light. But for the horses and a couple of cats who looked far too fat to be considered able mousers, the building was empty.

Lillie clutched the fabric of her skirt off the ground as she hurried through the central aisle, across the straw strewn cobbles, searching for the man she had seen from the window. As she did so she glanced at the stable clock. She wouldn't have long before she needed to leave for the church.

Emerging out the back of the stables she headed towards a small outbuilding to the left rear of the stalls. She would have a quick look inside before she made her way back up to the house. It was quite possible she might have missed the man, done a complete circle around him, and not seen him return to rejoin his catering staff. But what was she thinking? He wasn't really a caterer. Of this she had no doubt.

The door to the outbuilding was tall, heavy and unlocked. It creaked as she pushed it open and stood a moment inside the darkened space to let her eyes adjust to her surroundings. It was a one story structure but the ceiling was high, presumably to accommodate enormous bales of hay which were piled up now nearly to the rafters. Assorted pails and farm implements were hung and organized to the left of where she stood and to the right was an old wagonette with a missing wheel and faded paint.

The door slammed behind her and she jumped with surprise. Realizing it was just the wind, and that the building was empty, she reflected she was on a fool's errand and, frustrated, turned to leave.

As she spun around she felt the slightest whisper of a touch on her arm and out of the shadows stepped the man she had been looking for.

61

THE HUNTER

Oxford, Oxfordshire

The hunter wasn't pleased to see he had been followed and he wondered at his next step, fighting the urge to clasp his hand over her mouth and stop her from screaming.

Something in her face told him she would do no such thing and he realized with some satisfaction that she trusted him. She shouldn't, he reflected. Even though he had no intention of harming her, it didn't alter the facts of who he was or what he was doing there.

He wordlessly held a finger to his lips while he took her in. A dress of raw blue silk fell over her slim body, barely skimming her ankles. Her hair was drawn back from her face and hung down to the middle of her back in a softly turned curl. She was watching him, green eyes boring through his own, expectant—demanding even—and he admired her composure.

He motioned away from the door and she reluctantly

followed him towards the back of the broken wagonette. Here he held a finger to his lips, signalling silence, and pointed to a dark pocket between the wagonette and the wall. He crouched to his knees and crawled into it, then turned and wordlessly communicated for her do to the same. She looked skeptical but eventually did the same. With the two of them wedged into the small dark space, he felt a jolt of electricity run through him. He willed himself to get in control.

She could sink him, this girl, without even knowing it.

"Quiet, it's here..." The scent of her hair was on his lips and he felt his pulse quicken.

She was leaning into the back wall and when she attempted to adjust her position she brushed up against him—she didn't have much choice given the size of the space—and he consciously attempted to control his reaction.

"What is here?" she whispered back, turning her face so he could see her profile. Her small delicate nose was set off by her high cheekbones and the most magnetic mouth he had ever seen.

"It's a chemical compound, a weapon, and it is going to be used at the wedding. It's there, behind those barrels." He motioned with his chin.

"Well, shouldn't we go and retrieve it? Why are we hiding here? And will you please tell me who on earth you really are?"

"There isn't time for that now," he said, sharply. "And no, we shouldn't retrieve it. I know who stole the weapon but I want to make sure that is actually who is planning on deploying it. I don't want to assume it's just one person and then have three on our hands."

She had given up attempting to get comfortable and sat still. He relaxed somewhat. He was hot now, even though it was glacial inside the building, and a small trickle of sweat dripped down the curve of his back.

He could feel her breathing, in and out.

"Well," she said a few moments later. "No time like the present, and since there isn't anyone else here with us, you might as well answer the question. I am not inclined to sit here and do things your way unless there is some reasonable explanation for how you are involved. I'm quite serious."

"You don't want to know who I am," he replied softly, struggling to find the right words. "If you knew, you would run for the hills."

"Then you don't know me very well."

"No, I suppose I don't."

He realized then that he had finally stopped associating her with his old dead neighbour. What he was feeling now was something built not on memory but something new, something unexplained. His chest hurt—it tightened, wound like a ball of string, pulling tighter and tighter around its core, and he willed it to release.

"I've done something horrible. Two horrible things, actually—and in the past, so much more than even that."

She tensed. "You knew one of the men killed by the Summerdyne Committee, didn't you? A family member?"

She wasn't going to let it go, and he had grown tired of dodging her.

"Something like that," he answered.

"Who was it?"

"If you must know, Irving Guy Ries. He was a special person in my life. He saved me when I was young and lost. I owed it to him."

"To avenge his death?" She stunned him and he realized he had underestimated her. "He is why you are here." It wasn't a question. She knew. She just wanted confirmation.

He nodded, watching her eyes search his face. He didn't trust himself to speak.

"So you...you killed for him? For vengeance?" She surprised him by not wavering in the least. Her tone remained even, her eyes set firmly on his, when most would have been planning their escape.

"For justice," he corrected, "although if it makes any difference now—to you—I am filled with regret...I have only regret." His voice cracked and he could look at her no longer. His world was crashing in on him. He felt he was drowning, as though a mighty ocean was wringing out his soul and hurtling it against the rocks, over and over. For the first time since he was a boy he felt his face awash with tears.

She watched quietly in the dark as he lost control, his mask crumbling.

He wiped at his face with his sleeve, soaking it, then breathed deeply, trying to regain his composure. Reaching up she touched his cheek, just for a moment, and then removed her hand as quickly as she had put it there.

"Anyone can atone for their mistakes," she stated as plainly as she would the weather.

He nodded at her, not really knowing if he believed it.

"I suppose this explains why when you found me in the old watermill the other night, I didn't really believe it was an accident. It would also explain why you wouldn't go anywhere near my cottage—the police were everywhere."

"And yet you are here, unafraid of me, when you know it all, everything about me, about what I have done, about who I am. You should be terrified of me."

"Probably. But that isn't going to help me discover who is about to use a chemical weapon on my best friend's wedding, now, is it? Incidentally, are you going to tell me or do I have to guess?"

"You really are the most astonishing woman. I think you will be surprised when you hear."

"Go on, try me then..."

The sound of a door creaking open stopped her mid-sentence and he pulled her lower behind the wagonette, ensuring they were hidden.

The door slammed again and there, in front of him, stood his prey.

"It's not...who I expected. I don't recognize him." he whispered, so quietly he doubted she could hear him.

"Nor I," she whispered back and he realized he had his mouth so close to her ear she must have heard him.

He wondered if the crescendo of his beating heart was due to the risk of being discovered or something else entirely.

"Don't move. I want him to take it and *then* we can follow him—this isn't at all what I expected."

She shook her head in disagreement and he squeezed her arm harder than he would have liked to emphasize his instructions. Her head was tucked under his chin but they were both staring at the same thing. A short, stout farmhand who was now carefully lifting a wooden box out from behind a row of barrels. The man glanced around nervously, apparently unsure whether he was alone and, satisfied, he quickly stashed the box inside an oilskin bag he had slung over his shoulder. He carefully made his way back towards the door and in a flash he was gone.

Lillie jumped up at once.

"Hurry up! We have to follow him!" She was dragging him to his feet and was halfway to the door before he could grab her.

He swung her around to face him. "Slow down. If you go flying out there like that, he will be sure to see you. We know exactly where he is going so for Christ's sake, be careful and keep your distance. The last thing we want is him deploying that thing."

"I don't suppose you are one to take suggestions, but I think the sooner we catch that bastard the better."

"That 'bastard' is working for someone else, perhaps two

other people, and if you don't mind, I'd like him to lead us directly to them. I have no intention of botching things after all the work I've done."

The look on her face told him she would prefer to be giving the orders than receiving them, but she didn't argue.

"We are going to need a car," she said instead. "I am going to head back to the house and secure us one. You follow him. I'll pick you up on the way out, don't go further than the main gates though or I'll never find you."

"Don't bring a driver," the hunter warned.

She nodded her assent and slipped out the door.

He heard her footsteps like feathers over the gravel as she sprinted towards the main house leaving him with a trail to follow and an ache in his chest.

62

LILLIE

Oxford, Oxfordshire

The telephone was ringing again when she entered the foyer and, annoyed, Lillie snapped it up out of its cradle on her way past.

"Yes, hello?" She rushed, urging whoever was on the other end to get on with it. She really had no time to lose.

"Thank God! Lillie, it's Felix Petters. I have to warn you, there is a weapons grade chemical compound about to be deployed at Harry's ceremony..."

"Yes, yes I know! I am on my way there now, with a...a man who I haven't a clue about..."

"Presumably the same man who called to warn me of it. Careful of him Lillie, I have some theories on who he is."

"As do I, but we haven't time to talk of it now. Where are you? Can you meet us at the church?"

"I'm not far, about thirty minutes away or so. Get there immediately. Evacuate the building. I will call the Oxford

Police again, there should be a contingent there shortly to help."

"Got it, see you there."

She slammed the receiver down and raced down the hallway towards the west side door that would take her to the garage.

BY THE TIME she had commandeered Harry's new low-slung sports car and exited the garage, Lillie began to wonder at her own insanity. She was effectively partnering herself with a murderer in an attempt to stop what could be a hundred more deaths, assuming the man—*Daniel,* she remembered his name from the night at the water mill—wasn't actually leading her into a trap. But why would he? She wasn't the target, the Summerdyne committee was. Unless of course Basil Wilkinson had put him up to killing her in the process. She knew her upcoming story for the newspaper didn't exactly leave her out of the whole thing.

She thought about something her father had told her many years ago—trust your instincts. It had served her well over the years and her instinct told her now that she was about to pick up a broken, remorseful man who would serve today to be their greatest ally. The rest could be sorted out later.

He was standing half hidden behind the gates as she roared down the drive. He was certainly tall, and formidable, she thought as he opened the passenger side door. He folded his long legs into the small car then fixed his intense gaze on her.

"Well, did you see him?" She sat with the engine idling and he motioned for her to carry on. She put the car into drive and stepped on the pedal.

"He is on foot. We will have some time to get ahead of him, although he is moving quickly."

"I still don't see why we couldn't have taken him back there instead of letting him get within striking distance of the church and Harry's guests."

She took a corner in the road faster than she should have and felt the little car's rear tires slide.

"Perhaps I should drive?" the man suggested, ignoring her question.

Lillie shot him a frown. "Don't be ridiculous, I can manage a car perfectly well, thank you," she said, her voice clipped.

"Have you spoken to Superintendent Petters?" he asked, carefully reaching up to hold onto a strap to steady himself. He was folded up like a sardine in a can, his long extremities obviously terribly uncomfortable.

"Yes, he is en route now. He shouldn't be long. What is our plan, exactly, when we arrive? Obviously we need to get everyone out of the church immediately."

"Yes, pull up in front and together we will head into the building and move everyone out. We need them to scatter as far away from the building as possible and then I will remain— without you I might add—to take him down before he can deploy his weapon."

"Presumably the police will be there by now to help, Petters has been in touch with them apparently."

"Good." He looked thoughtful for a moment before he spoke again. "And you will be married soon yourself?"

She was surprised by his question, especially amidst the complete panic and chaos of their situation. "This seems a strange turn of conversation, considering our circumstances."

"Does it?" He had relaxed his hand from the strap and was staring straight ahead.

They were on the outskirts of Oxford now and she slowed the car as they encountered some traffic.

"You don't really seem the type to make idle conversation."

"Perhaps not, but I don't anticipate you and I will have much more time together."

"On this earth?" She felt panicked suddenly, the danger awaiting them finally sinking in.

He gave a little laugh. "As in, I must leave once we resolve this mess."

"Ah, because you are a wanted man presumably."

"Something like that..." He spoke softly and she could feel his eyes on her, dark grey and brooding.

"They will be gunning for you and Superintendent Petters is an astute officer. It will be difficult for you to slip away."

"But not impossible."

"I should hate for them to..." She didn't finish her sentence, realizing that contrary to what she should be feeling, what she really wanted was for the man to escape unharmed. She was actually rooting for a known murderer to flee. The world was certainly complicated.

"Shoot me?" He smiled and her and reached out with his hand then, but thinking the better of it, placed it back in his lap. "Can I say something to you—although under the circumstances you may think me...oh never mind, I've never spoken so much to anyone in my life, I must be under the weather."

"Go on, we are certainly through the looking glass now."

He seemed to be holding his breath, wondering whether or not he wanted to say it. "If circumstances were different, if I hadn't..." He paused. "Well, if I weren't in this situation, and you weren't in your situation, would you perhaps—*could* you perhaps, see anything in me worthwhile? Worth saving?"

They were on a side road now, carrying along at slower speed, one better suited to the quality of the road which was rutted and winding. Lillie pulled the car to the side and put her foot on the brake. She turned towards the man and grasped his hands. They were cold and smooth and they held on tightly to her own. She stared into his eyes so her words would have their maximum effect.

"Whatever you have done, whoever you are, you can make

amends. Do you understand me?" She squeezed his hands and watched as his stormy eyes filled with unshed tears. "I can't possibly understand your situation, where you have come from or the pain that has followed you, but I can see it. It's written all over your face. I know there is good in you—you saved me from a horrible situation when there was no advantage for you to do so. Pick a different path from here on forward and find meaning in your life. Move on from this. Change, grow. Find happiness."

His hands were wound tightly around her own, as though he were holding on for dear life and he startled her by letting go and placing his on either side of her face. She didn't dare to breathe and the thought crossed her mind that if he wanted to break her neck, he was perfectly poised to do so.

Ever so slowly and gently, as though he were handling a bird, he pulled her face toward his and kissed her. So briefly and deeply that she thought she must have imagined it. His lips were far gentler than she would have thought possible.

He released her at once, murmuring, "I am terribly sorry, I shouldn't have done that."

Stunned, she turned to look out at the road, her mind a swirling of thoughts. Jack. Harry's wedding guests. A chemical weapon and this man, a murderer, kissing her. It was outlandish. She put the car into gear and swung back out into the road.

Silence filled the air between them, the only sound the shifting gears and the howl of the engine.

"There is a speak easy on the upper east side in Manhattan. It's called the Red Ruse, do you know it?" He didn't look at her. He spoke as though nothing had happened between them, and she knew this wasn't without conscious effort.

"I can't say that I do," she replied, spotting the church in the distance.

"There is a bartender there, Charlie. Nice guy. If you ever need anything, anything at all, he can get in touch with me. Not that you would, of course, need anything from...well, from a man like me."

From where they were Lillie could see the last of the guests entering the church and hear the distant sound of an organ. She pulled in behind a long line of cars and carriages. She spotted Harry and Jack standing to the left of the church stairs and she felt her chest give a little flutter as they began to walk up the stairs and disappear inside.

Switching off the engine, she looked at the killer seated beside her, taking in his wretchedly sad ashen eyes and granite jawline.

"You just never know, do you?" she replied.

63

THE HUNTER

Oxford, Oxfordshire

The church was standing room only and smelled of fresh cut lilies and the parched pages of ancient bibles. An old woman dressed in an unfashionable lilac dress sat at the organ belting out music the hunter wasn't familiar with, not that he wished to be. Lillie had gone immediately to the bride's dressing room and he was standing now, at the precipice of the room, looking over a sea of turned heads and luxurious hats, awaiting her return. He searched the crowd for police and for the first time in his life realized he was disappointed not to see any.

They were on their own. Well, he was certainly used to that.

The groom and his best man were standing at the front of the church, murmuring quietly to each other while the vicar busied himself with something behind the altar. The hunter recognized the man as Lillie's beau and studied his appearance with the interested detachment of a surgeon. Attractive to be sure, able bodied, intelligent looking, capable. *Familiar? Somehow familiar.* He wondered if any man could ever be really worthy of her?

A rustle behind him caused him to spin around in surprise. The bride was moving quickly towards him, followed by Lillie and a flower girl. As they rushed past him, Lillie reached out to grab his arm, pulling him along behind them. By the time they reached the front of the church the congregation looked completely stunned. It was hardly the entrance they had expected of the bride.

They formed a circle around the groom, which the hunter carefully stood outside of. He could hear their urgent whispers and watched as the groom nodded and then moved to address his guests.

"Ladies and gentlemen, if you don't mind. We seem to have a bit of an emergency on our hands."

The hunter studied the crowd while he listened. He was scanning it for their weapons thief.

"We must clear the church immediately. I'm terribly sorry for this but trust I will explain it all later. There are two side exits and one out the back behind the altar. Please do not exit out the front. Quickly as you can please, orderly but with haste."

He watched the stunned faces as they began to mobilize themselves. He located the Professor, who was speaking to someone beside him and then saw him look up and lock eyes with the hunter. He recognized him. That wouldn't help the situation.

The hunter backed away from the wedding party and moved towards the side exit and out of sight of the Professor.

It was then he saw the man with the oilskin bag enter through the front door. He had made better time than the hunter predicted he would. The man stood, confused at the rush of activity, looking completely out of place as he fiddled with the strap on the bag.

Through the swarm of anxious guests, the vigilant eyes of the Professor and the distant glance of a woman he wished he could know better, the hunter finally saw what he had been looking for—the swish of an oyster coloured dress as it made its way towards the oilskin bag.

64

LILLIE

Oxford, Oxfordshire

What happened next Lillie knew she wouldn't easily forget. As she watched the man she knew as Daniel spring into action, she realized she had no earthly idea of what he was capable of.

He sprang into the fray, his long limbs as agile as a tiger's as he made his way towards the front door. It was then she spotted the man they had seen in the shed at Tynesmore, the same dirty oilcloth bag still slung over his shoulder. Florence was moving towards him as well and Lillie fought the urge to yell at her and tell her to go the other way. And then in a split second, Lillie saw the look that passed between them, and the realization dawned on her that *Florence* was their man. The other man was just her patsy, her soldier.

It swept over her like a sunrise. Suddenly, Jeremiah tugged at her sleeve, urging her to leave with them.

"Miss, please, you must come with us outside," he said,

looking back at the scene unfolding in the doorway of the church.

Florence was trying desperately to wrestle the bag off the man's shoulders as the hunter hit him again and again in the face, without remorse. He flung Florence to the ground with the slightest effort and began in on the man again, crushing his nose and cheeks with his fists.

"Stop, police!" Superintendent Petters burst through the open doorway trailing three confused looking officers behind him and Daniel reluctantly backed away.

"The bag," he murmured as he did, "...it's there, in the bag."

Petters knelt down and retrieved it off the body of the unconscious man, who was now bleeding profusely all over the vicar's carpeting. Florence was sitting up and another officer had her hands secured behind her back while Petters carefully opened the bag.

"It's here boys, good work. Let's get them outside."

Petters looked up at Lillie across the nave of the church. Bag in hand, he tipped his hat.

It was then that she noticed something odd, Daniel was nowhere to be seen. She hurried outside after Petters and Florence, her eyes scanning the wintry surroundings.

BEFORE DISAPPEARING BACK inside the church, Superintendent Petters had handcuffed Florence to the iron railing on the church steps. Her oyster coloured silk dress had been torn from the struggle and its hem soiled, but someone had taken care to throw a coat over her shoulders. Probably Rumple. Lillie couldn't help but think of the age-old saying that love is blind — regardless of the evilness in a person.

The stone steps on which Florence sat now must have been cold and unforgiving but it didn't look as though she cared, the miserableness of failure etched on her delicate features.

"I don't understand," Lillie said to her. "Why would you think setting off a poisonous gas inside a church was an acceptable punishment for the sins of a wartime committee of five? There are at least a hundred innocent people in there!"

Florence stared up at her with defiance. "I wouldn't have had to resort to these measures if that hired assassin had bloody finished his job," she said, and for the first time Lillie noticed a contempt in her eyes she must have missed before.

"And what exactly was his job?"

"To kill off the Summerdyne Committee, one by one, and then, when all that was finished, to murder that bastard Wilkinson. I couldn't have laid it out better for him."

"Murder? All of you? You included?"

"Of course me included. I only left the farmhouse that night with you because I wanted to lead him back to the Professor and give him a perfect chance to get all three of us at the same time. How can a professional hit man not pull that off? It was as easy as sliding off a log."

Lillie looked searchingly around their small circle of gatherers. Jack, herself and a couple of police officers. No hit man—no Daniel.

Was he really a murderer? She didn't understand how he could have been responsible for the first two murders in North Oxfordshire and yet also have saved her, and all of them from certain death. He was an unfathomable paradox.

Florence was muttering something, over and over, rocking herself back and forth like a wounded animal. *Atone, atone, atone.*

She was insane, that much was obvious. She needed to be treated for her illness, not locked up. The war had taken a toll on many. Some wore their wounds on the outside, for everyone to see, and others cracked, their minds unable to process what they had been told to do, and what they had done. The lives that they had ended.

"So this wasn't the work of Basil Wilkinson," Lillie said quietly to Jack, who had come to stand beside her.

He rubbed his hands together to banish the cold. "It doesn't appear so."

She didn't realize Florence had heard them, but she shot up and spat, "Oh he's a right bastard, make no mistake, but too stupid to put this together. I just used his name to write to that American jester," she said, jeering. "Told him I was Basil Wilkinson and fed him the names of the people who killed his friend. Unjustly of course."

Lillie looked back at her. "You mean Irving Guy Ries of course?"

"Ries was like family to him. A criminal family, mind you, but he wasn't a German spy, nothing of the sort."

Lillie sighed. "And to think I was having doubts about the Professor, yet all along it was you."

"He had his issues, I'll tell you that. They made him an easy accomplice. He didn't want that story of yours written for fear it would expose him so it didn't take much to capitalize on that."

"Expose what about him, exactly?"

"He is a homosexual. I guess you didn't know that."

"Does that matter?"

"Maybe not to you Americans, but it matters very much here in England."

"So you blackmailed him?"

Florence nodded.

"I suppose it was him who attacked me and locked me up at the Mill? I wondered how you would have managed that on your own. You aren't any bigger than I am."

"He was a reluctant participant. If I hadn't witnessed his grief over that violinist we executed I wouldn't have put it all together."

"He was having an affair with one of the accused?" Lillie remembered Petters telling her about the way the Professor looked when he told him of one of the executions in particular. Haunted, was how he put it.

Florence was nodding, her eyes glassy.

Jack gave her arm a squeeze, "I'll see what I can do to reroute this wedding party to Tynesmore. Harry and Primrose may still be able to have a wedding today."

"Good idea, I'll just wait here for Petters to return then join you all."

Jack leaned over and kissed her cheek and she watched him return up the stairs into the church.

When she turned around, she saw a man standing a fair distance away from her, amongst the bare wintery trees of the churchyard. Even from that great a distance she could see he was watching her, studying her. She could imagine his face as much as she could see it. Cool as ice, a competing mix of thoughts and emotions. A chameleon. An actor. An ocean. Churning, changing, revealing, then hiding again.

Lillie wondered at his confidence—and at his weakness.

She lifted her hand to wave goodbye and watched him nod at her in return.

He held her gaze for what felt like an eternity, then turned and disappeared into the forest.

65

THE HUNTER

Southampton, England

"**W**elcome aboard Mr...." The steward peered down at the ticket, raising his spectacles so they sat square on the bridge of his bony nose. "Mr. Underhill."

The man bowed slightly as the hunter re-pocketed his ticket.

"First class entrance is right this way." He waved with a grand gesture. "At your convenience, please proceed to the left and you will be taken to your state room. Your luggage will be taken care of from here."

He leaned forward and tagged the hunter's bag with a large manila flap laced with linen string which he then handed to a porter standing behind him. "Enjoy your voyage."

The hunter nodded and stepped onto the gangway. He inhaled deeply, turning to look at Southampton dock before he left it forever. He didn't expect he would be back in England again in his lifetime.

Despite the overcast sky and drizzle of the morning, the afternoon had turned out to be glorious. The clouds had parted, pushing away the moisture and warming the ground until it steamed like a smouldering peat fire.

A woman behind him struggled with her luggage as she followed him up the ramp. She was nattering something about getting sea sick and the lack of porters on the dock. Obviously she wasn't in first class, he thought as he offered to help with her bag.

"Oh thank you, that's kind." Her voice sounded strange after all his time in England. American South, he reflected, listening to her draw out her vowels. "I just can't wait to get home. I like traveling and all but there just ain't nowhere I like better than home."

The hunter nodded, even though he had no discernible impression of home.

"Are you American?" she asked, stopping to adjust her gloves and straighten her little hat. It was cheaply made of dyed mottled wool and, like her, it hadn't aged well. She wasn't likely a day past forty, but the weathering on her skin added at least a decade.

The hunter nodded again.

"It's just so nice to be around a fellow American," she gushed. The hunter thought that while she might have once been attractive, her blonde curls bouncing as she walked, her huge round blue eyes as honest as a sunrise, she really wasn't his type at all. He pushed back the memory of two women, one dead in a river, one alive in Oxford—neither of whom looked anything like the woman before him. He sighed.

"Here you are," he said, handing her bag to a porter at the top of ramp.

"Why thank you so much," she said, and her curls bobbed.

"Tell me, what brought you to England?" She seemed to be searching for a way to keep him with her. Talking.

"Work, but I'm retiring now."

"Oh! And then what will you do? You seem a bit young to retire?"

Before he even gave it a thought, the words were out of his mouth. "I'm starting a school for orphaned youth in New York."

"A philanthropist! I just knew you were a kind man when I saw you!"

The hunter looked down at her. "Did you?"

"Mm hmm." She nodded emphatically. "Say, how about a drink after we settle in?"

The hunter pondered this. He was making a change in his life, this much was true. A drastic about face. He searched her eyes, looking for something that could hold him. He so badly wanted to feel something again, like he had when he was eleven years old and his neighbour had led him away from his dismal life; like he had when he broke open the door to the Mill house and stared down at the nearly naked woman wrapped in the burlap blanket.

It was no use.

And so he smiled at her instead and told her truthfully, "I'm sorry, I have left my heart somewhere else. I won't be able to have that drink after all."

He turned and walked away from her, inhaling the scent of the ocean and his own rebirth. He had a new life to start.

EPILOGUE

"We will have to say good-bye soon."

"I daresay."

The boy's face was contemplative and Superintendent Petters watched him carefully. It was a loss for Jeremiah, and he had certainly had his fair share of those in his life.

"Of course it is the right thing to do." The boy set his mouth into a determined line, as if clamping his lips shut would stop the tears that threatened to spill over his alabaster cheeks.

"We may always take faith in that," Petters assured.

"Will it be all right?"

"Of course, you have done an exceptional job."

The boy nodded gravely, understanding but not yet at peace with it. He ran his slim fingers over the bird's feathers, the two pin sized black eyes looking up at him. Jeremiah put the creature back into the crate he had moments before cleaned and re-bedded. The bird fluttered his wings and it was obvious whatever ailment he had been suffering from was now healed. Petters knew it was time to release him but he wanted it to be the boy's decision. They should all have some control over their own destinies.

"Perhaps we should release him in the church yard? The old vicar would be pleased."

"I think that is a very good idea."

"Do you think I will ever see him again?"

"I expect he will see you. He'll have a much better vantage point for that."

The bird chirped, craning his little head around in search of his benefactor. Jeremiah obliged him by putting some seed into his hand and lowering his palm down so the bird could feed out of it.

"I'll miss him." The boy sniffed, beginning to lose the battle with his emotions.

"I know. But there are many more out there that need you. You must make room for them too."

"Good point, Mr. P."

"Call me Felix, please. Don't you think it's time?"

"What makes you think P stands for Petters?" The boy was mocking him. It always surprised Petters how quick he was.

"Oh?"

"Perhaps it stands for Poppa."

"Well then," Petters said, beaming and feeling a mistiness cloud his vision. "By all means, carry on then."

He felt a slim hand slide into the palm of his own. And the brush of an emerald green coat sleeve on his arm. He realized then that everything in their world would be all right. For he didn't mind Calista Hemny's germs, or Jeremiah's for that matter.

And then he knew, as sure as the snow would fall and the sun would rise, that for the first time ever he was about to have a family of his own.

∼

Lillie was waiting for him in his office when he returned from setting the bird free. She looked tired but satisfied.

"I read your article," Petters said, removing his coat and hanging it on a hook at the back of the door. "As always, very, very well written."

"Thank you."

"I would think it caused quite a stir in Wilkinson's department."

"Jack said it did, yes. They have asked him to take a sabbatical, at least until they can ascertain exactly how unjust his wartime decisions were. It will take time for the truth to come out, no doubt."

"And Harry and Primrose got off on their honeymoon?"

"They did, although in the end Harry couldn't part with Rumple so he ended up joining them. Probably for the best—at least now Harry can wear a tie to dinner." She smirked then changed the subject. "What will become of Florence?"

"She is being evaluated at New Bethlem Hospital in London, but I daresay she will be required to stand trial."

"And the assassin?"

She had a look that suggested she knew more than he did. He watched her carefully for a moment, wondering if she knew his whereabouts. "Gone. So it seems."

"Well," she breathed in response, pushing herself out of the chair she was perched on. "I better be on my way. I am due to give a statement to the police in Oxford regarding the Professor's role in my kidnapping. Not that I know anything; being unconscious means one tends to be an unreliable witness."

Petters hurried to open the door for her. "I hope we will work together again sometime."

"As do I," she said, grasping his hand and giving it a little squeeze.

He walked her down the corridor to the front door of the Chipping Norton police station. A handsome Lagonda sat awaiting her at the curb, and Jack, upon seeing them, got out of the car to give Petters a wave.

"I suppose your wedding will be next." Petters raised an eyebrow.

Lillie glanced towards the car and bit down on her lower lip. "I really couldn't say, Superintendent. I just couldn't say."

And with that, she was gone. He watched the two of them drive away into a fading winter sun until the car was nothing but a speck on the horizon.

AUTHOR'S NOTE

During World War I, the British government executed eleven men who were accused of being German spies. As is common practice during wartime, legislative parameters shift and change. In the case of the United Kingdom, the Defence of the Realm Act 1914 (D.O.R.A.) was passed just four short days after the war started. The Act would eventually give the government and its tentacles the authority it needed for social control, censorship, and the requisitioning of land and buildings. It was designed to assist in keeping public morale high and the enemy off British soil.

Unfortunately, wartime hysteria and spy-hunting, along with this new legislation, resulted in the probable execution of some men who were not acting in the manner of which they were accused. In many cases, the evidence cited was weak, circumstantial and tenuous at best. Some of these men were, in all likelihood, in the wrong place at the wrong time. Their actions in peacetime would hardly warrant a second glance, however during war they were deemed to be a threat to the security of the nation. Who they might have spoken to, or sent mail to, or in the case of one man—asking for sardines in the off season—prompted pernicious inquiry that sealed their fates.

This story, although entirely fictional, does use some situational anecdotes of those executed. It is my belief that the best stories derive their weight from historical interpretation, and in reading *A Willful Grievance* perhaps some light might be shed on the danger of censorship, mob mentality, and the misuse of legislation validated by wartime 'necessity'.

JOIN THE READERS GROUP

It's the best way to get up-to date details of new releases, special offers and news.

See details through my website at lisazumpano.com
Connecting with readers is my favourite part of being an author.
I'll look forward to seeing you there.